SPARROWS
IN THE
WIND

GAIL CARSON LEVINE

Quill Tree Books
An Imprint of HarperCollinsPublishers

Quill Tree Books is an imprint of HarperCollins Publishers.

Sparrows in the Wind
Copyright © 2022 by Gail Carson Levine

Library of Congress Cataloging-in-Publication Data
Names: Levine, Gail Carson, author.
Title: Sparrows in the wind / Gail Carson Levine.
Description: First edition. | New York : Quill Tree Books, [2022] | Includes
    author's note. | Audience: Ages 10 up. | Audience: Grades 4-6. | Summary:
    "Trojan princess Cassandra is cursed by Apollo with the gift of prophecy,
    and must try to find her place in a world that she knows to be perilous;
    years later, will her friendship with a young Amazon princess named Rin
    help her to avert a disastrous end to their war?"— Provided by publisher.
Identifiers: LCCN 2021063013 | ISBN 978-0-06-303907-0 (hardcover)
Subjects: CYAC: Cassandra (Legendary character)—Fiction. | Prophecies—
    Fiction. | Fate and fatalism—Fiction. | Gods—Fiction. | Amazons—Fiction.
    | Trojan War—Fiction. | Mythology, Greek—Fiction. | LCGFT: Novels.
Classification: LCC PZ7.L578345 Sp 2022 | DDC [Fic]—dc23
LC record available at https://lccn.loc.gov/2021063013

Typography by Catherine San Juan
22 23 24 25 26   PC/LSCH   10 9 8 7 6 5 4 3 2 1

First Edition

To David: Thank you for your company
in the worst of times and the best.

CAST OF CHARACTERS

TROJANS

Aminta	Cassandra's cousin
Andromache	Cassandra's sister-in-law, Hector's wife
Antenor	councilor to King Priam
Cassandra	princess
Conny	Queen Hecuba's little dog
Corythus	Paris and Oenone's son
Deiphobus	prince and Cassandra's older brother
Hector	prince and Cassandra's older brother
Hecuba	queen and Cassandra's mother
Helenus	prince and Cassandra's twin
Kynthia	Cassandra's cousin
Laocoön	priest of Apollo
Laodice	princess and Cassandra's younger sister
Maera	Cassandra's hound
Melo	Cassandra's cousin
Myrtes	palace musician
Pammon	prince and Cassandra's older brother
Paris	prince and Cassandra's older brother

| Polydorus | prince and Cassandra's youngest brother |
| Priam | king and Cassandra's father |

AMAZONS

Barkida	first bowyer (bow maker)
Gamis	second bowyer
Khasa	Rin's older cousin
Lannip	Rin's aunt
Pen (Penthesilea)	queen and Rin's mother
Rethra	Rin's younger cousin
Rin (Shirin)	princess
Serag	Rin's aunt
Short Black	a horse, one of a short horse breed
Tall Brown	a horse, one of a tall horse breed
Young White Chest	Rin's dog
Zelke	Rin's aunt

GREEKS

Achilles	warrior
Agamemnon	commander of the Greek army
Helen	wife of Menelaus
Hermione	Menelaus and Helen's daughter
Menelaus	king of Sparta
Pragora	Hermione's nursemaid

GREEK AND TROJAN DEITIES

Aphrodite	goddess of love and beauty
Apollo	god of truth and prophecy, protector of children
Ares	god of war
Athena	goddess of war and of the city
Eris	goddess of discord
Eurus	god of the east wind
Hera	goddess of the family
Poseidon	god of the sea
Zeus	thunder god, lord of the immortals

AMAZON DEITY

Cybele	goddess of the earth and sun, warrior goddess

PART ONE

CASSANDRA

A hound pursues a mouse
through the alleys of high-walled Troy—
a game for the hound; for the mouse, a dash for life.
Mortals are mice when gods give chase.

1

Helios, the sun god, was still asleep when Mother—Queen Hecuba—kissed my cheek and whispered, "Cassandra."

My hound, Maera, jumped off my bed. I squeezed my eyes shut.

Oh! The procession!

I sprang up. Maera was sniffing Mother's little dog, Conny. I rubbed Maera's neck and reached down farther to pet Conny too. Then I hugged Mother, whose growing belly pressed into my chest—another brother or sister on the way.

I breathed in the comforting, salty-sweet scent of almonds, which Mother herself pounded to add to our soups. Silence covered most of the vast women's quarters, but nearby rustling revealed that Melo, Aminta, and

Kynthia, who waited on me, were awake too.

Mother's smile was happy in the glow of the lamp she held. "My kanephoros. Troy is in your hands today."

"And on my head."

"Yes. Do well, love."

A kanephoros's task was to lead the whole city to an altar in the sacred grove, the altar of the god or goddess being celebrated. On her head, without using her hands, she balanced a heavy basket of fruit, honey cake, and the knife the priests would use on the sacrifices. Upon reaching the altar, she lowered the basket, and her job was done. A new kanephoros would be chosen for Zeus's festival two months from now.

I tapped my fingers nervously against my thigh. When I'd rehearsed yesterday, the basket had toppled. A mistake today would cause the entire city to suffer.

Mother had been kanephoros when she was my age and there had been no mishaps. Last year, however, the kanephoros for the festival of Artemis, goddess of the hunt, had stumbled. For six months, deer, wild pigs, and rabbits fled the land around Troy. Our archers could hit nothing.

Today's celebration was for Apollo, my favorite immortal. God of light! Healing! Truth! Prophecy! Guardian of children!

Especially prophecy.

What a relief it would be to see ahead and know I

avoided disaster today. Or, if something was destined to go wrong, I could correct the problem.

I'd warn other people too. Be careful on the stairs! Don't eat that scone! An asp will lurk in your sewing basket tomorrow!

Kynthia came to me, wielding a gilded comb. "Aunt Hecuba, we'll get her ready." She enjoyed attacking my knots and tangles—and giggled if I squealed.

Maera wagged her tail. She liked everybody.

"We've planned it all." Melo crowded next to Kynthia. "I'm in charge of jewelry."

Aminta, the shy one, hung back. "I'll drape the peplos." I barely heard her add, "The most important part."

Aminta probably couldn't see me smile at her in the lamplight. I wished I could be friends with her and Melo, but they were so close, there seemed room for no one else.

My handmaids and I were all cousins to each other. At seventeen, they were three years older than I was.

I bent over and held Maera's head in my hands. How shiny her eyes were. She was my friend.

Mother hooked her lamp's handle on the screen behind my bed and left, saying she'd send up porridge soon. Conny waddled after her. If I didn't disgrace myself today, my loom would be moved next to Mother's, where I'd weave in her sweet company.

"First, the hair." Kynthia waved for me to sit on my bed.

She knelt behind me, pushed my shoulders forward, and pulled my hair back with the comb, tugging on a knot.

I bit back a yelp.

Maera whimpered.

"Am I hurting you?" Kynthia yanked.

I gritted my teeth. "The kanephoros is above pain."

Finally, the comb glided easily. Kynthia patted the hair over my ears—sometimes she was nice.

Melo gave her the linen streamer, which would wind around my head and be plaited into a loose braid. This step was quickly accomplished.

"Your turn," Kynthia told Aminta.

A servant carried in a tray with bowls of porridge.

I directed her to put it on my low table. The others would help themselves, but I was too excited to eat.

"No!" I told Maera, and she backed away from the food. "Good dog!"

She wagged her tail. She was the best dog.

The ceremonial peplos filled Aminta's arms, causing her to trip and narrowly miss the porridge before she spread the fabric across my bed.

Let *me* not trip!

A peplos becomes a garment when it's draped and pinned, but, essentially, it's a rectangle of cloth that's wrapped around the wearer.

Unlike our everyday woolen ones, today's peplos was

linen. Mother had woven it, so it felt as smooth as the skin of a grape. Against the cream of the fabric, dyed purple triangles marched in a line a handbreadth from the borders. I'd never worn anything so beautiful.

Aminta folded it once, unequally. The longer side would fall to my ankles, the other just a bit below my waist. "Lift your arms, if you please."

I raised them while she wrapped the peplos around me. The fit was perfect, so that the cloth didn't bunch under my arms. I'd look graceful, not hulking.

Kynthia danced to me with the brooches that would be pinned at my shoulders. "Envy could cause me to accidentally prick you, Cassandra."

Only she would say such a thing, as if being kanephoros was my fault.

She inserted the pins and pulled them through the linen without even touching me. The pins were bronze, strung with pale blue terra-cotta beads. After I was pinned, she took a bowl of porridge and ate while reclining on her bed.

Aminta wrapped a purple sash around my waist, over both folds in front and under the shorter one in the back. If I felt chilly, I could lift the back fold over my head and shoulders.

Last of all, Melo fetched my jewelry for great occasions: a spiraling gold arm bracelet that ended in a tiny figure of Poseidon, god of the sea; gold earrings set with garnets;

a ruby ring. None of them mattered, though. What mattered was the necklace.

Holding it at arm's length, Melo carried it to me while we all recited the riddle: "What is brown, tan, and sticky, heavy as gold, cheap as air, common as clouds, loved by the gods?"

Melo hung the string of dried figs around my neck. She intoned,

> *"First a bow.*
> *Next a knot.*
> *This will hold."*

"Or we'll be full of woe," I said, making up another rhyme. The necklace presented another danger. The figs symbolized a bountiful harvest and prosperity. If the necklace fell off me, Troy would have to endure famine.

We loved the gods, who were kind and listened to our pleas—but were easily offended. Then they could be heartless and vengeful. We needed them—for the harvest, the weather, music, happy families—so many things! My fingers turned to ice when I thought about what could happen.

Melo stood back. "You're so lucky." Her father wasn't wealthy enough for his daughter to be kanephoros. She took her porridge and ate it standing up.

I felt a twinge of guilt.

When she returned the bowl to the table, she lifted her best peplos out of her chest.

Aminta arranged Melo's peplos around her, and I pinned it with her copper brooches, which had no beads.

Aminta murmured, "Didn't you ever fall when you were little?"

I probably did, but she had a scar across her right eyebrow. The kanephoros must be without a blemish. I *was* lucky.

Kynthia said, "Anger never sours Princess Perfect's words. She speaks only truth—in the kindest possible way. The opposite of a glutton, she barely eats."

I blushed. I hadn't touched my porridge. She wouldn't either if her stomach were turning somersaults!

And I did get angry—mostly at her.

Kynthia might have been kanephoros, when she was fourteen as I was now, if she hadn't been impertinent to Mother once too often.

Aminta took her porridge and whispered, "Cassandra, you're as beautiful as Aphrodite."

Aphrodite was the goddess of love and beauty. Embarrassed, I massaged Maera's neck. "You're the prettiest dog in Troy."

Anyway, today the only quality I wanted was good balance. I whispered back to Aminta, "Do you think I'll drop it?" The basket.

"You'll be fine."

Kynthia heard. "Maybe not. Anything may happen. You could sneeze. Someone else could stumble into you. A snake—"

"Hush!" Aminta and Melo said in unison.

Maera barked, ending sleep in the women's quarters.

Kynthia's damage was done. I imagined disasters: a fly on my nose; a blustery wind; Zeus's thunderbolt from the blue sky, striking the basket.

Melo and Aminta held my arms on the stairs—the stairs I'd raced up and down dozens of times a day when I was younger.

"The kanephoros mustn't take a tumble," Melo said.

Were they worried too?

Maera ran ahead and grinned at us from the bottom.

In the courtyard, stone benches surrounded a fountain. I collapsed on one, and Maera curled up at my feet. Melo and Aminta took another, where they whispered too softly for me to hear. From her own bench, Kynthia stared down at the mosaic floor.

Flowering laurel bushes grew out of clay pots that ran along the outer walls. Laurels were Apollo's flowers. I thanked the god for their smoky scent.

"Our Cassandra!" Father boomed, hurrying out of the living room, trailed by Mother. He stopped short a yard from me. A smile rounded his cheeks.

I swallowed over a lump. He usually looked solemn.

Sensing his good mood, Maera jumped on his legs. He patted her briefly, then straightened. "I want to remember you as you are today." He paused. "Those curving eyebrows that mean sweetness, your broad, sensible forehead."

I blushed, relishing his words—but how disappointed he'd be if I came to grief!

"A beautiful Trojan face." He reached behind him for Mother's hand as she came to stand next to him. "Darling, Cassandra has your rose lips that speak only kindness."

Mother blushed too. "I'm grateful for the health in her cheeks." She let his hand go and sat next to me. "Do you like her peplos, Priam?"

He turned his smile on her. "It's an achievement! Troy and I are lucky to have you both." He held out his arms for me, and I ran into them. He kissed my forehead.

I was near tears. Maera and I returned to Mother, and I leaned against her. In my mind, I thanked all the gods and goddesses for my parents.

Father held out his hands. "Come, both of you."

When we all, including the two dogs, stepped outside the palace, a shout rose. *"Loo lo!"* The plaza thronged with people, who spilled into nearby lanes and alleys too—the citizens of Troy, needing me to keep them safe.

Still holding hands, we descended the three steps to the plaza. At the bottom, Mother and Father let me go. Arms trembling, the old priestess Arethusa raised the basket. I stepped under it, and she released its weight. Ai! Heavy!

With a smooth gait but a bumpy heart, I began to walk, Maera at my side. Please don't trip me, Maera!

Mother and Father filed after me, though Conny wouldn't be able to keep up. Behind us, a dozen priests led four plump sacrificial oxen. Apollo would be given the gods' favorite treat, fat from their thighs. Later, Troy would dine on the rest.

Following the oxen strode the married women and the widows; then minced the maidens, alert to who might be observing them; then the young men, whose thoughts were almost certainly on the games that would come after the sacrifice; and, finally, the married men and widowers.

Flutists piped a melody that rose above the beat of our sandals. Men sang praises to Apollo, women to his half sister Athena, goddess of battle and protector of the city.

How grand, to be a Trojan!

From the plaza, the wide Way of the Immortals led to the east gate. Troy's famed inner walls lined the road— twice the height of my best brother, Hector, who was the tallest in the city. The walls were made of stones in shades of red, white, yellow, and brown, arranged to make pictures: athletes wrestling; horses galloping; women at their looms; Apollo's crows on the wing; thunderbolts of Zeus, lord of the gods.

The walls backed against Troy's grand upper city, where public life took place: the gymnasium; the market; the amphitheater, in which laws were passed and plays performed; and the courts, where laws were disputed.

At last, we reached the gate. I signaled with a quivering hand for Maera to stay, and she obeyed.

We left the cobbled street for the dirt road to the sacred grove. The ground was uneven here, and I couldn't tilt my head to see where to put my feet. Why had I practiced only on our cobblestone streets? Panicking, I slowed my stately pace to hardly more than a creep.

Behind me, a priest quavered, "Is something wrong with the girl?"

I made myself ignore him. Careful step followed careful step.

Finally, growing more confident, I walked a little faster. Minutes passed. Might we be a third of the way? Or just a quarter? Why had I wanted to be kanephoros?

A pebble wormed its way under the sandal strap across my toes and wedged there, digging into my skin. Ouch!

What could I do? I stopped. The basket wobbled. Ai!

2

The procession stuttered to a halt behind me. Someone called, "Why aren't we moving?" Someone else yelled, "Apollo, forgive us!" A priest began a prayer.

The basket steadied. I wanted to shake my foot to get the pebble out, but then I'd certainly topple the basket.

Had I angered a god, who was punishing me?

Ouch! I started walking again and somehow kept my steps even. In a few minutes, my foot felt wet. Mother gasped.

Soon, my blood greased the pebble so that it swam out, though the spot still stung. Would the pebble and my blood anger the gods, even though the basket didn't fall? Was I no longer without a blemish?

Feel the ground. Shift my weight. Good foot. Pebble foot. I didn't falter.

We continued onward to the altar, where I lifted the basket from my head and lowered it to the ground without spilling anything. I rolled my shoulders in relief.

Sacrifice and prayers followed while my toe stopped bleeding.

Still uneasy about being a bloody kanephoros, I waited in the front row of the stands just south of the sacred grove for the games to begin. Aminta sat next to me, not touching me but with her arm across Melo's shoulders. I wished Maera were here, pressing herself against my legs.

Kynthia, on my other side, congratulated me on my performance and added, "Last year, Apollo's kanephoros kept a steady gait. A whisper about your bloody foot ran through the priests to the mamas and then to us. The mamas may wonder what kind of wife you'll make, prone to scrapes as you seem to be. And the sons may have the image of your oozing toes lodged in their minds."

Hush, Kynthia!

My favorite brother, Hector, rushed to me and stopped abruptly. He declaimed in a big voice from his athlete's chest, "On Mount Olympus, the gods are praising *my* sister! The wounded kanephoros who didn't falter."

I smiled up at him, forgetting Kynthia. Hector was always my champion, but he wouldn't lie. If he believed I'd done well, then I had.

He bounced a little, always full of warm energy. His black curls bounced too. We had the same round eyebrows that Father had praised. If they meant sweetness in me, they meant a hive's worth of honey in him.

He raised his arms in a vee, then dropped to his knees. "Does it hurt?"

I tossed back my head, the wordless way to say no. "Not much."

Mother came to me from her chair next to Father. Hector jumped up and held her elbow while she bent down. "Let me see your foot."

I took off my sandal.

"Mm. Youth! Cuts don't last." She patted my knee. "People are marveling—your father and I are marveling too—that you didn't drop the basket. You showed remarkable determination."

She'd never described me as determined before. I wondered if I was.

Kynthia squirmed next to me. Good.

Hector said, "I would have stumbled."

"You wouldn't have!" Troy's best athlete.

"Since you don't mind pain," he added, "I could teach you to wrestle."

We laughed. Girls and women didn't wrestle. But it would have been fun.

"I can't stay. I have to take my place." He held out his arm for Mother, who leaned on him back to her chair.

I watched them go, the two tilting into each other. Father held his hands out to Mother when they were close.

Three young men rushed to us and saluted my cousins with raised arms. Their faces were scarlet. Melo and Aminta blushed too, but Kynthia pursed her lips as if she'd eaten a lemon.

My cousins were betrothed to the three and had two years left in their engagements. Married or not, they'd continue to serve me until I married too and went to live in my husband's house.

None of them had ever had a conversation with their intendeds. Kynthia, however, had listened to rumors that hers was dull. She often said, "Imagine me with a boring man!"

I pitied him.

Unless everyone really was disgusted by my bleeding toe, among the other contestants were young men who'd be put forward by their parents as my suitors. Succeeding as kanephoros took me a step closer from girlhood to womanhood. I'd cross entirely when I became a wife.

I watched the players intently. This one was graceful, that one strong, another easily distracted. Some seemed merry, some grim with concentration. What would be best in a husband? Hector, my ideal of a man, laughed and shouted to his friends. Once he waved to me.

But the games came easily to him. My best future husband might have to work harder and have no attention left over for waving. He might still be sweet and kind. How would I tell since I could only ever watch him from a distance?

Once again, I wished for future sight. Then I'd know which one I was fated to marry. If we weren't going to like each other, I might be able to persuade Mother and Father to choose someone else.

Hector won the wrestling. I snapped my fingers raw.

My twin, Helenus, won nothing, but he did better in every competition than our brother Deiphobus, which was all he cared about. Helenus couldn't stand to lose, and I'd learned early to let him win our little games. I preferred not to endure his angry silences and sometimes elbow jabs, which he pretended were accidental.

I loved him anyway. We were always together when we were very little.

At first, Deiphobus, older by four years, simply wanted to play fair, and he made allowances when Helenus was smaller and weaker. But now that they were evenly matched, Deiphobus wanted victory as much as my twin did.

After the competitions, everyone feasted on the sacrificial

oxen and the sacrificial fruit and straggled home. I asked Mother if I could linger in the sacred grove.

"Your toe is all right?"

"It feels just like my other toes." Not quite.

"You can stay. Don't worry if you fall asleep and don't wake up until morning. Apollo may send you a prophetic dream."

Maera would miss me, but I might glimpse the future! I'd pet her and tell her everything.

Gods could do more than send dreams. They might visit favorites and help them.

Or harm them. Zeus, ruler of the gods, sometimes carried off maidens he fancied.

But Apollo didn't behave as he did—or not often.

When everyone was gone, I sat on the bench in front of his altar and the marble statue of him under the branches of an ancient oak tree. In May in our warm land, the sacred grove was a wilderness of laurel shrubs, olive bushes, grapevines, and dwarf pine trees. A dove cooed. Leaves rustled. The scent of pine pleased my nose.

I smiled at the statue: the sweetness of the god's mouth, his powerful arms and legs, even the graceful fall of his tunic. His fingers on his lyre looked sensitive and purposeful.

The fingers plucked the strings, beginning a lively tune.

The statue plucked the strings!

My breath stuck in my throat. I blinked, but the vision continued. The statue tinted rosy with life.

After a little while, it—the god?—sat next to me. I trembled and shivered.

"They chose well when they made you kanephoros. I've never been so pleased."

His velvet voice relaxed me. For joy, I snapped my fingers over my head. "Thank you."

"You hurt your foot." He knelt in front of me—a god kneeling to me! Gently, he eased off my sandal.

How safe my foot felt in his hand!

"A valiant wound. You didn't drop my basket." He rubbed his finger across the scab. "There."

The cut closed. The last twinge of pain faded away. No sign remained that a pebble had cut me.

"You're the best god!"

He sat next to me again and mock frowned. "I'll tell Zeus you didn't mean that."

I laughed.

"Your brother Hector's wrestling pleased me. He will be beloved by the gods." The god of truth corrected himself. "Some gods."

"He's my best brother." Bravely, I added, "He's worthy of admiration even by the gods."

Three crows flapped over the grove and landed on a branch of the oak tree. They cawed words. Truly! Words!

> *"A minnow doesn't sense the rapids ahead.*
> *Apollo, god of light and truth (not wisdom)—*
> *Cassandra, the determined kanephoros—*
> *nothing bad has happened yet.*
> *God and princess, watch your step!"*

"Did you hear that?" I blurted. "Did they really speak?" Crows thought me determined too!

"They're just my crows." He waved a hand. Crows were his sacred birds. "Few mortals can hear them." He put down his lyre and stroked my hair. "Let me love you in a little while, dear, and right now I'll give you the power to see the future."

I already loved Apollo. How blessed I was that he wanted to love me too, which had to mean that, really, he already did.

"If you'd like something else, tell me."

I tossed back my head.

"You won't see my future or the future of any deity." Feather light, his hand caressed my cheek. "You won't see the near future of yourself or any other mortal seer because seers can act against their own predictions. You'll see only their more distant future. It isn't in my power to give you those abilities. Understand?"

I nodded. The enormous, important future! If I'd been good for Troy as kanephoros, how much better I'd be as a prophet.

And I'd discover which man I was destined to marry.

"You'll be the mortal of truth as I'm the god."

"I'll help people avoid their mistakes."

He corrected me. "Small mistakes, not big ones. The dread ship of fate is almost impossible to turn."

A sea breeze brushed my face. Why would the ship of fate sail to Troy? And why was it *dread*? Father was a good king, and we'd lived in peace for as long as anyone could remember.

Apollo's eyes shifted from me and then returned. He raised one eyebrow. "It seems I can't grant future sight to you without also bestowing it on your twin. Do you mind?"

I pitied Deiphobus, Helenus's rival, because my twin would certainly use prophecy against him. Still, I tossed back my head. I'd balance Helenus's mischief with my power.

Apollo told me to lie back on the bench. He spread his hand across my forehead. A cloud of shining dust motes collected around me. I gasped for breath as specks of the future in tiny instants poured into my mouth. My nostrils filled with them. They pounded in my ears. I gagged, then inhaled, and they tingled down my throat.

Deep within, they melted into me. Memories of the past joined visions of the future.

I could examine them later, but the god was waiting. I opened my eyes and sat up. That wasn't so bad. I smiled shakily at him.

He moved closer, so near I smelled the clove oil on his skin. He tipped up my chin. His face neared my face—his ageless, unchanging god's face! My stomach rose into my throat. He kissed my lips.

Ai! I swallowed the bile and pushed—no, shoved!—him away.

His face reddened. "You do this to me?" He stood.

I collapsed back. I'd angered a god. And I'd been a fool to think that loving me had merely meant I was dear to him.

Over the fear drumming in my ears, I heard him say, "I'll return tomorrow. Do not offend me again."

3

As soon as he left, the future unrolled as a bolt of linen sliding downhill on bumpy ground—fast, fast, pause, fast, pause. And so on. A blur, then a cavern with copper walls where a young man who reminded me of Father sat on a couch. Scenes flashed by. Stopped. Wide-sailed ships filled our harbor. How beautiful!

Behind my eyelids, red bloomed. A clamor rose: hoof-beats, war cries, screams. No!

Yards of cloth unfurled in a rush, a chaos of battling warriors. The fabric caught. I saw my beloved brother, Hector, curled on the ground outside Troy's wall, a spear through his chest, and knew that he had died. Ai!

My own chest heaved with sobs. The future rocked by in a sea of my tears, too blurry for me to see.

Eventually, I calmed. I would warn Hector. He'd live.

My spirit drifted above ashes that had been Troy. I knew the city had burned, but I had missed how soon the fire blazed—in three years or three hundred.

As I watched, Troy seemed to rebuild itself, as mighty as ever. An air current lifted me and bore me along. Cities punched up on the plains and mountain valleys surrounding Troy. An invisible stylus etched spidery lines—roads—between the cities. The lines widened. Dots moved along the roads, faster and faster.

Something crossed the sky above me, its passage too straight to be a bird. It disappeared over the horizon, but another succeeded it. They came and went, gaining even greater speed.

The breeze gentled me as the visions faded. Ordinary sleep claimed me.

Full daylight in the sacred grove. A crow cawed. I stretched and smiled at Apollo, who sat by my head with a bowl of grapes in his lap. His hand was soft on my arm.

I stiffened, remembering his kiss—and my visions. Yes, this was the gift I asked for, but the god of prophecy knew I'd see Hector die. He—protector of children— should have protected me. I was barely a child, but I still was one. Mother, if she were here, would be furious too, no matter that he was Apollo.

I jumped up. "Don't touch me!"

Apollo frowned, seeming surprised. "I gave you your wish."

"Do you think I *wished* to see my brother Hector"—I snarled—"*beloved* of Apollo, killed in battle—"

"I'll fight at his side."

"But he'll die. And you knew it!"

Apollo's voice was calm. "Every tale ends with the death of the hero, unless he becomes immortal, which happens rarely. It's the lot of mortals to die. What's important are their great deeds before they die. Troy will have many heroes." He held out the bowl. "Have a grape, love, and fulfill your promise."

I couldn't! I wouldn't! And Mother and Father would be disgusted with me if I did. "I don't want your grapes." I stormed away.

Behind me, the crows cawed:

> *"On a snowy night, the wolf*
> *smells the bone-white hare,*
> *and rage burns bright in the god of light."*

I'd run only a few yards before a wind blew back my hair, plastered my beautiful peplos against me, and lifted me.

A breathy voice whooshed in my ears. "Eurus, east wind. No harm meant."

The kind words lessened my anger and made me sensible.

Eurus returned me to Apollo, who paced between me and the bench. "This is how you repay me? This is how a worshipper serves her god?"

Eurus wafted away.

Mother came to mind again, sitting innocently at her loom, believing Hector would live a long life. My eyes pricked. I smiled shakily. "Thank you for the gift of prophecy"—I took a shuddering breath—"and for honoring me by wanting to kiss me." I swallowed. "I apologize for my anger." It wouldn't help Hector if the god remained angry at his sister.

Apollo stood still. "Dear, I honor very few by loving them." He smiled, seemingly fondly. "You know that."

"But I mustn't love you beyond what a worshipper does. My—"

His frown started.

"My p-parents would think ill of me."

The frown deepened. "Disapproval, *dear*, weighs little compared to a god's favor."

"I'd b-be d-disgraced." Against the god's tight mouth and red face, terrified, I went on. "I c-can't k-kiss you."

Apollo went back to pacing.

"I still revere you!"

"*Reverence* isn't what I want from you." He added after a moment, "I've discovered that a god's gift may not be withdrawn, but it may be cursed. I won't curse your innocent twin, however, who received the gift when you did." Apollo grew until he was twice my height, glowing, more beautiful than ever.

I raised my hands in front of me, as if I could ward off whatever my punishment would be.

"When you prophesy, you won't be believed. Your warnings won't be heeded."

I gasped out, "You may kiss me if Hector won't die."

One side of his mouth curled into a half smile. "I can't save him." He stared over my head and then met my eyes again. "But I can save you. In Delphi, you can be my oracle and I'll withdraw the curse."

What would happen that would make me need saving?

The god thought I'd desert my brother? Resentment made me brave. "You don't know the maiden you say you love."

"It was your choice." He mounted his pedestal and hardened to marble.

I staggered to the bench and sat. Would I die soon after Hector had? Or might I live a full life? Should I look?

I shouldn't.

But I could discover how far into the future I would find myself. Silly me, I still wanted to see my husband and find out how many children we had.

Did I have to lie back again to see?

No. The future was woven into me now.

Six years from now, I worked at my loom in the women's quarters. My expression had settled into sadness. I was unwed, or my husband had died—otherwise, I would have been weaving in his house. No baby's cradle rocked near me.

In six more years, I couldn't find myself. Troy was rubble.

Wisdom warned me not to visit my death, but I couldn't resist. A laurel branch lay on the ground near my foot. I held the branch in my lap as if it might protect me.

An older version of myself—but not old—stood at the prow of a ship, savoring the sea breeze. This me-to-be, whose tan face was tinted pink, looked prettier than I thought myself. The hem of my peplos had a green droplet design, probably woven by Mother.

At my side was a tall man, regal, almost as old as Father was now. His arm rested heavily on my shoulder. I felt iron dislike for him, but I dared not step away.

I squeezed my eyes shut. My death would be next.

In the living room of a palace I didn't recognize, a rageful woman I'd never met swayed before me. While my present self rocked back and forth on the bench, my future self heard screams, smelled blood, felt the bite of her knife.

I died.

I threw myself on the grass and sobbed.

Who was the angry woman? Why did she kill me? Did all the gods hate me?

Please forgive me for anything I've done! Please spare Troy!

When my tears finally stopped, I stood up and let the laurel go. I'd wept myself dry. I couldn't bear to look ahead again for the events that led to my death—I could guess. Troy must have fallen in the war I'd glimpsed. If my parents hadn't died, I'd have been separated from them—but probably at least Father was dead.

Another time, I'd see. For now, I wanted to peer just a minute ahead.

Soon, in the women's quarters, Mother would stretch

in her bed, roll over, and go back to sleep. How dear her face was, and her hand too, curled above the sheet.

In a minute, Aminta would sit up and wake Melo to ask where I was.

In the kitchen, a serving girl would scratch her arm. The kitchen air would be tangy with the scent of sardines. In his bedroom, Father would splash water on his face from the basin by his bed. He would straighten, his expression serious while beads of water coursed along his cheeks. He'd probably be planning the tasks of the day and what would be best for Troy.

Apollo hadn't cursed Helenus's gift, and Helenus loved our parents too. Together, we'd save them and the city. I was still lucky to be able to see the future.

The god said that the dread ship of fate is almost impossible to turn. *Almost* meant it could be done.

I left the sacred grove, remembering my yesterday self, who hoped to see the future to save someone from biting into a spoiled scone.

Troy loomed ahead, its white limestone wall tinted pink by the dawn. Though I'd seen it dozens of times from the outside and even more times from within the city, I saw it fresh now.

How bright it was! Above the shining limestones, the wall's height was doubled by a second wall, this one made of mud bricks and wooden beams, striped horizontally with green, purple, and coral paint. Father declared our wall stronger, better made, and handsomer than the wall of any city he'd ever visited.

What army could breach such a wall? Would Zeus himself destroy us?

The east gate arched over me. Inside, Maera wagged her whole rear half at me.

I crouched. "Did you spend the night here, Little Faithful? Whatever your future, I'll save you." I stroked her back, then straightened. "Come!" I started off along the inside of the wall, rather than entering the Way of the Immortals.

Maera ran ahead of me and kept looking back, her mouth agape in a doggy smile.

The god had said that I couldn't see the near future of myself or another prophet, which seemed to be true. I couldn't foretell where my twin would be in a few minutes, but I already knew that he rode out of Troy every morning to exercise his horse.

We turned right into narrow streets, winding along gaily painted but shabby houses. A knot of seven men turned out of a lane, arguing and laughing. A gang of girls and boys raced by, chasing a piglet. Ordinary Troy, but precious too.

Without foreseeing, I imagined what might come: this street aflame; these children, wailing; the air choking them, hot dust swirling around their ankles.

I stopped. Maera sat.

Hadn't the god of prophecy known I would push him away? He must have checked ahead to see.

My mouth fell open. When he looked, there had to have been a different future! In that one, I didn't refuse him. I might have chosen to be his oracle, or he might have *loved* me while I was still half-asleep, without me meaning to.

I had already changed the future, effortlessly. Now I'd put my whole self into it and hope that would be enough. "We can do it, Maera!" I set off again.

She barked once, an enthusiastic *Yes!*

Helenus slouched outside the stable yard's wooden gate. He was taller and stockier than I was and looked as old as his rival, Deiphobus, who was four years older at eighteen.

I rushed to him with Maera frolicking at my side. When I reached him, my olive eyes gazed into his olive eyes. His were red-rimmed, as I supposed mine were too.

Maera nuzzled his legs.

He gripped my hands. "You can see too?"

I nodded.

"I wondered." He gestured at a wooden bench under a spindly oak tree. Not a dog lover (or even liker), he ignored Maera.

We sat facing the stable yard gate. Maera lay at my feet.

Helenus was in all my earliest memories. We fell sick together from the same childhood ailments. We used to argue over the importance of the two-minute difference in our age. I was older, which he didn't like. When we fought, he was stronger but ticklish, as I was not. He hated the helplessness of being made to laugh.

He said, "I was walking back from the festival with our brothers—not including Deiphobus—when light seemed to pour into me. I groaned. Everyone looked at me. I stammered something and waved them on." He broke off. "You understand."

I nodded. "For me, it felt like dust motes."

"At home, I went to my room. I lay on my bed, where understanding came. Most of it was dreadful."

What I'd seen so far was, but most of the rest was dreadful too?

"Do you know why we have this power? It's from Apollo, isn't it?"

"I went to his altar after the games." I was too embarrassed to tell him about the god starting to kiss me. "I angered him somehow. He cursed my power so that no one will believe me, but he said they'll believe you."

"Oh. Ah."

After that, we were silent. In the stable, a horse neighed.

"I saw my death." I swallowed more tears. "And Hector's body lay in the dust. I know Troy burned. Then I stopped looking. How much did you see?" If his voice told me, rather than my eyes seeing it, the news might be easier to take in. "Did you see yourself die?"

"Yes. I'll survive the war and will live to be old."

I hugged him around the shoulders. "Oh, I'm glad you'll be old!" I laughed—I was eager to laugh. "Ancient, I hope! Others survived too?" I watched his face.

"Mother, but she'll be enslaved." His Adam's apple bobbed. He stared at the sturdy oak gate. "The survivors will be slaves."

Ai! I must have been a slave on that ship. "You'll be a slave?"

"No." He didn't explain.

I asked again, "How much did you see?"

"Everything. From now until your death and mine much later."

"Apollo told me that the ship of fate is hard to turn, but he didn't say it was impossible. We'll make a plan. You can warn Father and Mother."

He let my hands go and stood. "The war will be about a Greek woman named Helen. She'll come here, but the Greeks will want her back. They'll fight for her."

We had to stop her from coming!

He beamed despite his bloodshot eyes. "Cassandra, you've never seen anyone so lovely. Her lips! Her eyes, as big as . . ." He struggled. "Er . . . as big as eggs—but they don't look like eggs! They look like beautiful eyes."

I grinned at his awkwardness, but why was he telling me about her?

"It isn't just her beauty. It's the way she looks at people." His voice cracked. "She needs me. Only *I* can make her happy."

I swallowed a smile. How could he make her happy? He was my age, and wasn't she grown up? "How old is she?"

He waved the question away. "My important moment won't come for years. But now, just seeing her in the future, I love her."

I stopped breathing. He was going to tell me he wouldn't try to save Troy because of this woman.

He said it. "I won't do anything that could keep her away—or even make her leave quickly."

I reached down and petted Maera's head. "You were just pretending to be sad."

He fell back a step. "I wasn't!"

I stood too and so did Maera. "You can go to this Helen instead of waiting here for her. I'll help you." How would I help him? "We'll know where she's going to be. You can join her there."

He tossed back his head. "She's far away in Sparta. I

could die going there. If we don't meddle, her arrival is certain. Cassandra . . ." He came close and took my hand again. "Our gift can't answer the question, *What if?* I've tried. You can imagine helping me reach Helen, but we can't tell what will happen."

"I marched with a stone cutting my foot because I didn't want anything bad to befall Troy. Even without prophecy, we can create the future we want." I squeezed his hand, hating my next words: "Meanwhile, I'll help you against Deiphobus." I smiled the smile that always succeeded with Father.

He swung my hand away. "Keep your help. I want to bring my brother low myself. In the future, he's supposed to marry Helen. That's the part I hope to change. She should marry me."

He didn't care about altering the future to save my parents—or me.

"Cassandra, I believe that fate is stronger than prophecy, and chance is powerful too. You may live. I may die." He unlatched the stable yard gate.

I shouted, "The gods hate heartless people! You'll be punished." But I wasn't sure.

He entered the stable. I heard him speaking to his horse. I shouldn't have told him that no one would believe my prophecies.

Since changing Troy's future would be entirely up to me, I had to know all of it. I sat and clutched the edge of the bench at my sides.

I saw again the young man in the copper cavern and noticed a boy with him, his son, judging by the boy's features. The two sat on separate couches. I watched, listened, smelled. The man, called Paris, as I discovered, promised someone I couldn't see not to be tempted. His son—named Corythus—lowered himself sideways to recline on his couch. But his head didn't go all the way down. He seemed to be resting on an invisible pillow or lap.

Paris spoke to the boy and to a being I couldn't see, named Oenone, who could be a deity, since Apollo said my gift wouldn't extend to them. Or she could be a seer, like I was, since he'd also told me I wouldn't be able to see myself or any other seers in the near future, which this was, just two days from today.

The scene continued and moved on to other scenes with other invisible beings. Paris pronounced the names of three goddesses—Hera, Athena, and Aphrodite—and seemed to be addressing them.

Gradually, understanding came, though still with gaps.

I bit my cheeks and tasted blood. I foresaw it all, except my death. Why watch that twice?

My mouth felt dry. I opened my eyes and breathed

slowly, taking in the earthy smell of horses. My sandaled feet were gray from the dusty road. Maera whined. What would happen to her?

I hadn't looked at that.

I hugged her, and she licked my face. Then I gazed ahead. Hurrah! She was going to live to a great age for a dog. In nine years, a band of Amazons would come to Troy and the youngest of them would save her from being bitten by a snake. Not much later, before the fall of the city, I would entrust Maera to a shepherdess whose hut would be outside the city wall, who would keep her safe and be her last mistress. Giving up my dog would make me almost as sad as everything else.

But this vision, at least, augured well for someone— Maera.

I thought about the rest of what I'd seen and refused to cry again.

How rickety was the ladder that ascended to Troy's ruin! So many rungs seemed unlikely. If I took out just one of them, the climb would be broken. We'd be saved.

I had an idea.

5

In a few minutes, Father's columned palace gulped in Maera and me. On the top step to the women's quarters, I stopped and Maera sat. Our quarters wrapped around the courtyard below, which was open to the sky. Though the quarters had a roof, the sun gave us light.

My idea was to overcome Apollo's curse gradually. If I predicted little events correctly, people would have to begin to believe me. Then when I warned them of danger, they'd listen. Common sense would demand it.

Closest to the courtyard, along the balcony rail, where the light was best, were our looms, carding combs, and spindles—everything we needed to make cloth. Beyond them, separated by chest-high screens instead of walls, were the sleeping nooks of the palace women, including Mother, me, my sisters, my aunts, their children, and the women who waited on us. The nooks became darker the farther they were from the courtyard, some so inky that oil lamps were needed even at noon.

Most of the women were at their work. Their young sons and daughters played nearby. Dogs chased each other in the aisle between the looms and the nooks. Maera raced off to join her many friends.

How peaceful the scene was.

As I'd hoped before the festival, my loom had been moved next to Mother's. My cousins were on my other side, Aminta closest to me.

Mother's loom was empty. In future-sight, I saw her in the kitchen a moment from now, supervising the cooks, who were preparing lunch, which would be served in an hour.

Kynthia rushed to me. "Inconsiderate princess! To make us wait so long to hear what happened!"

Melo, Aminta, and I followed her to our sleeping cranny, where she sat me on my bed. She took one side of me and Melo the other.

If only we were friends! Then I'd tell them everything and how afraid I was.

Aminta sat on her own bed. "Did Apollo visit you?"

"He gave me the gift of prophecy." I'd try my idea out on them.

"No!" Melo bounced on the bed.

"Why to you?" Kynthia sounded indignant. "Did you give him something in return?"

I tossed my head back. "No. Apollo isn't a trader at the market." But he was.

"Everyone's future, or just your own?" Melo asked.

"Everyone's. I'll show you." My idea called for a prediction that would come true quickly. "In a minute, Dirce will announce that she finished her tapestry." Dirce was my older brother Pammon's wife.

"Apollo toyed with you," Kynthia said. "Last time I looked, she had a yard of bare warp left."

"Your sister-in-law is almost as slow as you are." Aminta touched my arm. "Sorry! Your weaving is beautiful."

"Done!" Dirce cried. "At last."

Kynthia shrugged. "Predict something important."

"Nothing important is about to happen," I said, "but Mother will come in with Myrtes in a moment."

I expected them to tell me this was hardly a prediction, because Myrtes always played his flute for us at this time, and Mother never missed a performance.

Melo said, "Not today."

Kynthia stretched. "This is the one day he won't play."

Had someone said he wouldn't?

Had Apollo tricked Helenus and me and showed us a false future? I hoped that future was false!

"I believe he has a stomachache," Aminta said. "I should get back to my loom."

The others followed her, so I joined them. Myrtes would bring understanding by coming or not coming. I'd barely begun spinning when Mother arrived with the musician, who started playing his usual stately songs.

I took in how lovely Mother still was. By the time Troy fell, narrow lines would run down her cheeks as if her tears had formed channels.

My eyes moistened.

Myrtes finished playing, bowed, and left.

I swallowed hard and whispered, "I told you he'd play!"

"He wasn't going to," Melo said. "I imagine his belly just felt better."

"Or your mother told him he had to play, no matter how sick he felt." Kynthia put down her spindle and yawned. "Maybe your prophesying doesn't include stomachs or mothers."

This was maddening!

Three crows flapped down from the sky above the courtyard and perched on the balcony railing. They cawed:

"Moles tunnel between Hades
and the roots of trees.
Trojans stumble from guess to error,
seeing only what they believe."

My cousins and the other women concentrated on their cloth making and didn't look up.

I whispered to Aminta, the safest cousin, "Look at the crows."

"Where?"

I pointed.

"No crows, Cassandra." She frowned. "You must be tired from yesterday." Her brow smoothed. "You should rest."

I put down my shuttle. Mother had begun weaving, arms and fingers flying.

"It's perfect!" I touched the finished cloth rolled at the top of her loom.

Her weaving slowed but didn't stop. "I'm making a longer peplos for Laodice. She's too old for her knees to be showing." Laodice was one of my younger sisters.

"She'll love it," I said.

"The music was especially fine today. I breathe deeper when Myrtes plays."

"Was he sick with a stomachache earlier this morning?"

"No. I asked after his health." She pulled her shuttle through her warp.

I stood at my loom and didn't move. If Melo had made either of my predictions, no one would have disagreed. Seemingly, my cousins had to disbelieve me, regardless of the likelihood that I'd be right. My fingers trembled as I picked up my spindle.

Kynthia noticed. "Apollo didn't make your fingers nimbler. Perhaps he wished someone else was kanephoros. Maybe he saw *me* in the procession!"

I didn't care about her teasing. She seemed to have shrunk since yesterday.

"Cassandra just has to get used to not being kanephoros anymore." Melo smiled at me. "I would have to."

Maybe I had to continue to predict and be right and eventually people would remember and realize I was a seer.

The monotony of weaving freed my mind to recall that the future could be changed, and that there would be many chances to change it before the Greeks came. The next opportunity would be in the cavern on Mount Ida, which was a mere twenty miles from Troy, but lions prowled between here and there, and I'd never been farther from the city than the sacred grove, the sea, and the Scamander River all no more than two miles away.

What else might I do? Could I persuade another god to

lift my curse? Or convince Apollo to forgive me and lift it?

I went back to Mother and asked her if I could go to the sacred grove again.

"You may always go to the sacred grove." She hugged me.

I hunched around her belly and felt better.

"My pious daughter." She let me go. "Did Apollo send you a dream?"

Ah. I nodded, planning my words. "In my dream, I saw a man and a woman enter Troy, bringing trouble. You and Father knew the man. You were happy to see him, so you let both of them stay. Then the dream changed." I squeezed Mother's arm, stopping her shuttle. "Troy was in flames." My voice broke. "If these people arrive, please send them away!"

She hugged me again and whispered in my ear, "Fire in a dream is cleansing. Visitors bring prosperity. The dream was a gift from the god, who loves you."

Who hated me.

"Before you go to the sacred grove, your father wants to see you. He didn't congratulate you yesterday."

As soon as I started for the stairs, Maera ran to me, sure I wouldn't want to leave her behind.

I crouched. "Do you believe me when I say you'll spend the day at the east gate waiting for me?"

She licked my face, wagged her tail, and grinned the happy face I loved.

The servants at the entryway to our living room let me in. I signaled to Maera. She whined but sat.

Among the many couches, his arms raised, my father prayed to Zeus at our home altar. Incense blessed the air. The tip of his sharp nose stuck out of the smoke.

Smoke! Father's sandals would be sizzling when he fought a Greek soldier with only his knife. The soldier would have a battle-ax.

I blinked and forced the future away.

He intoned, "All-powerful Zeus, I pray you to grant us sun and gentle rain." His eyes found me. "I pray you, give Hecuba and me a healthy baby who is as steadfast as our Cassandra." He backed away from the altar.

Pouches would puff out under his keen eyes after Hector died. I rushed to him and hugged him around his chest.

"What's this?" He led me to a couch. The webbing sagged when we sat. "Is something amiss?"

"A dream I had in the sacred grove." I described it and told him Mother's interpretation. "What if she's wrong?" I wanted him to promise to think twice about the couple when they came.

He returned to the altar, where he prayed for sweet slumber for me.

How kind he was, to trouble Zeus on my behalf.

He came back. "Your mother loves to interpret dreams, and she's usually right." He laughed. "Last week, I dreamed the baby will come out baby-size but with wrinkles and gray hair. Hecuba is sure it means the baby will grow up to be wise."

"What if my dream comes to pass as I dreamed it?"

He said what I used to believe: that Troy was mighty and had no enemies. "Your mother may be right about the dream's meaning. Or you may have been a little over-wrought by the festival." He kissed my forehead. "Darling, I congratulate you. That pebble!" He shook his head. "Anyone else would have stumbled, even a hero."

How wonderful he was. How lucky I was—we all were—but not for much longer.

6

Maera whimpered when we reached the east gate. I rubbed her soft ears and gave her the meaty bone from my offering basket, which I carried in my arms today.

Ignoring the treat, she watched me leave. When I was a few yards beyond the gate, though, I looked back, and she was eating.

A quarter hour later, not much after noon, I reached the sacred grove, where priests were tidying around the altar of Hermes, the messenger god. I nodded to them and went to Apollo's glade just as three crows landed on the god's statue.

I set a bowl of briny green olives on the altar, then prostrated myself on the grass. My voice was tight. "Apollo, protector of the young, please forgive me."

No answer that I could hear.

"If you won't forgive me," I pleaded, "save the others. Give my gift to someone else, who can warn my parents and be believed."

I waited, but when I peered ahead, Troy still burned. His crows cawed:

> *"The flea, the ant, the tiny creatures*
> *scrabble and scramble to stay alive.*
> *Men don't worry about their affairs.*
> *Apollo's lyre drowns out*
> *his worshippers' prayers and cares."*

After Apollo, I left gifts on the altars of Hera, Athena, and Aphrodite in their clearings. These three would be with the man Paris in the cavern. I spoke at length to each goddess, telling them how much I admired them, how marvelous Troy was, what a just king Father was. Then I begged them to leave Paris alone, which I believed would stop everything, though I didn't know why.

Not one appeared or sent a sign.

I continued to the other great gods and goddesses, leaving them grapes, raisins, dried and fresh figs, honey cakes, dried pork, and jars of goat's milk. I prayed to each to intercede for me with Apollo. The day wore on, and my only answer was a deeper quiet than usual.

Sound returned when I continued to the lesser gods and goddesses, whose clearings were on the outskirts of the grove. There, birds sang and leaves whispered. I had one offering left, a wool packet holding three heads of garlic.

At the altar to Eurus, god of the east wind, a breeze freshened the air. He was the god who'd blown me back to Apollo yesterday and had reassured me. Out of gratitude, I placed the packet on his gray stone altar near his statue, which was made of wood rather than marble. I'd have sat on his bench, but he didn't have one, so I just stood a few feet away from the altar.

How different he—or his statue—was from beautiful Apollo. Eurus was handsome in a rough way—stocky, with bulging muscles.

He stood, legs apart, arms out, as if for balance. The thick locks of his hair massed in clumps. A fringe of curly beard outlined his jaw. His nose was round, as were his cheeks. His left eyebrow was a little higher than his right, and the lopsidedness put me at ease.

I started to leave without a prayer for aid, because a lesser god probably couldn't influence Apollo, but when I heard laughter, I turned. The living god sat cross-legged on his altar, laughing. His tunic billowed in a wind I didn't feel.

I ran. He was lesser, but still a god.

As I was nearing the great gods again, a voice spoke in

the wind. "I'm a fool. I didn't mean to frighten you."

I stopped, unsure what to do.

A breeze spun slowly around my head. "You gave me a gift, and I terrified you. That's why I'm a fool. A buffard! A saddle-goose!"

This god was nothing like Apollo. I wondered if the god of truth had ever criticized himself, say, when he was truly—not eternally—young.

I returned to Eurus's altar.

He paced up and down where his statue had been. "She's back, and I'll probably do some dizzard thing again. She should know I won't mean to."

Still a little frightened, I said, "I'm not afraid anymore."

"You're not?" His frown turned into a smile. His eyes closed to slits, and his round cheeks became even rounder. I'd never seen anyone but Maera look so happy.

My fear evaporated. I smiled back.

"Oh!" He looked startled. "You're smiling."

I blurted, "Are you as old as Apollo?"

He tossed back his head. "No! I'm the youngest wind, not much older than you are. Notus got tired of blowing south and east and asked for another brother. The poets don't even know about me yet. My brothers call me a lesser lesser god."

We were as equal as god and mortal could be. My smile widened. "You're not lesser lesser!"

He blew out a stream of air. "I haven't thanked you by eating your gift. Buffard! As I told you." He popped a head of garlic in his mouth and chewed. He waved his arm, sending a gust that blew me backward a yard or two.

My eyes watered. I coughed and choked in a wind that seemed more garlic than air. The gale died. I could breathe again.

"I hardly ever get gifts. This is a good one."

"I'm glad."

"Why are you making offerings today when there was a festival yesterday?" He leaned toward me.

Even that sent a garlicky breeze. I wondered if he liked mint.

"The great gods won't care what you tell me. No matter what you say, I won't hurt you. How's that?"

He might think I deserved Apollo's punishment. He might change his mind and set his wind against me wherever I went.

"Your basket is big. You must have made many offerings before mine."

"I'll bring more! I can go now and be back soon."

"I'm not angry!"

He seemed angry.

He paced again. "I wouldn't hurt her even if I *was* angry! I didn't hurt her when I brought her to Apollo. Didn't she notice?" He stopped in front of me. "People don't pay attention to a lesser god. Even the god of Troy's own river, Scamander, has few worshippers. Do you think of us wind gods when there's a tempest?"

Blushing, I tossed back my head.

"You think only of Zeus and his thunderbolt. It doesn't occur to you that we might mind."

My mouth fell slack with surprise.

He yelled, "What did Apollo do to you?" He dropped his voice. "I mean, if you'd like to tell me."

I smiled again.

He sat on his altar. "The god of truth doesn't have much imagination."

Apollo failed to imagine how I'd feel when I saw Troy's future. I explained what had happened. "I should have understood his meaning."

"He should have realized you didn't."

"Because of his curse, you won't believe my prophecies."

"Apollo can't enchant me. He must have meant only mortals."

I wasn't sure. "There will be war between the Greeks and the Trojans."

"Go on."

"Do you believe me?"

"War is never a great surprise."

I laced my fingers together. That didn't sound like belief.

Maybe it was, though. My cousins had argued with me

when I'd predicted the almost certainty of Myrtes playing his flute.

I began, including my conversation with Helenus. Somehow, I managed not to cry again. However, to my astonishment, Eurus held his head in his hands and wept when I described my death. I unlaced my fingers. Here was a god who didn't think mortals' suffering was puny. A knot in my chest loosened.

I dared to sit next to him. The warm air seemed to warm even more. I didn't know how to comfort him, but I tried: "I'll save my dog."

"I'm glad." His voice was strained. He still held his head.

"It would be a good gift if it weren't cursed. I'd be glad if I could warn people." I didn't think he had the power, but I asked: "Can you make people believe me?"

"No." He looked up, eyes still wet. "I control only the east wind. If I tried and angered Apollo, he might ask Zeus to doldrum me, and the lord of the gods would. Then I wouldn't be able to raise even a wisp of a breeze. I'd be no use to you."

"Can you help me a little?"

"Maybe."

How? "I didn't understand the beginning, the part in the cavern with the man called Paris. I can't see gods and goddesses in the future at all. Or seers in the near future, including me."

"I may be able to explain some of what will happen in the cavern."

I twisted to face him.

"Last night, a mortal king and a sea nymph were wed on Mount Olympus. There was a banquet. I went, even though lesser gods are always snubbed at these affairs." He shrugged. "The food was excellent." He grinned. "Not just garlic."

"I'll bring other offerings!"

"We had chicken, lamb, and mutton. Plump and perfect."

He described every dish. The shadows lengthened.

Finally, he said, "The meal ended, as always, with drafts of ambrosia."

Ambrosia was the honeyed drink of the gods.

"When we put down our goblets, Eris rushed in."

She was the goddess of discord, nonpareil at making trouble.

"Eris was smiling, which soured my mouth. No one had invited her. Who would? She rolled a golden apple down the table and pranced off. When the apple stopped, by a platter of lamb bones, I saw these words etched into it: 'For the Fairest.'

"Everyone wanted it. I did too. I'm not splendid the way Apollo is, but looked at by an appreciative eye, I have an air and features that outshine the others." He slid off the altar and struck a pose, leaning forward, hurling an imaginary discus. Ropy muscles bulged in his arms. "Don't you think?"

I didn't giggle. He was far from ugly. His form had energy that the great gods lacked. He was a force!

Still, he was far from the perfect beauty of the great gods.

"Er . . ." Mother's politeness came to my rescue. "Judging between you and the other gods is like comparing the fig with the pear. Both are delicious."

"Exactly!" He laughed. "That Eris! But you understand."

His laughter lifted my hair.

He laughed harder. "We didn't even need Eris's apple. Hephaestus could make a golden apple with that inscription for any of us."

Hephaestus was the god of metalworking and sculpture.

Dusk was falling. I could hardly make out Eurus's features.

"But no one thought of that." His laughter faded. "Gods and goddesses yelled at each other. The banquet table was overturned. The bride and groom fled. Ares punched Poseidon. A brawl began."

Ares was the god of war and Poseidon the god of the sea.

"Finally, we turned to Zeus. He refused to pick a winner, but he narrowed the contest down to three goddesses:

Aphrodite, Athena, and Hera."

Aphrodite was the goddess of love and beauty, but people said that Hera, Zeus's wife, was even lovelier than she was. I'd never heard anyone praise Athena's looks. She was the goddess of the city and also Apollo's half sister. Her statue resembled his, though her cheeks were a bit doughy.

Eurus continued. "Zeus told them to make the mortal Paris their judge, because he'd been honest in a contest among bulls."

Ah. That explained why this Paris spoke their names.

Eurus snorted. "From bulls to goddesses. Didn't he think there might be a difference? The goddesses are spending today and part of tomorrow making themselves even more beautiful. Then they say they'll visit Paris together."

I began to fit the puzzle together. Paris would bring on the wrath of the two goddesses he didn't choose.

But what did he have to do with Troy?

"I know who Paris is," Eurus said, "but it's growing dark, and you should go home. I'll tell you tomorrow."

Couldn't he give me a hint?

"Tomorrow," he repeated.

He wanted to guarantee that I'd come back! I hid my smile.

He called after me, "I'll be hungry again."

I did smile.

7

I left Eurus, greatly cheered. With the help of a god, even a lesser one, surely we could turn the dread ship of fate.

In the twilight, I stumbled over a branch that lay across the path out of the sacred grove. I picked it up and broke off a length.

At Troy's gate, Maera leaped and bowed. I threw the stick for her as we entered the Way of the Immortals. The stars and a quarter moon were out. Maera dropped the branch and dashed away.

I peeked into the very near future and saw her with my brother Hector. Soon, I made out a tall shape ahead and a smaller one, jumping and prancing. Hector was on his way home too. I sprinted. Eurus and I would save him!

He straightened from petting Maera, and we hugged. How solid he felt!

When I'd gone to Helenus—before I knew he'd betray Troy—he and I had merely clasped hands.

Hector and I separated and set off again. Maera walked on his other side because she loved him too. Her nails clicked on the stone. Our sandals pattered softly.

"Brother! Why are you out late too?"

"I was planting in the new orchard. A ewe insisted on grazing wherever I was about to put a cutting. She slowed me down." He laughed. "I kept letting her eat."

He was kind to everyone, even a pesky sheep.

Troy was extending its olive orchard, a project Father had begun a year ago. All my brothers helped, but Hector was the most faithful to the task.

"Why is the brave kanephoros roaming Troy in the dark?"

"The former kanephoros."

"But still brave. A poet will write a ballad called 'The Princess and the Pebble.'"

"The ewe will write one called 'The Prince and the Piggy Sheep.'"

He laughed. "She's probably baaing it to her flock right now."

How I loved to be with him. A lump rose in my throat.

We crossed the plaza and mounted the palace steps. Inside, lamps had been lit in the colonnade. We stood together, and I believed he was as reluctant to part as I was.

He smiled down at me. "Helenus visited the orchard in the afternoon. He didn't work, but he gave me good news. Tomorrow will be a wonderful day for me."

I checked. It would be.

"He says he can see the future and I'll meet my wife."

Hector was twenty-five, eleven years older than I was.

I nodded. "Andromache. She'll come from Thebe with her father and brothers." Thebe was a city to the east of us. "Her father wants more trade."

"Did Helenus tell you too?"

Oh! I could use Helenus's uncursed gift!

"He said you'll love each other very much. He said she's as sweet as you are."

His smile widened. "He told me she's pretty."

I sat on a bench between two columns. Maera sat at attention by my knees. Hector lowered himself next to me.

"You'll have a son."

"Really? He said that?"

"Yes."

Doubt crept into his voice. "The babe may be a daughter."

My idea was probably doomed. When the words came from my lips, no matter if I claimed someone else had said them first, they weren't believed. Unwilling to give up, though, I added, "Not all he said was happy news. He told me you'll die young"—my lips trembled—"in a battle with the Greeks."

He regarded me for a long moment. "I've had a premonition of my early death, but now I think I'll be old when I die."

People thought me so wrong they believed the opposite!

"Helenus frightened me." I tried to gain something. "If there is a war, will you be careful and not risk yourself when the tide is against you? Andromache will want to keep her husband!"

"I hope so!" He laughed. "But she hasn't married me yet. I'm not an elegant eater. She may get sick of me."

"She won't!"

He sobered. "Be a coward? No. But there won't be a war. You should be careful about believing your twin." He kissed my forehead and stood.

I didn't want him to go. "Have you heard of someone called Paris?" Hector had traveled as far as the city of Mygdonia in Thrace. He knew the world.

He sat again. His voice was tight. "He was our brother."

61

Was?

A brother I'd never heard of?

"How do you know his name?"

I lied again. "Helenus mentioned him but didn't explain."

"I wonder how he knows." Hector rubbed Maera's shoulders. "I was too young to understand when it happened, but as I got older, I heard whispers. Finally, I asked Mother. Have you ever seen her look anguished?"

I tossed back my head. Only in the future.

"Paris was born three years after I was. A seer warned that the baby would bring down Troy when he grew up and said our parents should kill him."

My hand crept to my chest and felt my thudding heart.

"They believed." Hector looked at the painting on the ceiling, where Aphrodite's swans flew against a blue-sky background. "But they couldn't bring themselves to do it, so they told their chief herdsman to slay him. He took the baby and brought back his tongue. Mother said she wept for a year."

I wet my lips. "No! Mother and Father wouldn't!"

Hector stroked my back. "It's true."

Maera licked my hand. I petted her head.

He smiled grimly. "I'm glad the prediction wasn't made about any of the rest of us."

I could barely breathe.

"I've forgiven them. I'm sure they were thinking of me and their unborn children and everyone else in the city."

"Couldn't they have done something else? Sacrificed to Zeus? Gone to Delphi to see if a god or goddess could be appeased to save him and us?"

"They may have sacrificed to all the gods and gone to Delphi without changing the prophecy." He paused. "Can you forgive them too? They love us."

When Helenus and I were six and suffered a month-long fever, Mother never left us. She let us have honey cake three times a day if we could eat it. Father came often too and stayed to tell us long-ago stories of Troy. "I think I can forgive them. But . . ." I trailed off.

How was Paris still alive?

Hector left me. Maera and I mounted the stairs to the women's quarters.

This brother, Paris, would enrage two goddesses. If he was bitter because Mother and Father had tried to kill him, would he direct the goddesses' wrath at Troy?

Upstairs, Mother was the only one still weaving. I paused before she saw me. At her feet were a glowing lamp and a tray, the dinner she had kept for me, including two thick slices of honey cake. How good she was to me and my brothers and sisters! How frightened she must have been when she heard the seer's prophecy all those years ago. I loved her too much to judge her.

She looked up. "You've been at the sacred grove all this time?"

"I was talking to Hector too."

"My worthy children. Finish all the cake. Don't give any to Maera. The dog is plump and you're too thin."

I hugged her and pressed my face into her shoulder.

She said I could return to the sacred grove tomorrow. "Go whenever you like. Suitors' parents like a pious girl, but don't neglect your weaving. They want a skillful girl too." She laughed. "Suitors themselves don't care much about skill or piety if the girl is as pretty as you are"—she chucked me under my chin—"and has your smile."

I managed to smile back.

After I worked at my loom for an hour the next morning, I went to the pantry next to the kitchen and filled a basket with offerings and another meaty bone for Maera. At the gate, she seemed happier about the bone than sad that I was leaving her.

When I reached the sacred grove, I set a bowl of almonds on Apollo's altar and again begged forgiveness for offending him. "Please let me turn the ship of fate."

He didn't appear.

I'll do it without you, I thought.

As soon as I started for Eurus's clearing, a wind sped me along.

He was sitting on his altar. "All for me?" He grinned at the basket.

I lowered it to the grass and stepped away.

He crouched over it, naming each item as he drew it out. "Barley griddle cake. Sheep cheese wrapped in leaves. Sweet onions mashed with lentils."

I folded my arms. I had a question and could hardly wait to ask it.

"Pickled eel. I haven't had any in six years and twelve days. Mm. Walnuts. What's this?" He looked at me and lifted the last dish. "An entire baked chicken? For me?" He tore off a leg. With his mouth full, he added, "Help yourself."

I nibbled a morsel of griddle cake. "Can your wind carry me to Mount Olympus?" If Zeus favored me, everything would stop before it began.

He tossed back his head, and his wind shook me. "Uninvited? Zeus would be so angry he'd create a new Eurus to replace me."

Oh.

I let his wind carry my disappointment away. I'd think of other ideas, or we would. "I know who Paris is. But how is he still alive?"

Eurus held up a finger for me to wait. He finished the chicken drumstick, sampled the eel, and closed his eyes to savor it.

He finally wiped his hands on his tunic. "My wind goes everywhere. Like your parents, the chief herdsman couldn't bring himself to kill the baby outright, so he left him on the mountain to die of cold or be eaten by an animal. Instead, a she-bear nursed him. When the herdsman found Paris still alive, he gave in and raised him." Eurus grinned. "A prince of Troy brought up to be a shepherd!"

"What about the tongue the herdsman gave my parents?"

"A deer's tongue." Eurus shrugged. "A deer's tongue is big. Maybe it was a fawn's tongue."

"Does Paris know he's really a prince?"

"His wife told him." Eurus explained that my brother had married Oenone, a mountain nymph who was also a seer.

Nymphs were deities but not immortal, though their lives could span hundreds of years. I'd never seen one. There were no statues of nymphs in our sacred grove. Oenone hadn't been in my visions because she was both a goddess and a soothsayer.

Eurus added, "Paris makes a big show, but he isn't much. A coward. Lazy. He let a wolf get a lamb when he was herding."

I looked into the future an hour from now. Paris would be reclining on a couch in the cavern I'd seen when I'd received Apollo's gift, but unlike in that vision, he seemed to be alone. Had he already judged the goddesses?

I peered another hour ahead and saw the boy in the cavern with him. One more hour brought forth the scene I'd watched outside the stable after Helenus and I had spoken. I believed that during that scene Paris would declare his judgment. "Eurus? Can your wind carry me to Mount Ida?"

"I can carry an ox that far!"

I laughed, imagining him bearing an enormous ox on the palm of one hand.

"An ox wouldn't try to save Troy." I shrugged. "Though I don't know how to save the city any more than an ox would." I didn't understand what judging beauty had to do with Helen, the woman my twin said would cause the war.

"Come!" Eurus strode away from me, following the path to the far gate to the grove, which faced east.

I followed, pushed from behind. Beyond the gate, our grasslands began.

He stopped and crouched. His wind calmed. "Hold tight to my head."

His curls were feather soft.

"Grip my back with your legs. Ready?" He jumped into the air without waiting.

A whirlwind whipped around us. He said, "Mustn't drop her."

The sacred grove descended, as if it was falling instead of us rising. My head bucked forward.

"Keep her in place, you clod!" Eurus yelled at himself.

Let me survive this wind-riding!

I clung to him as tight as I could, but the gale strengthened. My grip loosened. We were torn apart.

Beyond his wind, the air was calm. I hung for an instant. In that moment, I saw in my imagination Mother, Father, Hector, Helenus, Maera. I dropped.

8

Below flowed the muddy Scamander River. I tucked myself into a dive. My fingers were inches from the brown water when Eurus grabbed my ankles. We thudded onto the bank. I came down on my left hip and shoulder.

In the distance, sheep baaed.

He sat up and bellowed, "You let go! You wanted to fly by yourself?"

I mustn't yell at a god. I yelled, "I didn't let go! Your wind blew me away!"

His fury flattened the grass, but it had veered away from me. "I'm a fool! I think I can do anything. I don't think! Her fate and a city shouldn't depend on a dawkin like me. How am I going to tell her she should find somebody better to help her?"

I was amazed that a god blamed himself.

What should I do? I had to reach Mount Ida soon.

It hurt to stand, but I discovered that I could walk, and my limp eased after a few steps. Maybe the lions would be too busy today to bother with me.

"Where are you going?" Eurus called, sounding surprised.

"If a lion doesn't eat me, I'll reach Mount Ida before dark." My voice had a *harrumph* in it. He'd let me down—in more ways than one. "Maybe I won't be too late."

He walked backward in front of me. "But you should go with me. Lions won't bother me." He saw my confusion. "You thought I'd leave you here?" He didn't wait for an answer. "We'll go slower, not very high, side by side."

He put his arm around my waist, and I clasped his waist too. I felt dizzy. Melo and Aminta and I sometimes danced this close, but they never made my head spin!

His wind lifted us gently and pushed us along. The tall grasses scraped my ankles. I raised my knees, and it was as if I was sitting in a chair. How wondrous!

The wind gained strength. He held me tight. My skin felt whisked as if with a brush. I grinned, and my teeth tingled.

We passed a spreading hazel tree. Sheep and bony cows grazed on the brown-green grass. We kept pace with a heron flying along the river not much higher than we were, until it landed. The horizon ahead grew lumps. One lump rose more than the rest—Mount Ida. Like Zeus's Mount Olympus, its peak was cloud-wreathed.

Soon, we were close.

Would Paris hate me? Did he hate everyone in our family? Did he hate Troy?

The mountain appeared in stripes: green meadows below gray cliffs below white clouds.

We came down gently on a ledge above a ravine. Far below rushed a frothy river. A palace was embedded in the opposite rock wall with only the facade showing. A bridge, lined with coral-colored columns, spanned the gorge.

"That was better." Eurus shook out his arms. "Wasn't it?"

"Much better. It was a marvel." I smiled at him. "Thank you."

He blushed. "Good."

Three crows weighed down a branch of a spindly mountain ash that grew out of a crevice next to us.

"Do you see them?"

"Gloomy birds."

He saw them, though Aminta hadn't. I supposed mortals couldn't, except mortals touched by Apollo.

I chattered instead of crossing the bridge. "Isn't the palace facade beautiful?" The entrance was topped by a white stone frieze carved with women diving off rocks. "I guess the women are nymphs."

The goddesses could have arrived by now.

"Very grand," Eurus said.

I nodded and gulped.

"If you ask me to," Eurus added, "I'll douse your brother in the river. I'll spin him until he sees dozens of goddesses instead of three."

How kind he was! I laughed. "I don't know if it will help Troy for him to be wet and dizzy."

A man emerged from the entrance and hurried toward us, smiling. "Sister!"

I smiled back, but I doubt I looked truly glad.

His wife must have told him I was coming and who I was. He seemed not to be angry. He opened his arms wide. "Welcome! Welcome! Welcome!"

Though he was making a show, he still might mean it.

"Oh, sister." He had Father's high forehead and chiseled cheekbones and Mother's large gray eyes.

When he reached me, he stopped short, reached out, and touched my hair and then my shoulder. "*Sister. Family. The family that had me. How I relish the words.*"

The crows cawed their alarm:

> *"On Mount Ida a pitcher flower*
> *cradles sticky syrup in its blossom cup.*
> *A single sip will kill its prey!*
> *Cassandra, do not taste your brother's brew!"*

He wanted his family, which made me think, despite what the crows said, that he and I might save Troy. I drank.

Paris seemed unaware of the birds. Nodding to Eurus, he said, "Welcome."

Eurus nodded back, curtly.

"Thank you ever so much for coming with her."

I introduced him as the east wind.

"Then thank you for blowing her here." He paused. "Please tell me: Do my sister and I share a chin, in shape if not size? Are we sister and brother in chins?"

I resisted an urge to touch my chin.

"Your sister's chin is more pleasing than yours." Eurus allowed that our eyes were alike in shape, though not in color.

"Ah. At least there's that." Paris took my hand and tugged me along the bridge. "You're my beautiful sister, who cared enough about me to enlist a god to help you journey here. I'm fortunate to be your brother."

This was promising.

"Come and meet Oenone and Corythus, the family I made."

I stepped onto the bridge, which swayed. "Er . . . brother, three great goddesses haven't come yet, have they?"

"No. Oenone says they will, but now I don't think so."

Because of me.

"She's vexed—I don't know why—but she's been eager all day for your arrival."

The nymph could see my future, though I couldn't see hers. Was she eager because her fate was terrible too? Did she believe we could alter it?

Eurus followed us to the palace entrance. "Cassandra . . ." His chin puckered, and he frowned—an unhappy face. "I can't go into the earth. I'm sorry."

I'd hoped we'd turn the ship of fate together, but I didn't want him to be sad. "Thank you for the wind ride."

He recovered. "I won't drop you on the way back, either."

"Come, sister!"

My stomach tightened. I clasped my hands together. Face the great goddesses!

Inside, the air smelled metallic. Paris took a flaming torch from a torchère and led me into a corridor whose rock walls sparkled with silver specks.

"Follow me, sister. How dear that word is. Sissster!" He sounded like a snake.

I shuddered. "If you were home, the word would soon stop being valuable. You have six sisters and eleven brothers and another brother on the way." Why was I saying this? I didn't want him to come home.

"Eighteen of us? Nineteen soon! An army!"

Ominous word—*army*.

He added, "It's not a brother on the way, though Oenone says you can see the future."

I sighed. Because I'd predicted a brother, he was sure the baby would be a girl.

We turned into a cavern on the left. Polished copper walls, gleaming in torchlight, rippled with the mountain's contours. Fresh air suggested an opening to the outer world.

"Cassandra!" A woman, probably Oenone, rose from one of four couches, where she'd been sitting with a boy of five or six who had been reclining with his head in her lap. The boy lay back and stared at me.

Amid the couches was a long, low table for dining.

"Sister!" she added.

"This is Oenone," Paris said unnecessarily.

Sister by marriage. The nymph dashed—shimmered— to me. Copper strands glinted in her dark hair, and her iron-colored peplos rustled as she drew close.

Her face was delicate, her small features as finely shaped as Apollo's lyre.

"You've come." Laughing, she reached up and brushed back my hair. "You should carry a comb when you ride a wind or people will think the Furies have acrazed your mind. Everyone will see you're lovely anyway."

The Furies were the three goddesses of vengeance, who sometimes punished wrongdoers by making them madful. Hastily, I raked my hair away from my face. I must have looked like a Gorgon—a monster with snakes for hair.

She changed the subject. "Paris can't believe your prophecies. Don't blame him."

I didn't, or I'd have to blame everyone.

"Paris, your sister was kanephoros and endured pain for her city."

I blinked in surprise.

"I foresaw it. What did I tell you, love?"

He smiled down at her. "You said you're proud to be part of my family because of her and my brother Hector."

She slapped his arm playfully. "I'm not proud because of *you*! If anyone has the doggedness to change the terrible future, she does."

Oh my! Another person who believed in my determination.

"I'll be guided by you, sister," Paris said.

I breathed so deeply my toes felt it. "Don't judge the goddesses! The two you don't pick will hate you."

"That's what I told him. Common sense, really." She sat and lifted her son's head back onto her lap. "Cassandra, you must be tired. Would you like to rest?"

"Thank you, but I'm not tired." How formal I sounded.

The boy sat up. "Who's she?"

Paris sat next to him. "Corythus, this is your aunt Cassandra."

Oenone straightened her son's tunic and kissed the top

of his head. "Cassandra, if we succeed today, please teach me to weave. I will be terrible at it."

I sat on the couch nearest theirs. "All of Troy will admire your work."

If Paris didn't judge the goddesses, he could probably safely come to Troy. How wonderful that future would be, the city unscathed and me with this sister-in-law for a friend.

Was Troy saved already because Paris had promised to listen to me?

No. "Brother, how—"

"I adore the word *brother*! Sister, ask me anything you'd like to know."

I liked him even if Eurus didn't. "How long have you been married?"

"I started young. Six years ago when I was sixteen. Corythus is five."

"He married me because he wanted the love of a goddess, and no one higher would look at him." She addressed him, smiling. "I'm not angry. I love you because I love you. I need nothing more." She gripped his arm across their son. "I will never stop loving you. I will cease loving *me* when you choose someone else." She added, "The goddesses will be here in a few minutes."

The air seemed to turn solid in my throat. I imagined running out to Eurus and wind-flying away.

"Cassandra," Paris said, "I keep telling her that I, who was abandoned, will never abandon anyone. I love only her and our son."

Oenone waved a dismissive hand. "You love everyone. You love your sister, and you met her just a few minutes ago." She winked at me. "I've watched you for years. When I foresaw I was going to marry Paris, I—Oh! Now!"

The cavern trembled. The table hopped on its legs.

The entire mountain seemed to thunder around us. My heart boomed with it. I flew up and slammed down on my couch. Oenone wrapped her arms around Corythus, who was howling.

Mustn't run. Troy, I thought. Save Troy.

The mountain stilled. Three crows flapped through the cavern doorway and perched on the table, and three goddesses appeared behind Paris and Oenone's couch.

9

I recognized each goddess from her statue in the sacred grove. *Beautiful* was too mild a word to describe any of them.

Hera, goddess of marriage and the family, came to sit between Corythus and Paris, who jumped up. He went to his wife and took her hand. His knuckles popped out. I stood too.

Hera kissed Corythus's forehead, which made him laugh and lean into her. Even seated, her back was straight as a spear. In complexion, she was darkest—brown-black—with her black hair captured in a beaded net. She watched Paris.

Athena's gray eyes fastened on me. Her clear voice sparkled with anger. "You! You're the maiden who wounded my brother! He's precious to me."

"As my brothers are to me." What was I doing, arguing with the goddess of war? "Most will die when Troy falls." She was also goddess of the city.

"Foolish girl! Troy will rise again."

"Mortals die." Instructing me, Hera added, "You see, that's what makes them mortals."

As Apollo had said too. As everyone knew.

I glanced at Aphrodite because Apollo was her half brother too. Did I have two enemies?

But her expression was pleasant. The goddess of love and beauty stood no taller than a mortal woman. Her edges were soft, made with a brush rather than a stylus. Her golden hair tumbled in ringlets to her shoulders; her eyes were orbs of honey; her smile made me smile back.

Athena widened her stance, as if she was address-ing troops. "Hear us, mortals! There is a golden apple." Without asking if we already knew, she told us about the wedding feast. "All the gods wanted—"

Hera turned to Paris. "My husband says you're honest." Instructing me again, she added, "I'm the wife of Zeus, ruler of the gods."

Every toddler knew that!

Paris blushed. "I hope I'm honest."

It was beginning. But what else could he have said?

The crows spoke:

"Which is more bitter: love lost
or love unsought? If Paris is a fool,
he'll choose among the goddesses.
If he's wise and doesn't choose,
he'll suffer too."

Would Troy suffer either way?

"He's *dis*honest." Oenone managed a laugh. "He calls *me* the most beautiful." She patted his hand that held hers.

Clever. If he chose one of them, he'd have lied to his wife.

Hera laughed too. "I've many times called my husband the wisest. He likes it. Flattery sweetens marriage. It doesn't make me a liar."

Athena raised her hands in a quick, impatient gesture.

I stalled. "What will you do with the golden apple if you get it?"

"I'll put it in a headdress with the writing showing." Aphrodite touched her ringlets. "It will become me, don't you think, poppet?"

I nodded. A warty toad in her hair would become her.

"The apple will be sacred to me," Hera said, "and apple cakes, golden with cinnamon, will be served at wedding feasts."

Glaring at me, Athena said, "I'll give the apple to my brother to comfort him."

She didn't even want it!

They all turned to Paris and waited.

I burst out, "His choice will cause a war! People will die!"

Together, they began, "Mortals—"

"They don't always die young!" I cried. "Children will die! Women will be enslaved. They aren't always enslaved!" Was I persuading them? "Troy will be rubble!"

Hera asked Oenone, "Why is the maiden here? She doesn't understand what's important."

Ignoring this, I pressed on. "We're your worshippers. We love you."

Hera just waited for Oenone to speak.

"She and I are trying to save my husband from a choice that will kill him."

Hera started again. "Mortals—"

"I can judge and that will be the end of it." Paris let his wife's hand go and cupped her cheek.

He said he wouldn't! He said he'd take my advice!

Oenone snapped, "Nincompoop! Sheep's head! It won't be the end of anything. You can't tell a seer the future and be right!"

Looking frightened, Corythus buried his head in Hera's lap.

"I'll show you." Paris looked first at Hera and raised his head to the two standing goddesses.

Athena leaned forward on her toes, as touchingly and

painfully beautiful as a new warrior going to battle. Her sandy hair flowed away from her face, in a wind I didn't feel. She had Apollo's strong jawline and his shapely mouth. Alive—rather than a statue—her cheeks were just a little plump, not doughy.

"You are three perfections." Paris threw his hands up. "Different in your ways but so beautiful that nothing can add to your charms."

Judging without choosing. The goddesses, by their expressions, were not satisfied. He'd accomplished nothing.

A thought struck me. "You can share ownership of the apple and each have it for a span of time."

Aphrodite nodded, her curls bouncing. "A sweet idea, precious."

Athena put a hand on Aphrodite's wrist in a gesture that seemed protective. "I'll accept that too. We'll declare a truce."

I held my breath.

"It's fine as far as it goes." Hera put Corythus gently aside and stood. "Aphrodite, you had the Graces dress you and perfume you before we came, but I left Olympus just as I was. Athena, dear, no one thinks you're even pretty. I'll share the apple, but my turn will be longest, because, after all, I'm the fairest."

Aphrodite softly and Athena vehemently said, "No."

My stomach cramped.

"So be it." Hera turned to Paris. "If you pick me, you will be the master of all of Europe and Asia. Parents will name their children after you."

Did he want that?

Paris took both of Oenone's hands in his. She brought his to her lips.

A fresh idea came to me. "Pray, hear my words. I'll sacrifice to you all just for listening."

At first, Hera frowned, but when she heard *sacrifice*, her brow smoothed. "Yes?"

I swallowed. "Who is more accustomed to assessing beauty than a woman? Shouldn't a woman be the judge?"

Aphrodite, who had been gazing at Paris, turned to watch me.

Oenone said, "This is why I adore your sister, love."

Encouraged, I went on, spinning half-truths. "We look in our dark mirrors and compare ourselves with other females. We're always making contests in our minds."

From their expressions, the three of them were considering my words. If I judged, two goddesses' fury would certainly fall on me, but Troy, Hector, my parents, and everyone else might survive.

"For example, I know that my younger sister Laodice outshines me. Her graceful neck alone is enough to prove it."

Aphrodite asked, "You admire me, don't you, dear Cassandra?"

"More. I worship you." A safe answer.

"I'll accept her judgment. You're a sweet girl, honey."

Hera agreed. "Better a female should do it. Women are the most discerning."

Were we saved?

But Athena refused. "Hera! You know my brother cursed her. She holds a grudge against me."

"I'll be fair! I worship you too! Didn't I bring you sardines yesterday? In salty and spicy brine?"

"A lesser god got the best of everything."

A kinder god.

It was slipping away. Before my chance closed forever, I shouted, "Hera, I choose you!" She was more important than the others. Use your power to make my choice *the* choice. "You're the most beautiful." They were all the most beautiful.

"But my soft lips." Aphrodite made kissy lips at me.

"No! Zeus said *he* should judge." Athena pointed at Paris.

"Do you think my lord will object to her decision?" Hera asked.

Aphrodite laughed. Zeus would let stand my choice of his wife.

I'd changed the future! I wanted to grin and dance, but then I looked ahead. Troy still burned.

It couldn't!

Hera said with satisfaction, "I will enjoy having the

apple. It will be my fruit, along with the pomegranate."

Aphrodite pushed my brother down on a couch and sat in his lap. "Dovey-love, which of us were you going to choose?"

Gallantly, probably believing that it no longer mattered, he said, "With you so close I can think of no one else. I pick you."

He was a blockhead! Didn't he guess that a choice no matter when would anger the other two?

"Villain!" Hera cried. "Fool! Bufflehead! To make an enemy of me!" To me, she added, "Many have suffered my wrath, always women. But I will make an exception."

Aphrodite laughed a burbling laugh. "Hera, love, you knew the truth all along."

Oenone stood. "Paris, the goddesses have received two judgments. Come. I have love secrets to share with you." Her lips were tight. She was afraid.

He slipped away from Aphrodite and put an arm around his wife.

Aphrodite stood too. "Zeus appointed you, so your judgment is the important one, apple or no apple, and I had a fitting gift for you if you picked me. Would you like it?"

"He needs nothing!" I cried. "His family is everything to him."

"What gift? Something I can share with my wife?"

He *was* a bufflehead! Or evil.

"This gift you cannot share." Aphrodite laughed again. "It is for the true admirer of beauty—the most magnificent mortal woman, desired by everyone. Behold Helen of Sparta."

The table vanished, replaced by a vision. On the edge of a meadow, a woman sat with her back against a gnarled olive tree. Across her lap lay an expanse of cloth. Her hand, wielding a needle, paused in the air. Her head was lowered to her task.

From the future, I recognized the woman's light brown hair, rippling down her shoulders. A gold bracelet circled her shapely upper arm. We couldn't see her face, but even without seeing it, Paris dropped his hand from Oenone's shoulder.

She rushed from the cavern. Corythus ran after her.

Paris called, "Wife!" but didn't move.

In the vision, as if hearing him, Helen raised her head: big eyes, brown with amber glints; a small, straight nose; smooth, ruddy cheeks; full lips. But Oenone was more beautiful than Helen, and neither of them could compare to the three goddesses.

Her expression won me over, though: smiling but wistful. Unfinished. *You*, it said, *will complete me.* I'd want to go to her, if Aphrodite would take me rather than my brother, offer her solace, be her friend.

10

I wrenched my eyes from the vision. "Brother! You said you'd never abandon your family."

"Sister? You're still here?" He seemed to recover from his daze. "Did you see Helen's expression? She needs me."

Those were Helenus's exact words too: *She needs me.*

He turned to Aphrodite. "Will you take me to her?"

"I'll do more, lovey. I'll make sure you win her." She led him out.

I called after them helplessly, "Don't bring her to Troy."

He said over his shoulder, "I won't."

He would. I had failed to break the lowest rung in the ladder to our ruin.

When Aphrodite's and Paris's footsteps ceased echoing, Athena vanished.

"The goddess of love can't resist herself." Hera laughed. "And I can't resist instructing people. Cassandra, a sparrow can't move the moon. A sardine can't stop a whale. A single mortal—or several of you—can't cause the enormous ship of fate to swerve. Think of the size of it! Even we gods and goddesses are on it! You may change the next ten minutes, but the rest of time doesn't budge." She paused. "Aphrodite gave your brother a gift for choosing her. I'll give you one for picking me. Would you like to be mistress of Europe and Asia?"

"Will that save Troy?"

"It will save only you. You'll emerge from Troy's ashes."

I threw back my head. "If you please, lift Apollo's curse." I went on despite her frown. "Let people believe me."

"I won't go against Apollo. What else?"

"Would you help Troy in the war?"

"And not punish Paris? All the immortals will take sides. Something else."

What? "Save Hector."

"Fate will decide that. I can't intercede."

I wasn't enough of a noddy-peak to waste her gift on a necklace or other bauble. "May I wait to decide? May I call on you later?"

She nodded.

That was something. "Thank you!" I smiled.

Her eyebrows rose. "I see why Apollo was taken with you. Farewell."

After she vanished, I tried and failed to find Oenone. Eurus carried me back to the sacred grove, where we sat together on his altar. While the sky darkened to dusk, I related everything that had happened.

"I should have blown your brother to the middle of the sea when I could have. Now Aphrodite protects him."

I feared he'd yell at himself again. "The goddesses would have found him there, and they would have been angry at you. I'm the one who failed."

"You were clever with Hera! Few mortals have won gifts from the gods."

He'd cheered me again, but he didn't know what gift I should ask for. "My wind may sweep away the dust and then we'll see."

I crossed my legs. "Paris will leave Sparta with Helen and bring her to Troy. My parents will be so happy to see him alive that they'll let them in. Menelaus, Helen's husband, will gather ships and an army and sail to Troy."

Eurus patted my arm.

"Will you take me to Sparta? If I can keep Paris and Helen from running off together, there won't be a war." This would be the next rung.

He frowned. "Don't you know I will?"

Was he angry? I jumped off the altar and looked up at him in the dying light. "I don't! I can't foretell what immortals will say or do."

"You already told me that."

"Then how would I know—"

"Because I carried you to Mount Ida!" He left the altar too and waved his arms.

My hair blew about. Would he freeze into his statue and leave me?

"My wind changes direction. I don't."

Tears stood out in my eyes.

"Don't cry!" His eyes were wet too.

I smiled. He smiled.

The next morning, after half an hour at my loom and another half hour playing with Maera in Troy's alleys, I brought offerings to the three goddesses, as I'd promised, and to Eurus, as he expected.

He ate and smiled at the same time.

Though the journey to Sparta by ship and on foot would take Paris a month, Eurus said that he and I would need only three days. Since Mother had given me permission to go to the sacred grove, I visited him daily. We spent much of the waiting time practicing flying without killing me.

I learned to cling to him with my arms around his chest and my legs around his waist, which made my heart fluttery.

The first time I clung, Eurus took my hands away—gently—and held up a finger for me to wait. After a few seconds, he breathed deeply and nodded. I clasped him again, and this time he seemed untroubled, but my heart still quivered.

He continued to worry about my safety. "You'll tire and loosen your grip." He vanished and reappeared a few minutes later, bearing a pale blue sash exactly the color of my peplos. "Hera wove it."

Was that her present? I could have gotten a sash from home.

"She said it didn't use up the gift she promised you."

Whew!

A line of tiny marks ran along half the length of the cloth. When I brought the sash close to my eyes, I saw that the marks were letters. "Can you read what it says?"

Father, several of his councilors, Hector, and Helenus could read, but few others had the skill.

Eurus read, "'All your attempts will be for naught, but this will not let you fall.'"

Thank you, Hera. "We have to prove her wrong about failing."

"You will! We will!"

We flew low for an hour, using the sash, and Eurus said it would do.

Hooray! We could go to Sparta!

I thanked Eurus a dozen times. His face reddened. Lesser gods seemed unaccustomed to a worshipper's gratitude.

I must have been unused to feeling this grateful. I didn't usually blush so often, either.

During the week after the festival, Mother was often called away from her weaving to join Father in interviewing parents who wanted me for a daughter-in-law. Each time, she told me the name of the young man in question. "Of course, you'll wait the customary three years before you wed."

Whatever the suitor's name, I'd peek forward to see what would happen to him in the war. Sooner or later, one way or another, they all died.

"Darling," she said once, stepping away from her loom and grasping my shoulders, "if there are any young men you've noticed at festivals—any you've fallen asleep thinking of—tell me. As long as the family is suitable . . . We want you to be happy."

I hugged her. "I know. Thank you."

She let me go and picked up her shuttle. "Think about it. You can name two or three. That will help us."

Since I couldn't foresee into a changed future, I wasn't

sure, but if Eurus and I succeeded, I would almost certainly marry. For my lucky future self, I should choose someone I admired.

While I wove, I brought the young men forward in my imagination as I'd seen them in games. This one was agile; that one was godlike in handsomeness; another was gracious in defeat; a few were friends of Hector, which spoke well for them.

But when I pictured their faces, I gave them a fringe of beard and mismatched eyebrows.

11

Before I let myself sleep that night, I suffered, envisioning young Trojan men. Since not one of those I liked would survive the war, I just chose three of them for Mother. All were brave, handsome, and kind to their sisters. In the morning, Mother thanked me and said I'd chosen well.

I couldn't ask her or Father for permission to go to Sparta because permission would be denied.

When I didn't come home from the sacred grove, my parents would be terrified. Mother would wring her hands red. Both would cry their eyes dry. By the time I returned, they'd believe I'd died.

If only I could tell them and be believed—but then I wouldn't need to go.

On the day of departure with Eurus, the sky was still dark when I gave Maera her bone in the women's quarters. I didn't want her following me and starving at the east gate until I got back. She lay at the top of the stairs, bone between her paws, and watched me descend.

I went back and knelt on the top step. "I'm doing this for you too. If we save Troy, I'll never have to give you away."

She thumped her tail. I rubbed her neck and continued downstairs.

Rain was falling and thunder rumbled when I stepped outside the palace. Eurus said he had nothing to do with this weather.

Ai! Had Apollo enlisted Zeus and his lightning bolts against me?

With trembling fingers, I tied Hera's sash around Eurus and me. I hoped that Zeus, if he truly hated me, didn't detest innocent Troy as well.

When we rose into the storm, I discovered that clouds didn't pile all the way up to Mount Olympus. Above them, the sky was blue-gray. Below, the clouds tinted dawn pink and looked like rippled ground solid enough for even a bull to stand on.

We could still go back. I wouldn't be missed until tonight. If we did, Mother and Father wouldn't suffer terror and grief caused by me. I'd stay at home and wait for the war, knowing that I probably couldn't have prevented it anyway.

The air above the clouds was cold. My teeth chattered. I'd worn my himation, but the rain had soaked the cloak, which worsened my shivers.

All day and through the night we passed over the sea. My himation finally dried. Warmer at last, I was able to think.

Might Greeks be able to believe my prophecies?

Probably not, but we'd find out.

Soon after Paris arrived in Sparta, Menelaus would leave to attend his grandfather's funeral on the distant island of Crete. While he was gone, Paris and Helen would fall in love. Before the king returned, they'd run away together.

What might I do? These were my ideas: Keep them apart. Tell Helen about Oenone and how much Paris loved her. Describe their son. Remind Paris how much more beautiful Oenone was than Helen and how lucky he was to have a goddess for a wife. Say how important his family was to him. Point out his weak chin to Helen. Repeat Eurus's opinion that Paris was lazy and a coward.

How could I fail?

For the next two days, we flew southwest. I grew so accustomed to flight and even to Eurus's closeness that

I learned to sleep while clinging to his back. When we were hungry, Eurus found spots to land where his wind could whip through a date palm, fig shrub, grape arbor, or almond tree and gather enough fruit and nuts for a meal. My favorite was the dates. At home, we usually ate them dried, but I liked them best straight from the tree.

During our first meal, when I worried that we were stealing from a farmer, Eurus waved a breezy hand. "I bring rain. Without me, farms couldn't grow dates. Most mortals owe me many more offerings than they give."

Still, the farmer hadn't meant for us to have this meal. Mortals and gods seemed to have different ideas about what was right.

We were in a sloping meadow on the edge of an orchard. The land here was moister and greener than at home.

I poked a date pit into the ground. Maybe a palm tree would grow. "How do you choose where to drop your rain and how much?"

He frowned. "When I don't blow hard or rain for a while, my ribs ache as if something is pressing on them. Then I have to, even if the rain is too much or my wind is too strong. Is that bad?" He brushed grapevine tendrils off his lap. "It *is* bad."

Apollo's crows landed and started to eat his figs. When he shooed them away, they perched on his head and shoulders.

"Wolves judge neither innocence
nor guilt when they pounce.
Tragedy is comedy to crows—
unless one of us is killed."

They flapped away.

"The crows know I'm terrible." He jumped up and paced. "Am I sending rain to unworthy farmers and denying worthy ones? How can I tell? Must I make their acquaintance, even though they never bring me offerings?" He stopped with a jerk. "What do you think, Cassandra?"

I was the wrong person to ask! "If I can't keep Paris and the woman Helen from running off together, I'll be happy if I just persuade them not to go to Troy. But then people somewhere else will die." I'd been worrying about this. "Do you despise me?"

He sat on his haunches and smiled. "You're like me, only without wind."

I laughed. He always heartened me.

He burst out, "If Apollo had given you the power to see the future of gods too, you could tell me what my weather would cause."

I'd love to do that!

I did know something of his distant future, though I was silent about it. Mortals would forget the gods. Their altars and temples would be preserved only to be gawked at. I was sure Eurus would be miserable, and I wanted to help his future self. "Will you visit me in Hades—whenever I go there?"

"Of course I will." He smiled.

"For centuries?"

He frowned. "Yes! I said I would."

"Good." I'd welcome him, and he'd be comforted. I would be too.

He said, "Our friendship will last forever."

We'd have bright happiness in that gloomy place. I said, "Beyond the funeral pyre."

12

On the third day, we arrived on a steep hill above Sparta. The afternoon was half over.

Sparta was little more than a village, watered by a broad river. From the air, I'd seen no majestic palace and no government buildings, not even a city wall, though I supposed the mountains on three sides and the hills we were in on the fourth kept the town safe.

Eurus said his wind told him that my brother was just a mile away. We sat on a mossy rock to wait.

If we failed here, only one rung in the ladder remained. I kept popping up and sitting again. I reminded myself that I had only to prevent Helen from leaving her home, her husband, her daughter—the people who loved her. This had to be the easiest rung to break.

"Should I come with you when you enter the city?"

I feared that Aphrodite might not like even a lesser god to be on my side. "Can I just call you if I need help?"

"Yes! I'll wait outside the city. You can whisper my name. I'll be listening."

Paris rounded a boulder and came into view. His hands flew up. "You pursued me!"

Such was his delight at seeing his sister.

Eurus and I leaped to our feet.

Paris seemed to recover. "Your hair is as tangled as a bird's nest, as if the gods made you madful."

I had forgotten my comb!

"Did Oenone send the two of you to fetch me back?"

"No," I said, "but Eurus can carry you home to her." Go!

"First I will accept the goddess's gift." He began walking again.

I joined him. "Then you'll bring Helen to your wife?"

"Oenone isn't my wife anymore. I left her."

This was custom. A husband had only to leave his wife for them to be divorced. A wife had to get her father's permission to divorce her husband.

"But if you return to her," I said, "you're still married, and this was just a trip." Father sometimes traveled on Troy's behalf, but Mother remained his wife.

"Why would I go back, when Aphrodite is giving me

the woman everyone wants?"

"What a villain you are!" Eurus called Paris every kind of rogue I'd ever heard of: lidderon, cokin, limmer, bricoun. He ended with, "You're no better than a smy!"

Paris just waved his hand. I grinned. *Smy* was a terrible insult. A smy praised you with his mouth and attacked you with his deeds, both at once.

Eurus looked fierce. "I mean it."

I reminded Paris that he'd promised not to go to Troy with Helen.

"Did I?"

The road changed from dirt to cobbled.

Eurus stopped. "May the great gods help you, Cassandra."

"Thank you!" I touched his hand.

We both blushed.

As Paris and I descended the hill into Sparta, Paris said, "Sister, do you think I could have left Oenone if I hadn't been abandoned to die on a mountain?"

Did Mother and Father start all this?

We passed a cottage on our right—clay walls, tiled roof, two stories, small—much like ordinary houses at home. Another cottage cropped up on our left. In only a few yards, the street narrowed; the houses tightened together, and soon they were attached, exactly as in the heart of Troy.

A pack of girls, just three or four years younger than I was, raced by, playing tag and shouting.

So much alike, and we'd be killing each other.

We passed intersections with other narrow streets. A herder used his staff to guide half a dozen goats toward us. The goats brushed me as they passed.

I planned what I might say to the king and to Helen and worried that I'd get it wrong or that it wouldn't help if I got it right.

After perhaps half a mile, our street widened. Soon, the avenue ended in a square, and we faced a freestanding house, which I'd seen when I received the future from Apollo. This house wasn't much, not compared with Father's palace, but it was grander than any I'd passed here. Marble columns made up the facade and supported a balcony fenced by a wooden railing. The tiled roof extended over the balcony.

Three crows landed on the balcony rail.

In Troy, a noble family would have lived in such a house, but here it was the king's home. A group of people came out, including Menelaus and Helen.

"Ah," Paris whispered.

Helen's lips parted. Her expression was unguarded, like a baby's at peace, big eyes watching the world. I saw the same longing I'd witnessed on Mount Ida: I beg you—bring me to my fullest self.

Could anyone grant her wish? Could I?

No. When her eyes reached my brother, they widened. She smiled, changing from moon to sun.

I looked at him too.

He was taller than a few minutes ago. Broader too. His weak chin had strengthened. His skin glowed, as if a lamp had been lit inside him.

This had to be Aphrodite's doing.

Helen began to reach for my brother but stopped herself. In seeming wonder, she spread her fingers and looked at them. Then, she twined her right arm around her husband's left and turned to him, her smile dimming to mere politeness.

Paris's eyes were on only Helen. Menelaus might not have been there for all the notice he got.

The king's face was handsome in a weathered way, with skin like the clay of a bowl after it's dried but not yet fired. He had a small mouth, deep-set eyes, and a curly brown beard, which would be gray by the time he entered Troy to reclaim his wife.

I struggled to breathe. Menelaus was going to kill many Trojans, including Helenus's bane, my brother Deiphobus.

But now he was simply a host who honored the tradition

of hospitality. He said in a booming voice, "Guests! Rejoice!"

The crows cawed about Paris and Helen:

> *"An empty sky gives nothing,*
> *and everyone wants a pretty bauble*
> *though within is only air.*
> *These two deserve each other!"*

Detaching his arm from Helen's, Menelaus came to us and clapped Paris's shoulder. "Many stare at my wife as you do."

My brother gulped. I saw his Adam's apple bob.

The king laughed. "Her beauty outshines the stars. Welcome to Sparta! Have you and the wild-hair girl eaten today?"

I patted down my hair, which probably made it more of a bird's nest.

"My sister has. I haven't. Poor misminded thing, she ate a handful of dirt."

The bricoun! He wanted to make sure no one would believe me.

I'd made everything worse just by forgetting my comb.

Helen's voice was so soft and breathy I had to strain to hear it. "Please come in."

If I failed, her cries when Paris was wounded would be soft too.

We entered, and a feast was quickly prepared. Helen and several servants brought dishes to low tables in the house's salon. We were dining with Menelaus and twelve of his men. I was the only female sharing the meal, and just because I was a guest. Here, as in Troy, women and girls didn't eat with men.

From his couch, Paris watched Helen as she went from table to table. The king asked him for the tale of his travels. No one asked me.

Paris introduced us as prince and princess of Troy and said that I had wandered away from the city. "I followed and let her lead me. If you force Cassandra to do anything, she weeps and wails. She was a good sister before the gods sent her beside herself." He favored me with a dewy smile.

Smy!

I wet my lips. I started to speak but no sound came.

Everyone watched me.

When I tried again, my voice was hoarse. Good. "This divine madness was sent by Apollo. You have my condolences, King Menelaus."

The king put down the ox bone he had been gnawing. "For what?"

"You plan to leave tomorrow morning to attend your grandfather's funeral."

Paris said softly, "Ah."

"Someone told you?" Menelaus said.

Spartans probably couldn't believe me, either, but I tried anyway. "I see the future. You'll ride a piebald horse."

He had probably chosen his horse already, so this seemed reliable.

"My mount will be a gray stallion."

"In the morning, the gray will be coughing." I added, as evidence that I could be trusted: "At Apollo's festival this year, I was kanephoros."

Menelaus raised an eyebrow and looked at Paris for confirmation—Paris, who hadn't been there.

"She hadn't been made brain-wooded then." He waved a morsel of mutton at the end of his knife. His table manners were dreadful.

"Disease isn't running through my horses, Cassandra. Your future sight is mistaken." Menelaus laughed. "Why do I bother to speak to a pebble head?"

My brother laughed too. "It seems kind to converse with her."

I hated him.

What else could I say? I stirred the porridge in my bowl and wished for inspiration. Mm. This wouldn't sound misminded. "Why not take your wife with you? She'll soften your grief."

It worked! Menelaus looked a question at Helen.

Sounding as if he had offered her a hairpin and not an adventure and the pleasure of his company, she said, "Very well."

Were we saved?

13

"Will we take Hermione too?" Helen told Paris and me, "Hermione is our daughter."

"As pretty as her mother," Menelaus said.

"Prettier!" Helen dimpled and appeared even more adorable than before.

I wondered if she always knew just how she looked.

Menelaus said, "The road is too perilous for a nine-year-old. I won't risk either of you."

A fresh failure. Trying something else, I asked, "King Menelaus, have you ever visited Troy?" He might have before I was born.

He said he hadn't.

"Our city is beautiful, especially its wall. The god of war loves Troy and has sworn that we'll always be victorious.

This is true, isn't it, brother?"

He couldn't know, and it would have seemed strange if he confessed that he didn't, so he nodded. I'd lied about Ares, but we had never been defeated, which I hoped the king would remember when he thought about attacking us.

Since they believed me madful I could say whatever I liked, so I went further. "King Menelaus, your wife always longs for what she doesn't have." My heart seemed to boom loud enough for Eurus to hear. "Doesn't she?"

His face reddened. I was right.

I went on. "My brother is foreign and very handsome *right now.*"

Paris choked on his food.

I hid my smile. "And he's youthful."

Menelaus's face deepened to almost purple.

I rushed on. "Diswitted or not, I warn you: Don't leave them alone together. Stay here in Sparta."

Menelaus signaled to two female servants. "Paris, I admire your patience."

I didn't want to be dragged away! I raced around and between the couches and tables. "There will be war!"

A servant reached, but her hand found only air. I was agile!

"Spartans will die!" I shouted as I ran. "My brother is a wolf that snarls at kindness. He's a snake! Beware!"

A diner could have snagged me, but astonishment

seemed to have frozen them. My brother rose to pursue me too, but he didn't know which way I'd go next.

"My words come from the god of truth!"

Menelaus lunged across a table and caught my hair. Ai! My scalp!

The servants took me away. I didn't fight them. I'd failed with Menelaus.

As I left, I heard Helen say in her soft voice, "I'm sure she meant no harm."

These women's quarters had no screened-off nooks. The servants led me to an empty bed farthest from the courtyard light, where they pushed me down and stood over me. Their fingers left red marks on my arms.

Three women were weaving and two sat on a bed, playing checkers. A young girl stared at me from another bed, where she was carding wool.

I tried to go to her, but my captors held me back.

She came to me. "They say the gods made you formad. How did it feel when they did it?"

"Are you Hermione, daughter of Helen?"

"And Menelaus."

"I have my wits."

"Your wits are gone, and you don't even know it."

I wondered if Helen's gaze had ever been as frank as her daughter's. Hermione's eyes were almost as big as Helen's.

Her mouth was small, like her father's. Her lips were the color of a dusky pink rose.

She tugged me to her bed. The servants continued to watch me.

I foresaw that she'd grow up to be as lovely as her mother, but she'd never teach her expression to entice as Helen's did.

Her thoughts seemed to be following the same track as mine. "You're pretty, but you should try to look happy."

What could I say to win this child for an ally? "Do you have a doll you love?"

She ignored this. "Did the gods curse you as soon as you were born?"

"Do you like brain-sick people?" I said.

"If they don't poke me. If they talk to me."

"I'll never poke you, and we're talking."

"It's interesting to talk to you." She whispered, "Do you see things that other people don't?"

"I see my city burning. It's terrible." Not meaning to, I shuddered.

She reached up and patted my disordered hair. "I once dreamed that I was chased by a monster. When I woke up, a spider was on my face. I screamed, and Pragora killed it."

"Your mother didn't come?"

"Pragora came. Her bed is still next to mine, even though I don't need a nursemaid anymore."

"Would you miss your mother if she went away from you?"

"Where would she go?"

"Perhaps to Troy, where I live."

"Is it far?"

"Yes."

"Who would take her there?"

"Maybe my brother would. Would you want her not to go?"

"Would Pragora go with her?"

"I don't think so."

"Mother can leave." She touched my knee. "Talking to you is like talking to anyone the gods didn't make extraught. It's sort of a game. Oh! There's the Minotaur in the doorway!"

I couldn't help looking. "There's no Minotaur." The Minotaur had a bull's head and tail and a man's body.

"All right. Ai!" She pointed at a window high in the wall. "A centaur is sticking its head in."

While Hermione tested me on a succession of creatures, I tried to think of a way to use her to save Troy.

"I like playing with you." She took my hand. "Will you stay here? Please?"

Ah. Excellent! "Yes, unless your mother leaves. If she leaves, I will too. You can help me by keeping her here."

* * *

114

A servant snored from the floor alongside my bed while I lay awake for hours, missing Maera, home, and Eurus, even though he wasn't far away.

In the morning, applause woke me. Everyone clustered in the middle of the women's quarters.

"Come!" Hermione rushed to my bed and tugged me to the front of the bunch.

Barefoot, Helen stood behind a low stool. In front of the stool was a double-handled bowl filled with water and a ladle. Everyone was smiling.

Hermione said, "Mother hardly ever does this. Watch!"

Helen tied the hem of her peplos between her thighs. She bent at the waist, placed her hands flat on the stool, and lifted her legs so that she was doing a handstand.

Though I'd done handstands, I always toppled quickly. How strong she was! Her legs began to curl backward over her head, farther, farther. She achieved an almost impossible arch and stopped.

Was she stuck? She was panting. Should I go to her? Could I help Troy by rescuing her?

But everyone was still smiling.

She recovered and continued curling. Her feet neared the bowl, then drew level with it. She turned her toes inward. With the big toe and the second toe on each foot, she lifted the bowl about six inches without spilling a drop of water.

If I weren't seeing it, I'd think the feat impossible.

"Come, Cassandra!" Hermione rushed to the bowl, crouched, dipped the ladle in the water, and drank. "Your turn."

I bent down. The bowl was steady.

The water tasted fresh. I drank.

Women and servants waited behind me. I passed the ladle and backed away.

When everyone had a turn, Helen lowered the bowl back to the floor, raised her legs again, hand-stepped off the stool, and stood—on her feet. I clapped with everyone else.

She smiled around the room. "I'm hungry!"

Everyone left, except my two guardians. One gave me a comb and hairpins. I tamed my hair, twisted it into a knot, and fastened it to the top of my head. Then they led me to the dining room, where a knife seemed to pierce my heart.

There, looming over his reclining younger brother, Menelaus, stood King Agamemnon of Mycenae, the future general against Troy, the man who would enslave me and take me to Greece, where we'd both be murdered.

Don't stare! Don't draw his attention!

I made myself look around. Paris and Helen stood together. Each held a slice of griddle bread. Apparently, men and women breakfasted together here. My brother, even puffed up by Aphrodite, was less monumental than Agamemnon.

The villain turned and saw me. "Here's the frenzied girl." He walked toward me.

Ai! What might he do to me now, such a man! I fell back a step, which made him smile. His face was both handsome and terrifying: thick eyebrows; flaring nostrils; large, square teeth; and a jutting chin. He stopped a few inches from me.

Too close! I moved back again.

"Paris, you didn't say your sister is pretty. A pretty girl doesn't need good sense." He chuckled. "Or any sense at all. She'll be a beautiful woman soon."

I wished for the courage to spit in his face. "I am a princess of Troy."

He reported to his brother. "Look! She knows who she is. She doesn't seem past herself."

"Er . . . Er . . ." My knees felt wobbly. If he hurt me, my brother wouldn't intercede. "I'll never be beautiful. Facial warts are common in our family. Mother has seven. Father can hardly look at her."

"I frighten you." His smile sharpened. "I have informants who don't lie. Your mother, Queen Hecuba, is a known beauty despite her years and her many children.

You'll have no warts, dear." He dared to stroke my cheek.

"Don't touch me!" Anger overcame fear. "You're a creature that kills its young."

The air seemed to turn solid.

Agamemnon would sacrifice his daughter to the goddess Artemis so that the Greek battle fleet could sail. Artemis herself would save the girl, but her father would believe her dead. He was a man who could do such a thing.

The daughter's sacrifice is the reason his wife would murder him and kill me for being at his side.

His hand circled my neck. Squeezed. "I love my children, but perhaps someday I'll make a meal of you."

I gasped for air. "Remember my prediction when you carry it out."

🖘 14 🖙

After breakfast, Menelaus, Agamemnon, and an entourage of warriors assembled outside the house. I stood with Helen, her women, and Hermione and tried to think of something to prevent the journey, even at this late moment.

Menelaus told his wife to entertain my brother and me.

Helen threw her arms around him. "Don't go! Remember that I love you, that you are my first love. Don't leave me alone with—"

My brother inhaled loudly, almost a gasp.

—"my sorrowing self!"

Menelaus patted his wife's back. "Darling, what's this about?"

It was about eloping with Paris—but also about leaving the door open for her to return eventually if she wanted to.

She shook her head, spraying tears. "I'm just a silly woman. You'll always forgive my foolishness, won't you?"

He chuckled. "I will. Take good care of our guests." He set her to the side and lifted Hermione over his head. "What would you like from Crete?"

"A baby bull!"

Her father laughed and put her down. Hermione smiled up at him. When he leaves for war, he'll be gone for ten years. Unless I succeeded, she'd grow up without her parents.

Agamemnon came to me again. I hated how afraid I felt.

But his expression was kind. "If your thoughts are jumbled, warm baths, massages, quiet sleep, and primrose oil on the eyelids are excellent remedies."

"My brother fancies himself a physician," Menelaus said. "Helen, my love, can someone do for her what my brother prescribes?"

Hermione said, "She won't be as interesting if she isn't a topsy-turvy head."

Menelaus laughed.

Agamemnon touched my shoulder. "I have an idea we'll meet again. I look forward to it." He mounted a white mare.

Menelaus climbed on a piebald horse. He told me, "The gray will recover."

As if my true prophesy didn't matter. "I'll be right about the rest too."

He spurred his horse. The street emptied. Hermione tugged me into the house to start Agamemnon's treatment, but after a massage, I persuaded her that we should help her mother entertain Paris.

We found them ambling on the bank of the slow river that ran through Sparta. My brother was talking and gesturing, brushing Helen's bare arms with his bare arms. She was laughing and not moving away.

Hermione ran to them, leaped, and tapped my brother's shoulder. "I'm a champion jumper."

He turned, smoothing away a frown.

"Do you think Corythus will be an athlete too?" Without waiting for an answer, I told Helen, "Corythus is Paris's son." I clasped my brother around his waist. "He may not have told you what a sacrifice he made when he left a wife whose beauty dazzles the sun."

There.

Paris squeezed me back, hard, meaning to cause me pain. "No decent brother would do less."

Probably quoting her father, Hermione said, "The evils of travel are made up for by the joy of homecoming."

"Already, I miss my husband. I can be comforted only by this—" Helen dived into the river. In a moment, she surfaced, laughing.

Paris surged in and splashed her, laughing too.

Hermione and I watched from the bank. She said, "Mother loves to swim and stand on her head. Pragora told me she doesn't like being a mother much."

I put my arm around her shoulder. "My brother may not like being a father."

"Mine does." She said I hadn't had my warm bath yet. "And I'd rather be alone with you."

I left with her. I'd have more chances.

During the next week, Helen and Paris were constantly together. My brother slouched near her loom when she was weaving. He stood in the kitchen when she supervised the cooking, or cooked herself, because she said she liked to.

I did everything I could think of to drive them apart. Even in Paris's presence, I warned her of flaws I saw in the future—he told long, meandering stories; the palace shook from his snoring; he was lazy—and flaws I invented—he was plagued by boils; he twitched when he was nervous; servants steered clear of him because of his bullying.

Helen listened, her expression serene. Paris just smiled.

Once, while they strolled to the stables, I related the prophecy that was made at Paris's birth. "Together, you'll bring about Troy's destruction."

Helen walked backward. "Poor Paris, to be treated that way by his parents," said she who was soon to abandon her daughter.

Walking backward too, my brother opened his arms as if embracing the world. "I think everything led me to this glorious moment, here in Sparta with all of you."

When they were saddled, I wanted to ride out with them, but Hermione insisted on playing tag with me instead.

"My daughter loves you." Helen laughed. "She never wants to spend time with her mother. Please indulge her."

I couldn't say no, and I knew they wouldn't run away quite yet.

That evening, I brought Eurus an offering from Menelaus's kitchen and asked him to send rain to keep Helen and Paris indoors where they'd be watched.

They went out anyway.

I examined and reexamined every minute before they were going to leave, hoping to find an opportunity—

And I found a desperate one—desperate and dangerous. I'd be imprisoned if Eurus didn't reach me in time.

It was a cruel plan, so terrible I was too ashamed to tell even Eurus. I tried to imagine something else, but nothing seemed as likely to succeed.

If Themis, the goddess of justice, weighed my scheme on her scale, Helen's suffering would rest on one side and Troy's on the other: thousands dead, thousands enslaved. Themis would call my plan just.

But she'd despise me, and I'd despise myself.

* * *

Cooking was done in Sparta as in Troy, in pots and pans set on coal braziers. Smoke exited through a hole in the ceiling, and the kitchen was always dark and smoky, lit by clay lamps, which produced more smoke.

It was late afternoon, and preparations for dinner were underway. Paris lounged on a bench, his legs extended. Hermione sat on a reed mat on the floor with a doll in her lap. I leaned against the doorframe. I may have looked lazy, but my heart was hopping.

Helen worked at a three-legged table bearing pottery jars of condiments. Acrobatic as always, she bent at the waist with a level back, her smiling face turned to Paris. "Sparta is famous for our black broth, which I haven't served until now." She laughed. "Today I will, though, since I'm running out of ways to impress you all. Remember my strategy, Hermione."

Hermione looked up. "Yes, Mother." She hunched over her doll again.

Helen went on. "The goodness of black broth depends on vinegar. Too much—you spit it out. Too little—you spit it out. Ah." She picked up a ewer and uncorked it. "I'll show you how it's done."

"May I taste it?" I went to the pot on the brazier. The broth bubbled. A clay ladle rested on a stool next to the brazier. My heart went from hopping to leaping.

124

"Of course you can taste it." Helen joined me. "Paris, it's all in the elbow."

I picked up the ladle for my taste, as they expected. Steady, hand. This is for all of Troy. My parents. Hector. Me.

Helen poured in whatever amount of vinegar she judged right. Before she could straighten, I dipped in the ladle and lifted it out full of boiling broth.

Do it!

I forced my hand and flung the broth at her face. Burns will disfigure her. Paris won't want her. It ends now.

15

Helen shrieked and ran out. Hermione wailed.

I felt dizzy.

The servants didn't move, as if turned to stone, too surprised to grab me. The floor seemed to tilt. I spread my feet wide for balance.

Paris rose, took a step to go after Helen, seeming unaffected by the rippling ground. He turned. "You spoiled her!" He raised his arm.

Would he strike me?

He didn't. "Oenone will take me back, I think." He sank down on his bench.

"Eurus, please come," I whispered and staggered to the door. After a yard or two, the ground steadied.

Behind me, a servant cried, "Catch her!"

I sprinted through the house while feet thudded behind me.

The future Troy did not burn! My feet seemed to grow wings. Eurus was right outside. I hugged him, which I'd never done before. He squeezed me back.

When we let go, his face was bright, as if a star were inside him.

"We saved Troy." Both of us. I wouldn't have been here without him.

In a moment, we were blowing north. I looked ahead. Father would continue his peaceful rule. Hector would succeed him. He and Andromache would have seven children. I'd have children too. I wouldn't be enslaved and murdered.

I watched the city's sturdy survival and didn't look ahead to my new, future death. It would be whatever it would be, come whenever it came.

Hera! See what a sardine can do.

But then Troy's wall reddened and glowed. Smoke rose.

I screamed, "Noooo!"

Eurus's wind stuttered. He brought me down on a hill outside Sparta.

"We have to go back."

We found Helen, as beautiful as ever, dripping wet on Sparta's riverbank.

Aphrodite was with her. The goddess of love and beauty had restored her. She wheeled on me. "Wicked girl! You're lucky I could repair her." She purred, "Perhaps improve her."

Helen pinched my chin in her hand and brought her face an inch from mine. "You are a wasp, shriveled with jealousy." Her eyes were sharp, as I'd never seen them. "Do you see a blemish?"

"No."

"Poor thing, who would be willing to lose everything for you?" She let me go. "No one would give up breakfast for you. You hate me, but I entrance you too." Her expression softened, became wistful. She tilted up her head. Lips parted, she smiled gently. Her eyes seemed somehow bigger than they were, and her gaze caressed me.

Aphrodite said, "Helen is unique."

Bile rose into my throat. I had become immune.

Aphrodite looked startled.

But Helen didn't notice. "No one will start a war for you. I pity and forgive you."

"This one is wise." Aphrodite touched Helen's satin cheek. "Anger mottles the skin."

I told Eurus I wanted to go home. In the air, I wept into his back. I'd done everything wrong.

He landed us in a field of grass and boulders. "I started a squall in the sea. You rattled my bones by sobbing."

"I'm sorry." I sat on the grass.

He lowered himself next to me. "How did we succeed and then fail?"

"You'll hate me."

He frowned. "You killed one of my sacred birds?"

"What is your sacred bird?"

"The greylag goose. They never recite annoying verses."

"I didn't kill a goose."

"You chopped down one of my sacred trees?" He saw the question on my face. "The hazel." His arms flew up. "Why don't you know which tree is sacred to me?" His arms came down. "Because I'm a minor god. Did you chop down a hazel tree?"

I tossed back my head. "No."

"Then why would I hate you?"

"If I murdered someone but didn't hurt your bird and tree, you'd still think well of me?"

"I don't know. Did you murder anyone?"

"I tried to ruin Helen's life, and being burned hurts. You may not know that." Not looking at him, I said what I'd done.

"For a few minutes, you saved many lives."

"But now they'll die again. All that's really changed is in the past, where I scalded Helen on purpose."

"Would you do it again if you thought it would succeed?"

I nodded, feeling sick. "Apollo sees the past and the future. At his altar, when he first spoke to me, he knew what I'd do today. Do you think he cursed my gift to punish me in advance?"

Eurus rose a few inches and came down hard. "If he had left you alone, you wouldn't know about Helen until your brother brought her to Troy."

"I might fear that war would come and throw broth at her then, to make Paris send her back to Menelaus. In every future I might do it."

Eurus stood on his knees and gripped my shoulders in both hands. "Then in every single future"—he brought his face close to mine—"you'd be a heroine. Brave Cassandra." He sat back.

A brave failure.

"You don't believe me. If I were a great god, you would."

I started laughing. "I'd believe it if my mother said it." Not everything was about being a greater or lesser god.

He smiled uncertainly.

I lay back, exhausted. "Helen suspects they'll start a war over her. She's proud of herself for it."

"I'd like to fly back there and scald her again."

"Aphrodite would be angry."

"Yes, she would. Sleep!" he commanded, as if he were Hypnos, the god of sleep.

Birdsong woke me. The notes were as bright as if tragedy didn't exist.

Eurus was standing next to me. A blade of grass pointed sideways from his beard. I smiled at it and him. My hair must be wild again.

Smiling too, he asked if he could take me somewhere other than Troy. "There are wonders . . . You don't have to be enslaved and murdered."

I sat up. "Would *brave Cassandra* desert her city?"

He shrugged. "A true friend would stay alive to continue being my friend."

"Wherever I am when Troy burns, I'll be too sad to be an enjoyable friend." I held up my hand to stop him from arguing, though his mouth was already opening. "Menelaus will be slow, gathering warriors and ships." I must have been thinking while I slept. "Before then, six weeks from now, Paris and Helen will arrive in Troy. If my father doesn't let them stay, we'll all be saved." I jumped up. "We need a plan."

"We'll make one. You're good at plans."

Not successful ones. "It will be our last chance." The final rung. "If we fail, everything will be in motion, unstoppable."

He leaped into the air with me, a lesser god sparrow and a girl sparrow, piercing the sky.

16

During the first day of flying, I regretted everything that had happened in Sparta. I plagued myself by asking endlessly, What if?

But over the next two days, I imagined my reunion with my parents, Hector, and Maera. I invented a story to explain what had befallen me and told it to Eurus. He called me a dreadful liar and said I should just be silent.

I couldn't do that! I added detail and pictured myself in the straits I described: an adder biting me while I prayed to Apollo, pain, delirium, finally awakening on the bank of the Scamander River near Mount Ida, finding my way home, walking only at night for fear of lions. When I tried again, I'd convinced myself so well that my voice broke.

Eurus wiped his eyes with his tunic. "That will do."

He was so sympathetic.

We reached Troy midmorning, fourteen days after we'd left. Eurus put me down at the west gate, and I rushed through the alleys on this side of the city, scraping by carts and donkeys and people, meaning to spare my parents more moments of grief.

Maera met me in the plaza outside the palace. I rubbed her all over while she licked my face and wagged her whole back half.

Indoors, I raced along the colonnade, foreseeing that Mother, Father, my brothers, and Father's councilors would be in the living room. I just couldn't tell if Helenus, my twin and fellow seer, would be there too.

On the threshold, I signaled Maera to wait. Then I hesitated myself. Father must have been praying recently because I smelled his incense. Clear light slanted in from the sky above the courtyard. Everyone stood and sipped honey water from pink and blue clay cups. Servants held pitchers in case anyone wanted a refill. Deep male voices thrummed in my chest. Home. Precious.

Mother and Father stood apart, each listening to several councilors, their expressions cordial. Why didn't they seem sad?

Mother's belly was enormous. My baby brother Polydorus

would come soon. When he was just ten, he was fated to die in the massacre inside Troy.

There was Helenus, standing near Hector and watching Deiphobus.

A councilor saw me, and it was as if a giant hand stirred the room. People turned toward me, then away, and then toward my parents.

"Father? Mother?" I ran toward them.

For an instant, Mother looked relieved, but then her face reddened.

I stopped short. Was she angry at me?

Father's lips tightened to a straight line. He *was* angry! He turned his back to me. My stomach hurt, as if someone had punched me.

Mother signaled a servant, who took my elbow and guided me up to the women's quarters. Whining, Maera came with us. I began to weep.

Voices and weaving hummed from above, as usual, but when we came into view, sound ceased, as if a god had snuffed it out. Through my tears, I saw that my loom was no longer near Mother's. I stumbled past the women to my bed and threw myself down on my stomach, sobbing. Maera jumped up and licked my neck.

Did Mother and Father hate me? Had they stopped being proud of me?

When I finally sat up, I saw my cousins crowded in

the entryway to our nook.

Melo looked curious, Aminta pitying, and Kynthia amused.

"Leave me alone!"

Melo and Aminta left.

Kynthia shifted her weight from one hip to the other. "Your brother said the shepherds would get sick of you."

"What shepherds?"

She grinned. "Sly, girl. That's what I'd ask."

"What did Helenus say?" It couldn't have been any other brother.

She was eager to tell me. At first, everyone believed that some disaster had befallen me on my way to or back from the sacred grove. Father assembled a force to find me, but Helenus met them as they left the city. He said he'd seen me frolicking with a dozen or more shepherds and shepherdesses in the fields between Troy and Mount Ida and predicted that I'd come home eventually.

They believed that I'd do that—make them fear for me without a good reason?

I refused to cry again until I was alone.

Kynthia said, "I'm enjoying your disgrace, Cassandra."

Clever Maera barked at her.

"Go away."

This time she did.

But I didn't cry again. I sat, stony-faced, furious as well

as miserable, furious over my parents' lack of trust.

Looking ahead a few years, I saw myself at my loom during the war. There would be extra space between it and the looms on either side. The chatter would swirl around me and not include me. But my head would be high and my face calm.

I decided to become that serene creature now.

I fetched my comb from my chest and attacked my matted hair. Maera went to sleep on my bed.

After a few minutes, Mother came in and took over, working gently at the knots. "Of all my children, I thought you the least likely to worry me and your father."

"There were no shepherds." How could they think there were? "I'd never forget your goodness to me, and Father's. Let me tell you what really happened." Please!

"Helenus saw you. Why would he lie?"

Because he wanted me to fail in whatever I might be planning. "You see how he is with Deiphobus."

"He had no reason to make up a tale, and you do." She kissed my cheek. "Your lot will be hard. Parents don't want a flighty wife for their sons. They've withdrawn their offers."

Good. I wouldn't have a husband and children to grieve for.

We were silent after that. When she left, my hair was free of tangles and held in a bun by a silver grasshopper pin, one of hers.

A few minutes later, I went to my loom and picked up my weaving. After a while, I asked Melo her opinion about the green I planned for the bottom, to go with my pale yellow cloth. She always had something to say about color.

But she just blushed. Was she embarrassed to speak to me? Did she worry people would think ill of her if she did?

"I don't know," she said at last.

Kynthia giggled.

Conversation was subdued throughout the women's quarters, as if they were all required to show their disapproval of me. By noon, I was trembling with rage at being misunderstood. I asked Mother if I could visit the sacred grove, expecting her to say no and thinking I'd leave anyway.

But she said yes. "You may go wherever you usually do."

My eyes smarted. "Come with me! Then you'll see."

Eurus would love a visit from another worshipper. He might be able to convince her of the danger of Paris and Helen. This was a wonderful idea!

"Dear, I can barely waddle ten steps. Just don't spend another night away."

I tried for second best. "I can take my cousins. They'll tell you where I go."

"Go alone. I won't let you tempt anyone into mischief."

17

In the sacred grove, Eurus was glad to see me and didn't instantly demand his offerings. He began pacing as I told him what had happened at the palace. "Don't the king and queen know their daughter?"

I laughed. "I'd been about to lie to them!"

"A heroic fib!"

My defender.

"Should I tell them there were no shepherds? They'll believe any god."

"Would you?" I put my basket on the altar and smiled at him.

"I won't tell it as beautifully as you would."

My champion. My eyes filled.

"I'll blow us to the palace."

I went to him and then backed away, unsure. "If you tell them, Helenus will know I have a god for a friend."

"Good. That will stop his scheming."

I tossed back my head. "It may *improve* his scheming. He'll have you in mind when he plans."

He nodded. "Too dangerous. Will your parents stay angry at you?"

"Mother isn't angry anymore. Father will probably forgive me."

"Good!"

But I'd stay disgraced.

He reached into my basket and drew out a honey cake. "Mm."

I sat on the ground and waited. After he finished eating, I said, "When Paris and Helen come, she'll be wearing pounds of jewelry." Rings, earrings, arm and wrist bracelets, and three gold necklaces—everything studded with precious stones.

"Father will meet them in the colonnade. He always wants more wealth for Troy, so the jewelry will tempt him." He'd also be taken with Helen's beauty.

My brothers and Father's advisors would be there too. The men would barely see Paris. Only Helen.

I stood up. "As soon as Paris asks, Father will say they can stay."

"Where do you think you'll be?"

"Probably on our balcony, watching with the women. Mother will almost fly down the stairs to embrace Paris. The women won't be charmed by Helen, not even Mother. While the men smile, they'll glare."

Three crows landed on Eurus's altar.

> *"The fox waves his plumy tail.*
> *The lioness perks her pretty ears.*
> *Pity Helen's prey*
> *and lament beauty's power."*

Eurus disagreed with the crows. "Beauty is fine. Helen isn't." Unaccountably, he reddened.

We began to talk about what we might do, but we'd settled nothing by dusk. Maera greeted me at the city gate.

I knelt and rubbed her back. "Do you remember that Hera owes me a gift?"

She licked my face.

"Don't pretend! You don't even know who Hera is." I explained about the gift the goddess had promised me. "She might keep Helenus from ever being near Helen." Grinning, I imagined his confusion and rage. "But that won't save us all, and I won't waste the gift. Do you trust me to dream up something that will help Troy?"

She barked.

* * *

During the next month, when I was home, I made cloth, with Maera lying at my feet. I prophesied constantly, praying that the correctness of my predictions would gather weight. I'd call out what was about to happen: that Melo would weave with blue wool; that a snake would glide across the floor; that Kynthia would yawn and five other women would follow suit.

My loom had no visitors except Hector. The first time he came after my return, he said, loud enough for everyone to hear, "I don't believe Helenus's nonsense. You wouldn't romp with anyone and frighten Mother and Father."

I touched his cheek. "Of course I wouldn't!"

Mother's hands slowed at her loom. She cried, "I love all my children equally!"

Hector and I said at the same time, "I know."

He visited me often. He'd pet Maera and praise my weaving. I'd ask him about his farmwork, athletic games, hunting. When those topics exhausted themselves, we'd lapse into a comfortable silence. Often, I'd inhale and exhale in time with his breaths.

Mother gave birth to her final baby, her nineteenth, my brother Polydorus, who was born with fat cheeks and a fuzz of black hair. She lay in state in her big nook, circled by Father and my brothers and sisters, all smiling down on her and the baby.

Father squeezed around Helenus and Deiphobus, who

stood side by side, linked by dislike. He patted Laodice's head and came to me.

"I'm too happy to stay angry, Cassandra." He put his arm around my shoulder and pulled me close.

"Father, I—"

He put a finger over my lips. "I wasn't sure when Helenus first told us, but he described everything. One of the shepherds picked his teeth, a shepherdess sounded like a sheep when she laughed, a shepherd had the worst bowlegs he'd ever seen. He couldn't have made all that up." He laughed. "Even our children aren't that clever!"

Helenus had probably met such shepherds and shepherdesses and wove his lie around them.

I just said, "The baby didn't come out old and wrinkled."

"What?" He remembered and laughed. "No, but I think he'll still be wise."

If he lived to be old enough.

A week later, Mother was back at her loom, with the swaddled baby in a basket cradle by her knee. Everyone came to coo at him. I went too and rocked his cradle while women (not Mother) watched uneasily, ready to save him from me.

Mother seemed not to remember that I'd predicted the baby would be a boy.

In the sacred grove, I proposed one way after another

that Eurus could use his wind—like blowing Troy itself to the land of the fierce Amazons, who would capture Helen for her jewelry—and he explained why he couldn't do whatever I suggested.

He said he wasn't powerful enough to lift an entire city. "You'd need all the winds for that, and my brothers and I never agree on anything." He wondered if Aphrodite would continue to help Paris. "I can blow him and Helen anywhere, but not if she doesn't want me to."

We agreed he shouldn't try.

Days went by. We turned over idea after idea, rejecting some, keeping others.

When I was sad, Eurus made his wind perform. Without seeming to do anything—even while talking to me about something else—he caused the trees to sway in unison, creating a whispering melody. Once, his wind wove a garland of leaves and flowers of myrtle, olive, and laurel.

"Your wind has fingers!" I cried. "It could weave at my loom!"

"Maybe."

The garland landed on my head. I pushed it off my right ear. "Thank you."

He adjusted it with his fingers. His face was intent. My heart picked up its pace.

"There." He backed away. "It doesn't disgrace you."

I blushed.

His face was ruddy too. "What would my wind weave at your loom?"

"A himation for you." I'd never seen him wear a cloak. "Red." The color would bring out the warmth of his brown eyes.

"With a border design of roast chickens."

We laughed. I resolved to make such a himation for him and surprise him with it.

Daily, we rocked back and forth from sadness and worry to merriment. But at last, we finalized a plan, which combined wind, omens, and, possibly, false predictions from me, depending on how matters went. Ahead of time, Eurus would blow Helenus across the Hellespont and a great distance to the west.

We were sitting on the bank of the Scamander River near a pomegranate shrub. I took off my sandals and lowered my feet into the mud at the river's edge.

His wind rippled the water. "I can waft you wherever you like."

I told him I hadn't changed my mind about leaving my family.

"If you go, you won't have to see them suffer."

I watched my feet, wavering in the water. "I see it whenever I peer ahead to the war." I didn't look often, but if I deserted everyone, I was sure I'd do nothing else, until future became present and then past and lost to me.

His wind whipped around my face. "She makes me use-less. Why am I trying to help her when she doesn't care about herself—or me?"

He vanished.

I gulped. "I do care!" Would this help? "If we don't succeed, your breeze can breathe on me when I sail away. We'll be together."

He reappeared, smiling. "I'll blow you to safety then. All your obligations will be fulfilled, and you can be free."

"Good." Maybe he could rescue me then, but I doubted my fate would let him.

Above the courtyard, the sky was cloudless, the sun bright. Hector stood next to my loom. Maera lay between us, watching each of us in turn. I hadn't been able to get my breakfast down. My hand shook as I drew the shuttle through my weft.

My kind brother noticed. "Is something wrong?"

In a moment, Paris and Helen would come through Troy's open west gate.

I shook my head and forced a laugh. "Yesterday, I made an enormous snarl. I don't want to do it again and spend more hours untangling myself."

"Oh." He went happily back to telling me the perfec-tions of Andromache, the woman he wanted to marry, the one Helenus had said he would, and I too knew he would.

"They say the children of Thebe crowd around her for stories. They say . . ."

In a moment, dogs would bark, announcing my brother and Helen.

Dogs barked. Maera jumped up and barked too. When she stopped, I heard tapping from the roof, which meant that Eurus had landed. He'd watch from there.

"Troy has visitors." Hector left and ran downstairs.

Maera trailed me to the balcony railing. Mother stood next to me and draped her arm across my shoulders, Conny at her feet.

Father, his advisors, and my other grown-up brothers came out of the living room into the courtyard. As one, they froze when they saw Paris and Helen—really, from their drooping jaws, they saw just Helen.

The other women came to the railing and saw Helen too. I felt them stiffen.

My brother was no longer huge and glowing. Helen, however, needed no goddess's help to light her up. She paraded while Paris merely walked along the colonnade toward the awed faces of the men.

When they neared my father, the newcomers stopped, bowed their heads, then straightened. Paris's resemblance to Father was clear.

Mother gasped. "Paris!" She almost threw herself downstairs to hug him.

When she finally released him, his head wagged grog-gily, like a bee after drinking too much nectar.

"He's our baby, Priam!"

"Are you our son?" Father's eyes remained on Helen.

Paris confirmed it. "This is my wife, Queen Helen of Sparta."

She touched the king's hand at his side. In her soft voice, she said, "We seek sanctuary. My former husband, King Menelaus, will pursue us."

Hector frowned—the first to seem to take in Helen's meaning.

Helen stroked Paris's cheek. "Love for your son caused me to flee the king." She touched her necklaces. "We aren't poor."

I saw Father notice the jewelry. "We'll honor you here. Troy will defend you."

"You are my new daughter." But Mother's arm hovered in the air before coming down on Helen's shoulder. She squeezed it and then stepped away.

I flicked my hand, my signal to Eurus, who blew a pair of dead ravens above Paris and Helen and let go.

A body landed on the heads of each of them.

"Ai!" Mother jumped back.

This was the moment when we feared Aphrodite might step in. She didn't appear.

Dead ravens were a dire, terrifying omen. As if she

knew, Maera barked. A few women screamed. I did too, for whatever good my voice might do. Father and the other men stepped back.

Paris tried to push the raven off Helen's head. But, delicately, using his wind, Eurus kept both birds in place—proof that a god was involved, as indeed one was.

One of Father's councilors, Antenor, cried, "They're cursed. Priam, we'll be cursed too if we let them stay."

Paris pointed at me. "A wind god is her friend. He's doing it."

My heart chilled. Would they believe him?

But Paris lacked Helenus's persuasive power, and not one of them had a god for a friend, so why would I?

Antenor added, "Wasn't it foretold that this son of yours would bring down Troy? Now here he is with an army at his heels."

No one spoke. I sensed their uncertainty and wished some other omen would appear. Eurus and I had planned only the ravens.

A yellow-bellied snake slithered from behind a column and glided over Paris's sandaled right foot, which he raised and shook. Seemingly unperturbed, the snake continued to Helen's dimpled feet. Its movements appeared natural, but I could tell that they were forced. The snake was pushed and guided by tiny puffs from Eurus—a surprise for me.

Everyone watched the snake, so, unluckily, they missed

seeing how ill horror became Helen. Her lips were drawn back; her teeth stuck out; her eyes bulged; blotches covered her cheeks.

The snake slithered toward the palace entrance.

"Woe!" Mother rushed to Paris, held him tight, then released him. "We have other children. A baby. You must go, at least until Sparta's king is satisfied. Then come back and we'll rejoice." She turned to Helen. "You'll be welcome too, if you come."

"Don't exile me again!"

Father's mouth tightened. "Leave, son, and take your wife." He softened it. "It's my heavy duty to send you away when we've just been reunited. Your mother . . ."

I gripped the balcony railing and fought not to fall. The future changed again. The sky above the colonnade seemed to pulse with light.

Helen took Paris's hand and led him out, while he still argued.

Troy would not burn!

18

While the others remained on the balcony, I wobbled dizzily away, Maera at my side.

I recovered on my bed, then stood. Softly, so the floor didn't groan, I danced while Maera wagged at me. Up on my toes. I raised my arms. Swayed. Right foot across my left, left foot behind my right, the length of the nook and back. I picked up Maera's front feet and danced her too, for just a moment because she didn't like it.

Ah, joy. Ah, peace such as I hadn't felt since before Apollo poured his gift into me. Relief so deep it touched the center of the earth.

Hector would live a long life. Troy's women would keep our freedom. Our beautiful city would become more beautiful, because Hector would extend the Way of the

Immortals to the west gate.

My own lot would improve as the taint of my disappearance faded. I thanked Apollo for his gift. The curse hadn't mattered.

The crows flapped into my nook. My heart seemed to freeze.

> *"Upon a lake, three ducklings sleep,*
> *their nest far from the storms that roil the sea,*
> *not virtuous, just favored by the gods.*
> *Cassandra, though, is punished for good deeds."*

What did they mean? I peered further into my future and saw myself at my loom in thirty years with grown daughters weaving at my side. You're wrong, crows!

Eurus would be waiting and wondering if we'd really saved Troy. I left my nook. Mother sat next to her loom, weeping into her hands at the loss of Paris, not knowing her good fortune that he was gone.

I rubbed her back. "Maybe it—" I cut off my prophecy. How could I comfort her? "Polydorus looks sweet." I crouched and rubbed his belly through his swaddling cloth.

Maera made a grumbling noise, resenting my attention to the baby.

Mother smiled at me through her tears. "You're a good daughter, regardless."

I sighed and smiled back.

In the kitchen, I filled a basket with offerings, including enough for Eurus and me. Maera whined. She knew what the basket meant.

In the sacred grove, I went from altar to altar, thanking the gods. When I finally reached Eurus and he saw my smile, we danced together, though Trojan men and women never did. I praised him again and again for the ravens and the snake. He preened and laughed.

At last, he sobered. "Is this the end of our traveling?"

"I'd still like to visit Delphi."

"That's all?" He pulled an apple out of my basket and sat on the altar.

"Where should we go?" I stretched out on the grass below him. Above me, his legs were muscular and shapely. "Where do you like best?"

"I like many places best!" He swept out his arms, still holding the apple. "The Rhodope Mountains of Thrace! You've never seen so many shades of green! In the fall, the reds and golds! The froth of the waterfalls."

We began to plan again. Eurus went on and on about our choices and educated me in the wonders of the world.

At home, I began to weave his himation.

If I went away with him, I wouldn't marry a man of Troy and have his children.

But I wanted to go! Eurus and I were happy in each other's company. I wouldn't be able to see him after I moved to my husband's house. Eurus would miss my offerings—and me. I'd mourn the loss of him.

So I'd go with him and be an outcast at home. I smiled and didn't pursue my thoughts further.

Two weeks passed. He and I were walking along the seashore when we settled on our first three excursions: to Delphi, to the Rhodopes, and to the palace at Knossos. I was at the edge of the water. Wet sand squeezed between my toes. I picked up a snail shell—pink, streaked with brown.

"See how perfect it is." I held it out.

"Lovely." He returned it to the sand. "We can leave for Delphi anytime." He paused. "Cassandra? Did you know that five years ago Boreas married Orithyia?"

I walked backward ahead of him. Boreas was the north wind, Eurus's brother. Why was he bringing this up? "Do they live near Delphi? And who is Orithyia?"

"She was a princess of Athens before they wed."

A mortal marrying an immortal.

"And"—his voice cracked, then deepened—"Eros and Psyche have been married for years."

Everyone knew the story about the god of love and the

mortal girl. Heat began to travel up my neck. I stopped and stared down at my sandy feet. If he was saying what I thought he was, this would be too much happiness.

Nervously, I said, "Before we go to Delphi, we should make sure Paris and Helen won't go there for advice during our visit. I'll look a little ahead to see."

"Cassandra, we—"

"Ai!"

"What's wrong?"

"Paris and Helen are about to enter my father's palace! Helenus is with them!"

"Should I find more dead ravens?"

Helenus must have met the pair on his way home. He would have foreseen where they'd be.

"Any dead animal." I had a new idea. "First, bring Oenone and Corythus." They might remind him he once had a more beautiful wife than Helen—and a son by her.

I rushed off. On my way home, I decided what to do and say, though I doubted I'd matter. The outcome would almost certainly hang on Eurus's omens, Oenone, Corythus, Paris, Helen, and my twin.

Maera met me at the city gate and ran with me. In the salon, Father and his councilors stood a few yards from the returned couple and Helenus. My mother hovered between the groups, her arms held out to her sons. As before, the other palace women leaned over the balcony railing. Maera and I stood on the edge of the men.

Helenus was in the middle of saying something: "—them just in time, or they—"

"Brother Paris! Sister Helen!" People turned. I ran and embraced Helen, who was limp in my arms. I kissed her smooth cheek and released her. Growling, sensing my true feeling, Maera jumped up on her legs.

I made Maera sit. "How glad I am you've come back, brother. Since you left, I've heard Apollo's crows cawing in my ears. I'll tell you what they say."

No one interrupted me—they were probably too bewildered by the unfolding drama.

By now I knew how the crows phrased their messages:

> *"Dew on grass at dawn,*
> *in each shining drop a mirror to the sky.*
> *When has beauty ever augured ill?*
> *Helen is heaven-sent to Troy!"*

I hoped people would disagree with Helenus when he argued for keeping the pair, since they always disagreed with me. And I was giving Eurus more time.

From the balcony, Melo called, "The ravens were sent by the gods to warn us."

Helenus put his arm around my shoulder. His fingers dug into my flesh. Maera growled again.

My twin said, "When bees hum and dogs bark, mortals listen, though the meaning is unclear. Who knows what deity put truth on my sister's tongue today?"

I decided the next thing I'd say would be clearly false and strange. "How gray and aged you are, brother. Oh, see! A ship sails into the colonnade, its sail—"

All heads turned to the entryway, where Oenone stood with Corythus.

She came in slowly, dignity in her bearing despite Corythus tugging her along.

He pulled free of her. "Father!" He ran to Paris and leaped.

Caught off guard, my brother stumbled backward, barely managing to hold his son and not fall. He looked weak, almost overmastered by a little boy.

"Our grandson!" Mother took him and held him easily.

"Husband," Oenone said, extending her hands. Unlike Helen, she wore no jewels, suggesting her person was enough.

Paris didn't take her hands, and she lowered them.

Corythus wriggled free of Mother. "Pretty." He hugged Helen around her hips.

She stroked his hair, and there was something in the slowness of her hand, the dreaminess of her face, that made me feel as if my own hair were being caressed.

The men smiled vaguely, looking as dazed as I felt. I

wished that Eurus would rain down a few omens, but he must have still been collecting them.

"Have you missed me?" Oenone's voice was honey and butter. "I've missed you."

"Oenone—"

"Come home! Weren't we happy on our mountain?"

"Oenone—"

She went to him and rose on tiptoe to kiss him on the lips.

Let her kiss taste sweet, I thought, though I felt embarrassed to be watching.

He kissed her back.

I looked at Helen, who gazed at the air just below the balcony. Her peaceful face suggested that none of this concerned her.

When Oenone and Paris separated, he wiped his mouth with the back of his hand, as if her kiss had been distasteful.

My father coughed and introduced himself and my mother to Oenone.

The nymph ignored him. "You'd wound the mother of your son, Paris?"

"Oenone—"

"Yes, darling?"

"The past is gone. I loved you then." He turned to Helen. "My queen, what shall I tell my former wife?"

There was no feeling in Helen's polite tone. "Tell her that fate governs all. If the gods had willed it, you'd still love her." She nudged Corythus toward his father. He went, stepping backward, watching her.

"Paris, you want her only because other men do too." Oenone moved close to Helen. Her finger circled Helen's eyes and mouth. "The age lines are thin, but they won't be in five years. I have no lines, nor will I. Which of us is more comely?"

Oenone was as far above Helen in beauty as a butterfly is to a moth. The delicate shape of the nymph's nose, the gentle slope of her jaw, the roundness of her bare arms were surpassed only by those of the great goddesses. She smiled. "Decide, my love."

He stepped back. In the moment he did, Helen leaned toward him. Her eyes widened; her gaze sweetened; the corners of her mouth curled up; her lips opened. She was as I first glimpsed her: unguarded, tender, unbearably precious.

Helenus whispered, "Oh. Ah."

What could I do?

Oenone, unaware of what Helen had done, smiled brilliantly, radiating certainty of her charms. She was complete in herself, meant for someone who wanted an equal.

Helen sought completion. Her face promised that she and her darling would be fused in their love. Each would fulfill the other.

Paris's Adam's apple bobbed. "I prefer my now-and-forever wife, Helen."

I rushed to Oenone and caught her as she started to collapse. Holding her under her arms, I hoped no one could see she wasn't supporting herself.

For an instant, Helen's expression registered satisfaction before it dulled. Maera growled again.

The future Troy still didn't burn, but I thought it would.

Oenone gathered herself and stepped away from me. "Paris, my love, you're welcome to your fluff-over-wood woman. Corythus, come!"

"I want to stay with Father."

"Come!"

Reluctantly, he did.

The two left the palace.

Helenus coughed.

All eyes went to him.

He addressed our father. "Paris told me of dead ravens falling on him and his wife, but no priest or prophet interpreted their meaning, though everyone knows the gods speak in riddles."

Father rubbed his eyes.

"Apollo gave me the gift of future sight. Isn't that true, Cassandra, my dear?"

"As much as I have it."

"This is the future I see: Menelaus will come with his fleet of heroes to besiege the tall towers of Troy, but we have—"

Eurus dropped a two-headed calf at Helenus's feet.

Everyone gasped, even Helenus.

From the balcony, Aminta said in the quiet that followed, "This portent needs no interpretation. Troy will suffer if these two stay."

"My children," our father began.

I started to hope.

The monstrous calf was still alive. It lowed pitiably through two throats.

"I will not risk—"

Helenus, who seemed to have recovered, held up a hand. Father stopped.

"Which god do you imagine sent the monster? We all know Poseidon adores the Greeks. Achilles' mother, Thetis, wants her son to be safe, and everyone knows he's to die young if he goes to war."

I saw where this was going. What could I do?

Helenus listed gods and goddesses who were more friendly to the Greeks. Then he said, "They fear us. Our heroes surpass theirs—Hector, Aeneas, Agen—"

Eurus dropped a dead raven on him, but Helenus used it to fuel his argument. "One of them wants to frighten us."

The calf moaned again.

161

When it stopped, Helenus said, "I prophesy this with the power that Apollo gave me: Troy will defeat Greece. Tribute will pour in from the city kingdoms."

Three crows flew down—real, living crows. From their flight, Eurus couldn't have blown them in. They landed on Helenus's shoulders and pecked his cheeks. Everyone saw them. I know because Mother ran to him and bravely shooed them away.

Speak, crows! Tell my parents that Troy will fall!

They flapped away.

Father said, "Son, if you're right, then the seer who foretold about Paris at his birth was wrong. If you're wrong and Troy will be destroyed, those events will happen. No one can evade destiny." He turned to Paris. "You and your wife may stay."

I saw Troy burning.

Eurus didn't finish what he might have meant to say to me on the shore. We doubled each other's sadness. I stopped visiting him, because I reasoned he'd be happier without me, but I sent a servant with offerings every day and continued weaving his himation.

I played with Maera and predicted small moments just before they arrived. I didn't look further into the future than a few minutes ahead. My gift allowed me to spend more time with Hector than I would have without it. After he and Andromache married, I smiled at her working at her loom across the women's quarters. I rarely visited her there because I wanted her to have friends.

In a year, the Greek ships sailed into our harbor.

When Agamemnon and Menelaus entered the palace after the Greeks made camp, I didn't hang over the balcony to see them. They had come to negotiate for Helen's return, but she wouldn't be returned. Why watch it happen?

The next day, the war began.

PART TWO

RIN

A hoopoe fans its feathers in the dust;
mares race across the plains.
A proud Amazon draws back her bowstring
and shoots her arrow,
thinking she can wound the moon.

1

I ride Short Black into the mountains long before daylight, as I'd been doing for a week. Young White Chest, my hound, trots along and stays with me after I dismount to climb among boulders and rockfall. I hope not to turn an ankle in the dark. As the sky lightens to gray, I make out a rivulet, cutting between two crags. Grass pokes up from cracks in the stone.

The boulder we'd hidden behind before seems unlucky, so I choose again, an overhang where three rocks meet. I pull my bow and five arrows out of my gorytos, the case that holds my bow and arrows, and stand still. A hoopoe calls, *Oop-oop-oop*.

After a few, slow minutes, Young White Chest's ears prick. I hear irregular taps. The hound watches me. I wait.

Wait. Clench my fists. Wait.

I hear lapping.

Wait.

I raise my bow and jump out while nocking an arrow.

The ibex, a big male with magnificent horns, looks up. I loose my arrow, which pierces his shoulder. That won't slow him. He flees upward, fast for such a big beast. I shoot again, and Young White Chest gives chase.

My second arrow goes wide. Cybele, I pray, thank you for bringing him to me. I'll reward you by keeping him.

I reach for more arrows and clamber, seeming to bounce from rock to rock. Young White Chest is with the goat, nipping his ankles and slowing him. I shoot from below and pierce his stomach.

In the end, he takes fifteen arrows before he falls, and one more finishes him. A lump rises in my throat when life leaves him. Why am I sad since I wanted him?

Soon, though, pride and happiness take over. I spend a while admiring him. I'd never managed more than small game before. "All of you will be used," I promise his carcass.

Then I run for Short Black and gallop to our wagons for help bringing my kill home. Young White Chest trails us, falling behind.

My mother, Queen Pen, promises not to let Barkida find out what I've brought down. Though she's our queen,

Pen does everything we all do, and she's a fine butcher. I spend half the afternoon scraping blood and skin away from the horns.

When I finally finish, I hide the horns behind my back and stand over Barkida, where she's kneeling in the dirt on the other side of the wagons from the rest of us. I bounce on my toes and grin.

"You again." She doesn't look up.

I don't say anything.

She goes back to rubbing dried horsetail sprigs along one side of a length of oak to smooth it. When she's finished, the wood will be as slick as dewy grass.

In my imagination, her big hands are my hands. I feel the rough bark cradled along my left arm. In my right hand, the horsetail is scratchy.

Barkida won't let me try this task, though I'm convinced I'd do it well. Only she and Gamis, our second bowyer, perform all the steps to produce a bow.

With the hand that holds the horsetail sprigs, Barkida pushes her red hair away from her forehead. We're all redheads. The Greeks call us Flames of Rage and are cautious in their dealings with us.

"You're in my light, Rin."

I step to the side, even though she's already in the late-day shadow of her wagon. Her gorytos leans against a wheel. Mine still rests at my left hip on the strap across my shoulders. An Amazon—woman or girl—keeps her best weapon close. Our favorite possessions are our bow and arrows, and we never know when we'll need them.

Over the *sh, sh* of her scraping, Barkida says, "Be useful. Get a skin ready."

She wants me to make glue, but I don't move.

Finally, she turns. "Rin?"

I shake my head.

She frowns, but it's a mock frown. "Why not?"

"My hands are full." I'm making her ask.

"What do you have?"

I bring them out.

"Rin!" She groans as she stands to take the ibex horns from me. One she puts on the ground and the other she turns over in her hands. "I haven't seen a pair as good in years."

Happy tears threaten to spill. "Let me help you work it when it's ready." In a few months, after the horns dry, long strips will be cut from each one for a bow's limbs. The strips will be scraped smooth, steamed, and gradually shaped. Making a bow is complicated and slow.

Instead of answering, she asks, "Did you take down the goat?"

I nod.

"Rin, you might make a mistake and waste part of the horn."

"I'd be careful!"

"Thanks for your gift." She goes to her wagon and takes out a length of felt. "I'll use one of the horns for Rethra's bow. You'll have a place in the rites when she gets it."

Rethra is my cousin. She'll receive her bow when she's big enough and strong enough for it. I got mine at the beginning of the past winter.

Barkida puts the horns in the wagon, atop a pile of felt sheets, then returns to me. "They'll be dry enough by . . ." She calculates. "Midsummer. We need glue now."

I don't move.

She takes my face in both her hands and smiles into my eyes. "You want to learn to do everything, right?"

"Every single thing." I'm almost as tall as she is. "Already, I can hunt and shoot." I went out with Pen on our band's last raid, when we cut a dozen sheep out of a flock and herded them away with us. Along with everyone else, I shot backward at the villagers who came after us, who never got close enough to be hit.

I continue my list. "I gave Rethra her first tattoo." With her mother supervising, and the sun in the tiny sun-burst is more oval than round, but it looks pretty on her left calf. "Also, I etched a fawn into my gorytos gold." We hammer flat the gold we get from spoils and tribute. Then we engrave designs on the sheets and cover our bow cases with them.

I pinch out a bit of my leggings, which collapses back when I let go. "I've made more felt than this. I can do every step. Can't I make just Rethra's bow?" I don't want to actually *be* a bowyer, because bowyers aren't allowed to hunt or fight. We can't afford to lose them.

Groaning again, Barkida kneels to resume her polishing. "If she understood anything," she says, "she wouldn't make such a stupid request."

She is me.

"I would spend four years teaching her to make one bow. I could die in less than four years."

Barkida isn't old, just an adult, but anyone can die at any age. People sicken or are killed in battle. In a skirmish, another cousin of mine caught an arrow in her shoulder and was gone in two hours. We poison our arrows with snake venom. So do other bands.

My nose is suddenly stuffy. I stand over Barkida, remembering my cousin. I feel as heavy as the ibex carcass.

Barkida goes on. "*She* could die, and then I would have wasted my time."

I remember that Cybele honors my cousin, and she's fighting now in whatever wars the goddess wages.

I give up. "I'll prepare the goat hide." Glue-making starts by boiling scraps of hide in water.

My ibex's skins make an awkward bundle. I heave them into Barkida's wagon, saving a single length in my hands.

Aunt Lannip bellows, "Zeeyaa!" It's the dinner shout. My ibex is cooked.

I go to our wagon, where we keep our things and where I sleep at night with Pen. I climb in and put the skin on top of a pile of felt. Then I find my willow-wood bowl, which is light as a handful of grass. My gazbik—spoon on one end, ladle on the other—is harder to locate, because it's small and likes to dive between blankets. Pen says I'm untidy. When I have it, I head for the blankets and skins that are spread around the cookfire.

Pen and my aunts and older cousins take turns cooking. Tonight, it's Lannip, so everything is sure to be good. Pen waves to me to join her and Young White Chest on a lion skin rug as soon as my bowl is full. When Pen cooks, I help her. I'm learning cooking too. People still tease me about the weeds I once added to a stew in hopes of making it more pungent.

Away from the fire, strips of meat hang from branches of the only tree here, an oak. Now, in early spring, the tree is bare except for ribbons of ibex, dripping blood. Lannip didn't put the whole goat in our deep iron pot. Once the strips are air-dried, we'll eat them for months, whenever we don't have fresh kill. Amazons never go hungry.

Lannip limps to the pot. The others have served themselves, but she takes my gazbik from me and ladles stew into my bowl. "I buried the best for the hunter."

The tastiest part is the back meat.

"And I saved the biggest carrots. Here are dandelions and bulrush hearts." The gazbik goes back in. "And juice." She pours on the gravy. "Now yogurt." From an open leather bladder, she spoons a dollop of yogurt on top of the stew.

I thank her and take a silver cup from the jumble of silver cups around the silver pitcher—all plunder from raids on villages. The pitcher holds fizzy koumiss, fermented mare's milk.

When I sit, Pen rises to her knees. "Ouch!" She rubs her hip.

Every Amazon past early womanhood has aching hips or knees or both. Already, I feel twinges when I stand up. When we meet other bands in autumn to worship Cybele, everyone—men too—limps. Cybele gave us horses, and horses bounce us into pain. We spend as much of our lives on horseback as walking on earth's belly.

I manage not to spill my meal while Pen hugs me, musses my hair, takes my face in her hands, shakes my head back and forth, and, finally, kisses my cheek. "Another hunter for the band."

Young White Chest, the beggar, uncurls himself and sits up, staring at me. With the knife from my belt, I spear a morsel of meat and hold it out. Young White Chest eats and lies down again. He knows better than to expect more.

In a big voice, Pen says, "Rin will be queen after me, and my next daughter will be her lieutenant, and the daughter after that will be *her* lieutenant."

Some laugh. Some cheer. No one is unhappy.

Pen had a son last year, but she gave him to his father, who leads a band of men, to raise. We keep our daughters and teach them to be riders, hunters, and fighters (or, occasionally, bowyers). The fathers do the same for their sons.

We're a small band. Pen is queen over forty adult subjects and twenty-seven children, all of us women or girls and all blood relatives. Everyone loves my mother. Anyone who doesn't, leaves or is chased away.

Aunt Zelke says, "How many daughters, Pen?"

"As many as I can make!" She sits again. "I'm proud of you, Rin." She laughs. "Before you killed that enormous ibex, I had to content myself with loving your shining hair, your endless freckles, your big hands."

We all have freckles, but mine are so crowded together, I expect fighting to break out.

I protest. "I went on the raid!" My first.

"Did you hit a villager?"

"No one hit anyone!"

She's laughing again. "Exactly."

I taste the ibex. Succulent, tender, juicy. I had gotten it when it was full grown but not so old that it would be stringy.

Pen and I settle in to steady eating. People murmur. A light breeze blows from the north, fresh, chilly, but without winter's bite. The first star comes out. My older cousin Khasa takes out her bone flute and starts a melody.

In unison, we sing, "We've eaten meat. One of us hunted. One of us cooked. We have music."

We fade out until a high pure voice comes in. "We have our horses . . ." The voice quiets.

Aunt Serag: "Our flocks . . ."

"Our grassland . . ."

Pen, with laughter in her mellow voice: "Our daughters . . ." She puts her arm across my shoulders.

I sing, "Our queen . . ."

"Our sky . . ." As if we own it. How confident we are.

"Our bows . . ."

In turn, voices name our weapons as the sky blackens. The stars brighten, and my eyes get used to the dark. People name events of the day. Barkida sings, "Ibex horns . . ."

Finally, our ideas peter out. We stop to take a breath before the usual ending, but Rethra pipes in. "Our tattoos."

Yes, it was good to mention them.

We all join in for the end. "We're what you mean for people to be: riders, fighters, hunters, roamers. Cybele, this is our song for you. Thank you, Cybele, for smiling on us."

Everyone stands. Young White Chest follows me as we bring our bowls to the dying fire, where the dogs lick them speckless. Tomorrow, we'll wash them in the river.

Young White Chest growls, barks, and rushes away. All the dogs are barking.

Two men ride straight to the crowd of us and rein in their horses. Slung across their chests are ridiculously enormous bows. Their quivers hang from their belts. Even though they're on horseback, I can tell both are shorter and stockier than we are. Darker too. They're the brown of oakwood to our yellowy white of mare's milk.

One man says, with an accent, not pronouncing his l's, "We're 'ooking for Queen Penthesi'ea."

Pen goes to them. "Yes?"

The man, who seems to be the speaker for both of them, says his name is Pammon, and he's a son of King Priam of Troy, where war has been raging for years. I press my hands together and wish on my bow, my arrows, my strong body.

The man's voice takes on the cadence of a recitation. "Mighty Troy hovers between defeat and victory. Renowned is the courage of the Amazons. Warrior women and their immortal deeds will propel us to success. Will you come to our aid?"

Pen says nothing.

Say yes! Please!

Pen! Why are you waiting?

The man's eyes travel from one of us to another and pass by me quickly.

At last, Pen says, "We'll take what spoils we want and as much as we want."

Pammon thinks for a moment, then nods.

"I'll command us. No Trojan will tell us how to fight."

Pammon agrees to this too.

"We'll rescue you." Pen turns to me. "Yes, puppy. You can fight with us." Back to Pammon: "We'll stop for a day at Cybele's rock to worship her."

My true life is beginning.

2

Pen chooses eleven others to fight with us, among them
Lannip, Serag, Zelke, and Khasa. The Trojans seem satis-
fied. I'm untested, but everyone else is a seasoned warrior.
The unchosen in the band will wait for us to come back.

At dawn, we're ready to leave, though the others are
just beginning to sit up in their wagons.

Each of us warriors—including me!—has a skin flask
of koumiss, a sack of dried meat: rabbit, deer, squirrel—not
my ibex, which is still fresh. We'll hunt as we go and drink
raw milk when the koumiss runs out.

My gorytos is slung across my shoulder. From my
wide leather belt hang my shield and my other weapons:
battle-ax, spear, and sword. I used the spear once to fend
off a lion, which I failed to kill—and vice versa.

Pen gives me Tall Brown to ride. We have two kinds of horses: tall and short. Short are best for milk and are fine for rides when speed doesn't matter. Tall Brown, no longer in first youth, is fleet and used to battle.

The morning is more winter than spring, and I'm glad for the felt lining under my leather tunic. Scales made of bits of horses' hooves are sewn into the leather. Amazon tunics are as good as metal armor for turning swords.

I'm not so cold, though, that I want the leopard skin blanket that's draped behind my felt saddle.

The two Trojans are wrapped in wool cloaks they call himations. We set off at a trot. I pull my felt hat down to cover my ears. The sunrise is behind us. The sky is pale, cloudless, broken only by a circling hawk. How lucky I am. Thank you, Cybele.

Pen says the Trojans and Greeks worship the same gods and goddesses and are forever begging for favors. When she says this, she makes her voice whiny: "Zeus, please win this war for me. Ares, please give me a beautiful shield. Demeter, please keep the rain off my head."

We thank Cybele for what we have and don't ask her for anything. After all, she already gave us our grasslands, our horses, our strength, and our roaming natures. The rest is up to us.

When an Amazon is dying in battle, Cybele comes. The Amazons nearby see her, a huge, granite-colored woman with thick, curling red locks. Pen has seen the goddess three times, and Cybele has always said the same words, in a rich, warm voice: "You will fight on my side now. Thank you for your courage. Your friends will miss your arrows."

Once Cybele has spoken, we know our warrior will be safe, though we mourn her. If he's still alive, we slay her killer.

Pen trots to me. "Rin . . ." Her face is serious.

We ride together silently before she speaks. We're all spread out, except the two Trojans, who ride shoulder-to-shoulder as if they were yoked together.

"Rin . . ." She's silent again.

Is she going to tell me she's changed her mind about letting me go to battle?

"Rin, how was it when you killed the ibex?"

I don't know what she means. "I used up fifteen arrows before he fell. I didn't think he could keep going so long."

"That's right. How did you feel?"

"Sad." Was that wrong? "He was beautiful. I'd taken his life away from him." I'm feeling bad again. He would never graze anymore, never mate or grow old.

"And later. How did you feel?"

"Happy." Was that wrong? "He was the biggest animal I'd ever brought down. I was proud. I knew you'd be proud."

Pen reaches over and touches my shoulder. "It's the same in battle, though the thinking and feeling happen later—you'll be too busy at the time. Later, it will be a jumble, regret for the man you killed, who probably had a wife and children, who loved life as much as you do—mixed up with joy that you survived and spared us mourning you. The spoils will be especially precious, won at such a cost."

I nod, feeling uncomfortable. I want victory in battle to be pure joy.

Surprising me, Pen says, "I prefer hunting to fighting. We don't eat our human enemies." She laughs. "I like a good, young ibex."

I think of the principles we live by: fight for spoils; hunt for food.

Otherwise, we become village women.

Pen guesses where my thoughts are, or she wants to remind me. "Village women are mice, who do what they're told. Villagers plant wheat and eat bread."

Of the possible fates, being a farmer seems a terrible one: tied to a scrap of land, begging the sky for sun and rain, starving if the right amounts of each don't come.

But farming isn't the worst destiny.

In battle, if victory is impossible, we choose death. We contrive to be killed, open our chests and invite the spear, rather than be captured and enslaved.

"Before my first battle, Lyte told me what I've just said to you. Otherwise, I might have been too shocked to keep fighting."

Lyte is Hippolyta, Pen's mother, who died before I was born.

Pen kicks her horse and rides to Lannip.

Pen took away the pleasure of anticipating my first battle. I spur Tall Brown into a gallop. We race ahead of everyone. I turn to see the startled expressions of the two Trojans.

Pen will be right about what she told me, I'm sure. Fine. I want to learn everything, so I'll learn this too: both liking war and being saddened by it.

I face into the wind and stick out my tongue. Ah, the tingle! Here I am. The future can't change the present. I pat Tall Brown's rough mane. Thank you, Cybele.

We ride for three days, due west, then south, then west again, following the sea. Troy is to the southwest, but our first destination is Cybele's island. We want to thank her for the fighting to come, and I have special thanks to give her before my first battle.

Rain falls rarely in the grassland where we roam, but here, so close to the sea, we ride through a chilly mist. I pull the leopard skin over me, and it makes me almost warm and almost dry. And nothing can dampen (ha!) my pleasure in this journey.

The Trojans don't mind our delay. They say fighting

has been halted for a while for both sides to do their spring planting.

Pen and the others tease. She begins it. "Do you stop fighting to wash your face?"

Lannip pipes in: "To trim your toenails?"

"To throw a stick for your dog?"

"To eat your pasty bread? To be gluttons?"

The Trojans are as lean as we are. They smile fixedly at our fun.

I can't think of anything to add. And I'm sure I'm too young for a remark of mine to be welcome.

Lannip comes in again. "To beg your gods and goddesses for the courage you lack?"

I gasp at her brazenness.

The Trojans don't let this stand. Pammon says, "We also pause in the fighting for the tempests that Zeus sometimes sends, and to bury and honor our dead."

We can't ridicule those. The heckling stops.

That night, around a sputtering fire, as we chew on dried meat, Pammon tells us the reason for the war with the Greeks. The war is over a woman. A Trojan stole her, and the Greeks want her back.

We have no questions, because inquiries are silly when nothing makes sense, but Pammon adds that she was taken because she's the most beautiful woman in the world.

What good does it do to seize a woman because she's

beautiful? Her beauty still belongs to her. No one else can own it unless she's a slave. Pammon says she's a queen, but, really, she must be a slave.

We Amazons are beautiful too, with our bright hair and features that are—as Pen was once told by a Greek artist—a vase painter's dream. But no one would dare steal one of us, and we wouldn't live long in captivity anyway.

On the fourth morning, rain lashes us. My hat, which can absorb a lot of water, is soaked and useless. As we ride, I wring it out and slap it back on my soaked head, because I don't know what else to do with it. I wonder how I'll climb Cybele's rock in this weather. But I must! Every Amazon must before her first battle. (Raids don't count.) If I fail, I won't be allowed to fight.

Midmorning, we come to the skiffs that all Cybele's worshippers share, gray lumps in this gloom. They number about fifty, because some bands are much bigger than ours. The boats are far enough onto the beach that a flood won't float them away. The oars lie wind-tossed here and there.

Amazons aren't seafarers. We dislike bodies of water bigger than a puddle, but we can row the short distance to Cybele's island—unless the wind has another plan for us. My heart is hopping. I want to fight for Troy and die if I must. I don't want to drown.

We dismount. The horses will wait for us. We turn

three boats over, put in oars, and push the skiffs to the water's edge. Six of us get in one boat, seven in another. I'm one of the rowers, which pleases me. I've always been too young to row before.

The Trojans say they can manage their skiff without help.

We don't ask Cybele to stop the wind. The Trojans don't ask Zeus's help, either, because, I suppose, this isn't a bad storm to them, who live close to the sea.

As soon as we begin to row, Cybele or their Zeus stops the wind. The rain still pours down, vertically now.

On a clear day, the island is visible from shore. Now it's hidden. I hope we won't be forced east or west by currents and miss it and row until we die. It's a tiny island.

We don't miss it, but we don't see it until we're almost upon it. We bump onto the rocky shore and haul in the boats.

The island seems to be part of a mountain under the sea. I know from memory, since I can see only a few feet in front of me, that a forest lies about a quarter mile ahead, seemingly growing out of stone. Cybele's rock—shaped like a fist, roughly three times Pen's height—rises between the shore and the trees.

Cybele lives in a cave at the bottom of the stone. When she wants to come out, she lifts the rock and exits, but most of the time she's in there. She's always there when Amazons visit.

Together, we approach her rock. I wonder, although I feel wicked about my doubting thought: What if an Amazon dies in battle at the same moment other Amazons visit the stone? Which will Cybele pick?

A voice roars between my ears. "Gowk-head! I can be in a hundred places at once."

Am I about to die, since she spoke to me?

I continue to breathe.

When we're a few feet from her rock, we stop and begin the ritual. Pretending to be horses, we paw the ground with our right feet then our left. We shake our wet heads as if we were shaking our manes. We prance in place.

Human again, we stretch our arms across one another's shoulders and begin our thanks, much as we did after the ibex dinner. We go on for so long that Pammon walks away, and the other Trojan sits on the ground and draws in the mud with a stick.

Feeling that I have to make up for my doubt, I go beyond anyone else. I thank Cybele that there's land beneath my feet, that my toes number ten, that my ankles are strong and my elbows bend.

Pen snuffles, and I realize she's laughing. I stop.

We prostrate ourselves and kiss the wet stone because Cybele is the earth goddess. We rise and shoot arrows into the sky because Cybele is the sun goddess.

Pen's wet lips kiss my wet cheek. "Go, darling."

As I walk to the rock, the wind picks up again, even more than before, seeming to roar. Rain stings my cheek and hands. I run back to Pen and give her my leopard skin, which may hinder my climbing.

Long ago, people drove spikes into the rock. I put my right hand on one above my head. It's wet, slick, and cold, but my grip is strong. I hold tight, place my left boot on a spike at knee height, and ascend. As I rise from spike to spike, I review my prayer for when I reach the top. I decide to improvise a little in case Cybele is still angry.

Halfway up, I'm panting from the effort of holding on. At last, I reach the summit, which is flat but dented with small craters. I bend over with my hands on my knees to catch my breath.

When I can stand up, I spread my arms. "Thank you, Cybele, *who can be in many places at once.* Thank you, goddess of earth and sun, for giving me strength in battle. If you grant me victory, thank you for that too. Thank you, Cybele."

Pen starts the battle shout, and everyone from our band joins in: "Kiikiikaa!"

I begin to descend. The wind picks up, and the roar rises to a shriek. When I'm halfway down, a gust tears me loose.

I fall.

3

I feel as if Cybele slapped me with the entire earth.

"Rin!" Pen cries.

I open my eyes. She and Lannip crouch over me. The others, including the Trojans, circle me. I have no breath to breathe. Cybele, did I offend you?

Finally, I can speak. "I'm all right." Arrows of pain pierce my right side, where I landed. I try to stand but slump back.

Gently, Pen rolls me onto my left side. She presses cautiously on my right shoulder and watches my face. I don't wince.

"Good." She continues to probe.

I clench my teeth, but when she barely touches me below my armpit, a groan escapes. She moves her hand down, testing. Groan. Groan. After that, less pain.

"Do you feel this?" She pushes her thumb into my right thigh.

"It doesn't hurt."

"But do you feel it?" She pokes my other thigh. "This?"

"I feel them, as always."

"Could have been worse. Three ribs." She pats my belly. "You won't go to battle for a while, Rinny-Rin." She tells Pammon, "Miracle girl. Never broken anything before."

I struggle against tears. "I can fight. I don't mind pain."

"Those ribs will get you killed. You may die in battle someday, as I may, but not for being foolish. I say no."

I know better than to argue out loud, but deep in my mind, where no one can see or hear, I'm shouting my disappointment. "How long?"

"Until I decide."

"When will you and the Greeks finish farming?" I ask Pammon.

"A week or more after we get home."

With help, I manage to stand. On the skiff back to the mainland, I'm a passenger, not a rower. I need help to mount Tall Brown. When we set off, I feel like a pile of stones. Whenever the mare takes a step, the stones pound each other.

I wonder if stones really feel pain. Might I have hurt Cybele's rock and that was why she blew me off?

* * *

At night, Pen paints her sleeping remedy (cedarwood resin, oil of chamomile, roses, lavender, frankincense) on my temples and under my nose and leaves the vial open next to me for the scent to escape. I fall asleep quickly and sleep deeply. We all do. Even the Trojans are drowsy in the morning.

During the day, we ride through our grasslands, following the sun, which has returned, bypassing occasional villages. The weather warms. The Trojans shed their cloaks, revealing thin garments they call tunics that are pinned at the shoulders, leaving their arms bare.

Pain replaces enthusiasm as my companion. Sharp on the first day, it dulls to a constant ache on the days that follow. I tell Pen it's gone, but she knows better.

On the third day, near sunset, I see a rabbit. Dinner. Barely thinking, I squeeze my knees. Tall Brown breaks into a canter. I reach into my gorytos for my bow. Ai! Ouch! Ai! I pull Tall Brown in. The rabbit is gone.

Pen rides to me. "When your face stops turning gray, I'll know you've recovered." She waves a hand across my face from ear to ear.

As the pain diminishes, my shame grows. King Priam expects Amazon warriors—and one of them is just an injured girl.

Two days later, since my eyes are sharpest, I'm the first to see the hill that Troy rises from. Soon there's more than a hill, but I don't know what. Not a forest. Not a mountain atop a hill.

"Pen?" I point.

"I don't see anything."

It grows until everyone sees.

Pammon shouts, "Troy!" He kicks his horse.

If the villages we raid have walls at all, they're made of mud, but Troy's wall, from the ground to half its height, is white stone that makes me blink in the sun. I wonder where the stones came from, since all around is grass. Painted mud brick continues above the stone. As we approach, I calculate that if four Amazon women stood on one another's heads, the top person might peer into Troy.

The carved wooden doors to the gate ahead are open. Although the gate is big enough to ride through four abreast, we dismount and leave our horses to graze. I'm sure they'll be happier here. I would be.

We stand outside in a clump. Pammon and his companion remain on their horses.

The wall is twenty feet thick, so the gate is really a tunnel. Pen takes my hand. We're used to the sky as our ceiling, and we don't move to go in. Why do we have to? I think. The fighting will be outside the city.

The Trojans are laughing. Pen ignores them.

Pammon says to us all, "King Priam is eager to meet you."

I'm not eager to meet him. Shame over my injury clasps hands with my fear of the tunnel.

Pen and I lead us in. I count a dozen strides as we go through. The stones glisten, and beads of water stand out on them. I smell mold. My ribs don't slow me or make me limp.

The Trojans, it seems to me, could just stay behind their wall and wait for the Greeks to give up.

But then they wouldn't get any spoils. Amazons wouldn't let plunder go untaken, either.

I blink in the sunlight when we emerge, and my heart returns to its normal rhythm. We enter what I believe is a road—impossibly straight, coated with flat stones.

Pen doesn't let my hand go.

The road is wide, which I like, but walls rise on our left and right, which I don't like. It doesn't matter that they're wonderfully made, with colored stones forming pictures. Since the walls are so marvelous, they could come together and squeeze us to death.

The bottoms of my boots grow hot from the sun on the stones.

How do people live here without melting?

The walls and the road end in an open area in front of an enormous building made of white stone. I find out later the building is called a *palace*. A woman sits on the top step of the three that lead inside. She's the first female we've come across. Only men, mouths gaping at us, were on the road. An old tan hound lies on her side next to the woman. The dog's long teats tell of many litters.

The woman's back is straight, her head held high. She has courage, I think. But I don't see even a knife tucked in her sash. She's as defenseless as a tadpole!

She doesn't stand as we approach. Her mouth and eyes are stamped with sadness, caused, I suppose, by the war. How outlandish she seems. Her head is bare, her black hair thick and wild, almost snakelike. She doesn't care how she looks, an attitude I sympathize with.

Her pale green robe leaves her arms bare and falls in loose folds, like syrup, pooling in her lap before descending to the ground, mounding over her feet. The neck and hem are bordered by embroidery in gold thread. So little gold says these people aren't wealthy. I hope the Greeks are richer than they are, or our spoils will be meager.

Her arms reveal her to be slender, but her billowing robe reminds me of snowdrifts.

How do we appear to her?

We wear our scaly leather tunics and our felt leggings plated here and there with gold. Etched into the gold plate are animals—eagles feeding on goats, deer running, hawks circling.

My hat is tall and is embroidered with strutting lions. My forearms below my sleeves and my legs between my leggings and my low boots are tattooed with signs that Cybele loves: sunbursts and wavy lines that stand for wind blowing through grass. This woman's skin is unadorned.

I don't envy her, except in one way: she appears cool, while my scalp is soaked, and sweat drips down my thighs.

She regards us all until her gaze settles on me. When we reach her, I stop while Pen and the others go in. I'm in no hurry to be introduced to Priam as the useless girl with the broken ribs.

"I'm de'ighted to greet you," she says, speaking with the same accent as Pammon. "I don't care about your fate, so we'come to Troy." She smiles brilliantly.

Why would she care?

She adds, "Maera will stand up and go to you."

If Maera is the dog, it's a silly name.

The dog exhales deeply.

I exhale too, just because the dog did. The deep breath hurts my ribs.

The dog raises her head. She won't stand. Too much effort at her age.

The woman must be misminded to predict what a dog will do. Cybele shattered her poor arrowhead.

Creakily, the dog rises, and, stiff-limbed, comes down the steps to sniff my leggings.

The woman must have signaled the dog in a way I failed to recognize.

"You will rub Maera's neck."

I pull back my hand. I had been about to. Everyone pets a friendly dog.

The woman laughs. Her laugh is airy and pleasant. "I can change the future in small ways."

"Is the dog's name *Maera*?"

"Yes. Do you like it?"

I don't, but I don't want to hurt her feelings, so I tilt my head, which could mean anything.

"What would you name her?"

"Old Tan."

The dog curls up between us on the paving stone below the first step.

"She wasn't always old."

I explain the obvious. "First she'd be Young Tan, then Tan, now Old Tan."

She laughs again. "Do they call you Young Freckles?"

I grin. "We don't name people that way. I'm Princess Shirin. My mother is Queen Penthesilea. We call her *Pen*, and everyone calls me *Rin*. We're Amazons." In case she doesn't know.

"I'm Princess Cassandra, Youngish-But-Soon-to-Be-Middle Cassandra."

Making this joke, her face smooths and appears hardly older than mine, but when she first stared at us, I saw thin lines of age. I decide she's a little younger than Pen.

"Everyone calls me *Cassandra*."

Another joke.

She squints. I think she's judging me. "Apollo gave me the gift of seeing the future."

I say the first thing that comes to mind. "Is Apollo another dog?"

Her shoulders shake with laughter. She reaches out to rub Maera's rump. "You'd like it if Apollo were a dog, wouldn't you? You could play!" She straightens up. "Apollo is the god of healing and prophecy and many other powers. He gave me my gift of prophecy and then cursed it so that no one believes me. In a moment, a crow will land on your head, and one will land on each shoulder, but you won't see or feel them."

She's crackbrained.

Or all Trojans believe nonsense.

"I'll tell you what they say."

We wait in silence.

"Ah. Their words are worth heeding." She stands without groaning, as easily as a six-year-old, and pulls her shoulders back. "This is what they said:

> *"The tempest is but a breath now—*
> *the volcano merely simmers.*
> *Rin should persuade her mother,*
> *whose lips still shape hello,*
> *to bid King Priam farewell."*

197

"Crows see the future too?" Instantly, I regret the words. I don't want to mock her.

She doesn't seem insulted. "They're Apollo's birds. If you stay here, your mother and the rest will die in battle."

I feel my face redden in anger. "We won't die." Maybe one Amazon will, but I doubt even that. "Greeks will die. No one withstands us." I calm myself. Cassandra is a city woman and probably doesn't go to war.

"Greeks will die too," Cassandra says, "especially at your mother's hand. You'll stay in Troy, waiting for your ribs to heal, but when she's killed, you'll fight to avenge her death and will die too." She crouches to pet the dog's head. "Maera, I shouldn't befriend her."

I didn't ask for her friendship! "How do you know I'm hurt?"

She rises. "Soon, your mother will tell my father that you broke three ribs and won't join the battle immediately."

Mother won't mention me, as if an untested girl would make a difference in the outcome. "My name won't come up."

She comes down the step and tilts her face up at me. "You will die in less than a month."

4

I can't help laughing. "When Amazons are outnumbered, our horses carry us away. We shoot at our enemies as we go. Do the Greeks cast spells on horses?"

Her placid, sad expression doesn't change.

She shouldn't waste her worries on us! "We're the best archers." I pat my gorytos. "Everyone envies our bows. Our arrows are poisoned with asp venom. Our foes weaken before they can even raise their spears. But should one get close, we fight with our battle-axes too."

She doesn't argue. "In a moment, brave Hector, my favorite brother, will come out. He'll die an instant before your mother does."

"No one will come out until my mother returns." It would be rude to. "Pen commands attention." Pity softens my tone. "Your brother won't die." I don't know why I believe this. The brother may not be skilled in battle, but I don't question my certainty.

She looks up at the sky. "He'll die three days after the fighting starts again."

"When will it begin?"

"In fifteen days. He's my best brother out of many. You'll like him. Everyone does. He's called Tamer of Horses."

Amazons are all horse tamers, but here it must be unusual.

She continues. "He's killed more Greeks than any other warrior."

Maera barks and wags her tail. A man leaves the palace carrying a young boy on his shoulders. The man, I suppose, is Hector, who must come out at this time every day. Cassandra didn't say he'd have a child with him, proof, as it appears to me, she doesn't see the future.

He smiles down at us from the top step, a wide smile under a slightly crooked nose, which makes his face friendly. Cassandra smiles back. She introduces me to him as he descends the steps.

He raises his right hand in greeting. This seems like a solemn moment. I raise my hand back, though I've never done so before.

He's my height, tall for a Trojan. When he sits on the lowest step, he doesn't groan. He must not spend his life on horseback, no matter how many horses he trains. Cassandra sits next to him.

His eyes go to my gorytos. "Your mother told us what a warrior you'll be." He lowers the toddler to his lap.

The boy squirms away to Cassandra and stands on her thighs. He tugs her hair, laughing. She catches his hand and kisses his fingers. Her face is sad. Does she think this child is going to die soon too? He won't be fighting!

Hector says, "Your mother told us that anyone else would have been crippled by the fall you took."

I wonder if that's true. My mind passes over Cassandra's correct prediction that Pen would speak of me.

He says, "I'll be proud to go into battle at your side."

I like him. Most others would say *with you at MY side.*

I return the compliment. "We'll keep each other safe." I hope to reassure Cassandra.

"Would you mind . . . May I . . . see your bow?"

I pull it out of my gorytos and give it to him.

He stands and holds the bow by the riser. "Isn't it beautiful, Cassandra?"

"Mm."

"Oak, right?"

I nod.

"Cassandra, it isn't all wood, though. There's goat horn and sinew and glue, a little army assembled to help the archer."

Soon, he'll be my favorite of her brothers too.

"Very nice." She makes her nephew sit.

"Cassandra! Listen!" Hector hasn't finished his enthusiasm. "An Amazon's bow compared to ours is like Father's palace compared to a mud hut."

He probably wouldn't admire the wagons we sleep in.

He draws back the string. "So flexible you can feel it gathering its power."

I'm won over. I confide, "I could shoot when I was just eight."

"The bow helped you, right?"

"Yes, but I couldn't hit anything."

"It taught you!"

True. I hadn't expected to find understanding among these barbarians.

He returns the bow, sits, and takes the boy again. "This is my son, Astyanax. He won't be strong enough to pull back our bows until he's ten at least." He lifts the boy's chin. "Nax, call on the Amazons when you go to war, and stay in Rin's shadow."

The boy leans against his father's chest, regarding me solemnly.

Maera puts her head in Cassandra's lap.

"I'll come if you need me, any of you." I've never felt so important.

"As will I."

This, I think, is what it means to be allies. We've just made a compact. I'm behaving as a future queen. Pen will be proud—I hope.

Hector's hand keeps petting his son's head while Cassandra does the same to Maera. I half wish I had a brother.

"My sister says I won't live much longer and Nax won't survive to grow into a man." He turns to her. "You might have spared me that foolishness, love."

At least one Trojan doesn't believe her or make such prophecies.

Her voice is level. "Achilles will kill you, and Rin here won't be alive to protect Nax. Rin's mother will die the same day you do." Her hands pause in the air above Maera. "Leave Troy! Now! Save yourself and Nax."

Nax propels himself out of his father's lap and runs away from us, windmilling his arms, laughing as he goes. Cassandra goes back to stroking Maera.

"She speaks nonsense, Rin, but I wish she'd make up more pleasant lies."

"Helenus will become a king eventually—not of Troy—after he betrays us. That will be pleasant for him."

I don't know who Helenus is.

Hector sobers. "He'd never be a traitor."

"Helenus is my twin," Cassandra tells me.

"Rin, I'm sure I have more life left than she says, but I don't expect to be an old man. This war will finish me."

Now I don't want to fight near him. Foreboding will slow his arm. If the Trojans are all like these two, no wonder this war has dragged on.

He raises his eyebrows. "How serious we are! Not always." He stands. "Nax!" He runs and picks up his son, holding the boy around his middle and gliding him in the air. While the child shouts with laughter, Hector sings, hitting high notes and plummeting to low, "Up. Down. Round around. Swimming like a lark. Flying like a trout."

I smile. Cassandra does too, while a few tears trickle down her cheeks.

Hector brings Nax back to us. He sits and stands his son next to him. Then he wipes Cassandra's tears away. "Rin, my sister may be strange, but there's no one more loving or worthy of love. Will you befriend her as well as fight beside me?"

I laugh nervously. "I think I know how to be a comrade in war." Even though I've never fought. But I don't know how to be a friend—only a daughter, niece, or cousin. "I've never had a friend."

His eyebrows rise. "There's no difference. If we're comrades in war, I'll keep track of you and watch out for your enemies. You'll guess what I may need and be ready. If we're separated, we'll try to reunite. We won't linger on our missteps. That's friendship too." He turns to his sister. "Will you be Rin's friend, sister?"

She sounds resentful. "I already tried to persuade her to leave Troy and not be killed."

"Not that!"

"A friend is someone you weep to lose." Cassandra shakes out her hair. "Rin is a worthy child, but I already have too many people to grieve."

Her head is stuffed with felt.

"I'll be your friend. You don't have to be mine." I'd learn to be one by doing it, just as I'd learned to hunt and ride and make glue.

They both smile at me.

Cassandra says, "Hec, when we were her age, did either of us have such an open, unguarded face?"

Embarrassed, I crouch and pet Old Tan—Maera. I feel a twinge in my hip, and my ribs hurt.

Pen and the others come out of the palace. Feeling strange and liking it, I introduce Cassandra and Hector to them. I've never introduced people before.

Cassandra doesn't predict everyone's death, which I'm glad for. I don't want my friend to be laughed at.

As we start off, she calls after me, "Rin—friend—I'll welcome your company tomorrow and every day until you fight."

Another prediction that won't come true. Pen will want me at our camp to help with chores. But I promised to be Cassandra's friend, which means being with her. And I would like more time with the Trojans. Maybe I can make the prophecy come to pass.

We stride through the streets and endure the gate again. As we make camp, I tell Pen about the alliance with Hector.

To my delight, she *is* proud of me. "When you're queen, we'll be up to our horses' bellies in plunder and tribute."

At night, I bed down near her on my leopard skin blanket. The air is mild and smells of the sea.

"Pen?"

"Mm?"

"Can I go back to Troy tomorrow? Cassandra, the princess, told me things—mostly foolishness, but not all. I want to learn about the Trojans."

"Go. You can stay with them until you're well enough to fight." She sounds sleepy. "Such a queen you'll be."

Cassandra's prediction that I'd return to Troy tomorrow will come true, but not because she foresaw it. The other prophecies coming from her madful mind won't come true at all.

5

When dawn is just beginning, I dash through the gate tunnel. My ribs scold me for running. As I approach the palace, Cassandra steps outside, followed by Maera. I can't read her face. Is she glad to see her friend? She doesn't look surprised. I bid her good morning.

She points across the plaza to a crooked house. "A baby will cry."

No, it won't, or it will from a different house.

A baby cries from that house. Babies often cry.

Cassandra waves her hand at two paving stones. "A black viper is about to slither out of the crack, and you'll kill it before it hurts Maera."

I don't reach for my knife. There can't be snakes so

close to where people live. The Trojans would have gotten rid of them long ago.

Maera barks and rushes to the crack. A snake emerges. Maera lunges. I whip out my knife and chop off the creature's head. Maera sniffs the body.

"Thank you." Cassandra pets Maera, who wags at her, even though I'm the one who killed the snake.

"Don't you have a knife?"

"Only for eating. It isn't a weapon, but I would have remained inside if you weren't going to be here."

How has she managed to stay alive this long? She didn't know I was coming, since I got Pen's permission only last night. Why does she want to convince me she sees the future?

"Come. You can sample our food and taste bread." She grins. "The food that enslaves us." This is funny to her.

I defend our belief. "Farmers are yoked to their land just as their oxen are hitched to their plows."

She repeats, "Come."

I swallow my fear. The gate to Troy was the closest I'd ever been to being indoors.

We enter a corridor lined with marble columns. Cassandra calls it a *colonnade*. I see sunlight ahead and grit my teeth.

The colors soothe my eye: soft pinks and browns swirling through the marble; pastel greens, tans, and blues in the floor tiles. There are no rugs, such as we cover the bottoms of our wagons with, and the floor is hard. Cassandra's sandals slap; Maera's nails tap; my felt boots whisper. Amazons are stealthy.

The colonnade is empty, except for a man hurrying ahead of us.

I hear male voices ahead on my left and female ones coming from above.

Cassandra wheels to the right after we pass the third column before we reach the sunlight. Stairs rise above my head, make a square turn, and rise again.

"Prepare yourself, Rin." Cassandra stops on the third step. "What you're about to see will make you want to bolt."

My ears heat up with anger. "A lion chased me once. You think I'm easily frightened?"

"By this, yes." She starts climbing again.

I follow. The women's voices grow louder.

Cassandra is right. I'm afraid. How does she know me so well?

I clench my fists and force my foot up to the next step and the next. The women's low voices drum in my ears.

As soon as my head is high enough to see, my heart bangs against my ribs.

The voices fade. Everyone stops moving.

Too many strangers! Many too many!

I'll find out later that sixty or so women are staring

at me, not six hundred. Most are the wives of Cassandra's many brothers and their ladies-in-waiting. Some are widows. Some are my friend's sisters, not yet wed. I don't take this in immediately, but they're arranged along the balcony, sitting or standing next to wooden frames—looms, as I learn later.

They work by sunlight that slants in from open sky above a courtyard downstairs. Thank you, Cybele, for the bright sky. My legs feel shaky.

"This is Rin, princess of the Amazons." Cassandra announces as she climbs the last step.

I follow her up. Maera trots away from us.

"Rin," Cassandra says over her shoulder, "we call ourselves cultured because we eat our breakfast long after sunup. Food will come soon. One of the servants with a tray will stumble on the stairs, but nothing will spill."

I'm sure no one will trip.

A sharp voice agrees with me. "They're too afraid of the cook's wrath to fall. Another absurd prediction."

Though I believe it won't happen, I want to defend my friend—but I don't know who was speaking. There are so many of them!

A stately woman comes toward us. "Welcome, Princess Rin. I'm happy you're here." She smiles warmly at me, and I feel that she really *is* happy.

I stammer that I'm glad too.

"This is my mother, Queen Hecuba. She regards every-one under twenty as her child."

I smile back at the queen, understanding this at least. Every grown-up in the band mothers every girl.

Hecuba is the same height as her daughter, with the same tan coloring. Unlike the wildness of Cassandra's hair, however, the queen's black waves are tamed by a net that sparkles with tiny silver balls.

"Please don't worry about the servants," Hecuba says. "They're sure-footed."

No one seems to put stock in my friend's prophecies. I'm glad most Trojans aren't madful, because then fighting at their side would be too risky. But I'm sorry that Cassandra has to endure their disbelief—and mine.

The queen puts her arm around Cassandra's shoulders. "Rin, you're with my sweetest daughter."

Cassandra leans into her mother. Her expression is more peaceful than I've seen it. "My parents are kind."

Hecuba excuses herself. "I must return to my loom."

Cassandra leads me past a wooden frame on my right and left. One has strings running up and down and a nar-row band of cloth at the top. The other has cloth from the top to halfway down, vertical strings below.

We turn and walk along an aisle between women and a wall of screens that ripple in a faint breeze. The screens hide the extent of the women's quarters, which take up the entire story.

At last, we reach two empty chairs next to a loom. A low table stands between the chairs. Cassandra sits in one chair and gestures at the other. I lower myself into it, glad to become less noticeable.

Minutes pass. Cassandra says nothing and does nothing. Maera comes and curls up at her feet. Gradually, I calm. The women start chatting again.

Three other women, who turn out to be servants, rise from the stairs. I hear a clatter. One cries out, "Ai!" Then, with relief, "I'm fine!"

The sharp voice cries, "Wrong again, Cassandra! Only a misstep. A stumble is greater than that."

I don't like the voice or the teasing.

Cassandra just shrugs. "I'll bring our breakfast, Rin." She leaves with Maera.

I'm grateful. I don't want to have to pass everyone again.

The roof isn't very high above us. I feel it press down despite the sky over the courtyard.

I'm too shy to watch the women around me, who might not like to be stared at anyway, so I turn my gaze to the screens across the aisle instead, which display tapestries of beautiful women, also making cloth.

Cassandra returns with a platter on which rest two

cups of a pale liquid, two roundish brown things, two flat
tan things, and a mound of shelled hazelnuts. She sets the
tray on the table. I eat a hazelnut.

Maera sits expectantly.

Cassandra grins. She points first at the tan thing and
then at the brown thing. "Bread, which you'll hate. Honey
cake." She points at the cups. "Honey water."

She may know that Amazons don't usually eat bread, so
this isn't much of a prediction. I take a bite and do hate it—
tough and then mushy without much taste, eaten only for
the sake of a full belly. I swallow and ask, "Do *you* like it?"

"As much as I like anything."

The honey cake glistens. I like honey.

Mushy, sweet, and moist. I enjoy the honey, and moist
is better than dry. Since I'm hungry, I finish both bread
and cake and half the nuts. The honey water is pleasant but
not as good as koumiss.

Cassandra eats half her bread and feeds the rest to
Maera. "Soon Helen will come to meet you. She's one of
the two mortals who've set in motion your death, and then
mine two years from now."

Helen is the woman Pammon told us about, the cause
of the war. I don't believe she'll approach me. Why would
she?

Cassandra continues. "She always leaves her bed a
few minutes after breakfast arrives, and she'll go to you,

because her servants will have told her that someone new has come."

Oh. That isn't a prophecy. Cassandra is just explaining Helen's nature and what she's likely to do.

She adds, "If Helen were a flower, she'd be a sundew."

Sundews are pretty, but if you're an insect, watch out! If you drink their sweet nectar, you'll be stuck, and then you'll melt from the poison.

"She wants everyone to love her, and she devours them."

"I'll be careful." I'm eager to meet the human sundew. This is why I'm here: to study the strange foreigners and their ways.

Cassandra says, "I'm full." Maera gobbles down the honey cake.

No wonder her dog is plump.

The women fall silent again. The hunter in me recognizes this quiet as different from the one when I came in. That silence was surprised. This one is angry.

I hear scraping and turn. A woman slips out from between two screens.

"Helen," Cassandra murmurs.

The woman is tiny. How can she be the most beautiful? If I were standing, her head would reach my chest. She's wearing more gold than I am: rings, necklaces, bracelets. Jewels too. If the Greeks conquer Troy, they'll win excellent spoils from her alone.

She rushes toward me. "An Amazon!" She seems to be shouting in a whisper.

I brace myself.

She halts a few yards away in the aisle, as if someone pulled in on a rein. She smiles brilliantly at me, showing perfect teeth. I resist the impulse to smile back, remembering the sundew. Her smile wavers. I notice that she's older than Cassandra.

"Horsewoman!"

She knows about us.

To my surprise, she makes fists, bends at her waist, and puts her weight on the fists as if she were a four-hoofed creature. She shakes her head and scrapes the tiled floor with her right fist. With her weight on her hands, she kicks her back legs—I mean, her legs!—in the air. Then, for an instant, all her legs—her arms and legs!—are in the air with her legs kicking. She's bucking, as excited horses do. *Exactly* as they do. I wish Pen could see this. Thank you, Cybele, for letting me be here.

She comes down fists first, then legs, and straightens. Smiling still, she says, "I am Prince Paris's wife, Queen Helen."

I stand and greet her in return and say my name.

She continues to smile.

I can't keep smiling! I relax my face and sit again.

After a moment or two, she stands on her hands with

her body straight in the air. She lets go with her right hand and hops in a circle on her left. Another feat of strength. Her hair drags on the floor. Her face looks strange upside down, red, with her cheeks bulging.

She changes hands and hops in the opposite direction. Then she lowers herself to the floor and rises with her head at the top. Smiling yet again, she stares at me until she bursts out, "Did you like it?" As if she were the child.

I'm not sure how to answer. "You're very strong."

She laughs. "And very hungry." She leaves me, then turns and adds, "Paris says the Amazons will turn the tide for Troy and then he'll never have to give me back."

She heads in the direction of the breakfast trays. Something about her unsettles me. She brings to mind a wingless fly I once saw crawling in our wagon.

"Is Paris one of your brothers?" I ask Cassandra, who nods.

"Was she a slave before she married him? Isn't she really a princess if your brother is a prince?"

"She was never a slave. Why do you think she was?" Cassandra goes to her loom and begins to pass a rod of wood that has thread attached to it between the up-and-down threads. I learn later that the wood is called a shuttle and the vertical thread the warp.

"She said she'll be given away if Troy loses the war."

"Before she left with Paris, she was married to

Menelaus, king of Sparta in Greece. That's why she's a queen. He wants her back."

"I don't understand."

"He'll take her back when Troy is destroyed. He could kill her if he wanted to, but he won't want to." Her shuttle reaches the end of her row.

"If Troy really were to lose, she'd be a slave then, right? The women would be spoils?"

"All the other women will be slaves. Not Helen."

I ignore the prediction. "How could he take her if she didn't want to go with him? Why couldn't she go somewhere else?"

Cassandra's hands stop moving. "Can your hat refuse to let you put it on your head?"

I smile. "Helen isn't a hat."

"Trojan and Greek women belong to their husbands as much as your hat belongs to you."

No! I feel like I'm drowning in a river of nonsense. A question swims to me. "Do you have a husband?" Is she a hat too?

"No. Because Apollo cursed me."

These people are *all* felt heads, and their gods may be felt heads too.

6

The Greeks and the Trojans continue farming for two weeks while I stay with Cassandra. My ribs continue to ache, though less and less as the days pass.

We sleep in her nook in the women's quarters. I sleep in a bed! Under me is a thin mattress made of reeds on top of mesh webbing. The webbing sags and hugs me. In the middle of the night, I wake up sweating.

Village women and Amazons sound alike when they snore!

I eat bread, scones, and thin porridge at meals and continue to dislike it all. One evening, we're served slices of roasted ox. That's better!

Every morning, Cassandra sends a servant to Troy's sacred grove to carry offerings to a lesser god, as she tells me. When I look puzzled, she says, "The great gods are never neglected. Everyone gives them gifts. I favor one of the lesser gods, who"—she smiles wistfully—"feels hurt if he gets nothing."

Another strangeness of these people is their many gods.

Cassandra spends a few hours every day at her loom with the other women. I don't know why the Trojans need so much cloth. Cassandra is weaving a tapestry of Hector doing battle outside the wall of Troy. In her worried imagination, the war is going ill, because the Trojans are up against the city.

I don't know how she did this, but the air shimmers between Hector and the wall. He's in full armor, wearing his round iron helmet. Only his feet aren't woven yet. His visor is up—which it wouldn't be during battle. I think Cassandra loves him too much to hide his face. He's thrusting his sword at someone outside the tapestry. I feel his energy, his strength, the force of his lunge. His expression is calm.

We Amazons have no fabric as elegant as woven tapestry. But I prefer our felt for its usefulness—warmer for the weather where we live and easier to make, because felt almost makes itself.

While they work, the women compliment one another on their weaving. They talk about the weather or how tall some child has grown. Their children are with them or are playing in the streets. The older girls help their mothers, who tell them what to do. Soon, I stop hearing words and their voices become the bubbling of pigeons. I cease listening to Cassandra too, who, rather than joining the conversation, murmurs a stream of predictions: who will speak next, who will leave her loom to card or spin, who will stretch or scratch an itch.

It seems like coincidence that she's always right. The women's actions are so limited that they are sure to do one of the things she names.

The women never praise Cassandra's cloth or Helen's, whose loom is two away from hers. Unlike the others, Helen weaves lazily, as if she were moving through honey cake.

Men visit her so often that chairs are kept in a semicircle around her loom. Sometimes a dozen crowd in. I wonder if anyone is farming.

We're close enough to hear the conversation. Some men shower Helen with compliments; some boast about themselves; some relate their latest doings; some sit in silence. Some come daily. Some stay for a few minutes, some for hours.

Occasionally, the wife of this man or that one leaves her loom to ask her husband to see her weaving or to go somewhere with her.

Among those who come early every day and stay late are Cassandra's brother Deiphobus and her twin, Helenus. Except for a narrower forehead with deep frown lines on Helenus, Cassandra and her twin have the same features. Deiphobus has all the forehead Helenus lacks and more. Neither one sits. Occasionally, one of them speaks to Helen, never to each other. Helenus's voice goes down at the end of each sentence, making a thud. The brothers always leave together, as if there were a signal.

Cassandra sometimes giggles when they come and when they go. Once, she says, "Hate binds them. If they could endure each other, they'd be apart more often."

I don't understand.

Helen smiles, gazes into the faces of the men around her, drags the shuttle slowly through her warp. Her husband, Paris, isn't there nearly as often as Helenus and Deiphobus are.

Cassandra says Paris was once enchanted and was exceptionally handsome then. "Helen followed an illusion. Now she has to follow a mere man." She chuckles. "A very mere man."

Although I hardly know him, I guess what she means. He's more or less handsome, nothing extraordinary. His skin looks spongy, like felt when it's wet. If I push a finger into felt, the cloth doesn't bounce back. I haven't tried poking Paris!

He tells rambling stories about herding goats and sheep on a nearby mountain, interrupting himself to ponder details, such as whether three lambs or four had wandered away or if the shepherd who searched with him was named Rocus or Nisus. During his stories, I look away to yawn. Helen yawns openly. Once, one of the seated men fell asleep and almost slid off his chair.

Hector, my comrade-in-arms, is never dull. He comes to the women's quarters daily, sometimes with his son, Nax. He does no more than wish Helen a good day before he heads for Cassandra and me. Helen's eyes follow him, as they follow no one else.

I always jump up. He's older and should sit if he likes. When Nax is there, he puts him in the chair instead. Otherwise, he keeps standing, and the seat stays empty.

I often think I'm hearing a poem when he speaks. He tells us of farming: the slow rhythm of the oxen at the plow, the scent of the breeze, the idle clouds, the circling hawks. And he regales us with Nax's antics.

Hector is the only male I've ever gotten to know or even spoken with. If our band might make an exception—which we won't—and let him in, he'd be a credit to us.

Andromache, Hector's wife, sometimes joins us. She's the only woman other than Hecuba who is friendly to Cassandra.

Once, when Helen's visitors are joking loudly, Hector

says to his wife, "Cassandra is as beautiful as Helen, don't you think?"

I wonder how these people judge. To me, Helen has the showy beauty of an iris, while Cassandra reminds me of my favorite flower, the shy winter rose with its soft colors and long bloom.

When she's feeling affectionate, Pen calls me her pear tree, because, she says, I'm hardy, strong, and, above all, useful. Sometimes she adds as an afterthought that I'm pretty.

"Cassandra is much lovelier. What's more, she weaves cloth, not webs." Andromache touches her husband's cheek. "Helen seems to have no power over you, my love."

He smiles at her, and I feel happy.

After Hector leaves us, Cassandra always brushes at her eyes.

I grow irritated at her gloominess. "If you're sure he's going to die, why don't you *do* something?" What might a Trojan woman do? What would work on Hector? "If you ran away, I'm sure he'd search for you. I'd help you find a good—"

She waves away my idea. "I can't save anyone." Her voice is hoarse. "It's my curse that I'm just a sardine."

How can I be her friend when I don't know how to help her? Or understand half of what she says?

She tells me that she and I are the only females who

can leave the women's quarters except on extraordinary occasions. Even her mother, the queen, who often goes downstairs to the kitchen or other rooms, rarely steps outside.

Cassandra takes me through the streets and alleys of her city, where boys and girls toss balls and chase one another. At least Trojan girls have freedom when they're young. I'm only a little too old for their games.

As we wind through an unpleasantly narrow lane, Cassandra tells me the history of Troy. "Really a legend," she says. "We believe my father and his children are descended from Zeus himself"—their main god—"and Electra, a goddess who became a star after being a mother."

I say, "Our first mother—"

"—was born of a she-wolf, and her father was a lion. The beasts didn't like the hairless creature, so she raised herself, thanks to Cybele." Cassandra winks.

I scowl, thinking through what just happened, which seems proof that she can't prophesy. "If you can predict the future but can't change it, how could you stop me from saying what I was about to say? If you really can see the future, wouldn't you know that you would interrupt me?" I'm getting confused, but I keep going. "If you interrupted me in the future, how would you know what I was going to say? Someone told you about the first Amazon."

She throws up her hands. "It's complicated. I can

change little things that don't matter."

Silly!

She says, "The Amazons' beginning is as remarkable as ours, and your ancestress is more laudable."

True. I smile, glad she's my friend.

Sometimes we leave Troy and walk half a mile to the lazy Scamander River. The distance hardly troubles my ribs. I'm healing. I take off my leggings and wade in up to my chest while Cassandra swims. She says she'd teach me to swim if I weren't injured.

I'm not eager. Amazons don't swim. "Maybe after my first battle."

"Your first battle will be your last."

Annoyed, I splash her.

Treading water, she says, "I wanted to stay indifferent to you."

How sad she looks about my death that won't happen.

7

War resumes for the Trojans and begins for us, though not yet for me. From outside the western gate, Cassandra and I watch Pen and our band and Troy's warriors ride to battle. The other women are allowed out for this. They stand together near a knot of elderly men.

The battle is three miles off. When the Trojan army disappears in the distance, everyone but Cassandra and I reenter the city. I stand still while she throws a stick for Maera, who runs stiffly after it.

The sun is low when a messenger comes to say that the army is camping on the plains for the night. They've driven the Greeks almost to their ships and hope to finish the job tomorrow.

I think, Yes, because our band killed so many.

Among us Amazons, according to the messenger, no one was wounded and no one died. The Trojans lost five warriors and the Greeks lost more. Our band and the Trojans managed to strip six bodies of their armor. Our first spoils.

Matters don't go as well on the second day. By dusk, I hear hoofbeats and battle cries, especially our *Kiikiikaa!* I put my trust in the skill of our band. When fighting ends for the day, Pen and the others come to me. Again, no one is even wounded.

The Trojans lost ground, but they're happy because Hector killed some important Greek warrior.

Cassandra tells me to sleep with the band tonight and until I go to fight. "Hector will die tomorrow. Achilles will kill him. I'm not fit company."

I pity her. I'm certain Hector won't be killed, but should he be, my friend will have suffered both before and after his death.

Over a meal of three spitted rabbits and not a crumb of bread, Pen and my aunt Zelke describe the fighting.

"Galloping at their line," Pen says, "we dropped the first row of Greeks. A dozen or more spurred their horses after us, thinking—"

"Foolishly," Zelke says, "that they could catch us."

Pen grins. "Not knowing we shoot backward and forward."

Perfectly each way.

"They didn't make that mistake again." My aunt Serag joins in, waving the air with a hare leg. "Their plan after that was to pull us off our horses and test our battle-axes. They regretted that too."

"When we could, we remounted," Pen says. "They didn't expect our horses to linger on the field. Rinny-Rin, when you come with us, I want you to stay far enough away that they can't unseat you. You'll watch and shoot, but you're not ready for ax warfare."

I agree with her. I have more to learn. "I'll shoot the ones who are attacking us." I laugh. "If one comes after me, I'll give him a chase."

Pen stretches. "The Greeks are numerous. Like mice."

"Are the Trojans good fighters?" This is something a future queen should know.

"Excellent at close fighting. Your comrade Hector doesn't stop for breath. No one can withstand him. We surpass both sides at archery."

I feel proud of Hector and us.

My cousin Khasa laughs. "One was good only at dancing."

Pen laughs too. "He pranced away from every attack and just wiggled his spear above his head."

I'm curious since I know some of the warriors. "Did you find out his name?"

Zelke says, "The Trojans teased him. I heard the name *Paris*."

Helen's husband.

When we lie next to each other on the dry grass with only the stars for a roof, Pen asks me about living in Troy. I want her to have enough time for sleep, so I don't tell her all I'd like to. I just describe Helen's acrobatics and what Cassandra said about Trojan women being like hats.

She hoots over the hats, but she wishes she could see Helen perform. "I don't think I'm strong enough to do her tricks. We might learn from her. It's good you stayed in that palace."

"Paris—the coward on the battlefield—is her husband."

"Then she's the one with strength in their family. Maybe she'd like to join the band." Pen yawns. "I need sleep."

We don't need a human hat!

I'm not as tired as everybody, so I fall asleep after all their breathing has deepened and Zelke has started her rumble-snoring.

The clouds are thick at dawn when we wake up. Pen pokes my rib cage here and there. "Another week, Rin, and we'll ride into battle together. Your arrows can protect us and your comrade Hector."

I shout my delight. Everyone smiles.

* * *

As we ride to Troy, I remember that Cassandra predicted that not only Hector will die today. She said Pen will too. But he and Pen are the best fighters Troy has, the least likely to fall. Cassandra torments herself with ridiculous worries.

The Trojans are assembling when we trot to the western gate. I dismount and stand with my friend.

She says, "I hugged and clung to him. He kissed the top of my head. I still feel his lips. Andromache isn't here because Nax has a fever."

I pat her shoulder as I think a friend would. "You'll laugh with him tonight."

She seems not to notice.

Hours pass. At noon, servants come with baskets of scones and fruit. When I offer Cassandra an apple, she seems not to recognize me. Her eyes bulge. Whites surround the irises. Finally, she waves the apple away.

I hear thuds.

Cassandra grips my arm. My bones hurt. I don't expect her hands to be so strong. She tugs me through the city gate. Maera follows us, barking.

"We have to hurry or there won't be room for us." She leads me up a ladder to the ramparts.

I climb after her. Maera whines at the bottom.

At first, I see a cloud of dust. Then shapes emerge of Trojan warriors galloping toward us followed by Trojan foot soldiers. My heart gallops too. Where are Pen and the band?

Except for Priam, the watchers below hurry into the city.

Last of all, on horseback, come Pen and the band, dashing back and forth behind the fleeing Trojans, loosing arrows at the line of Greeks, allowing the Trojans to retreat without more deaths. Greek warriors fall but the pursuit continues. I marvel at the number of Greeks. I don't see the end of their army.

Women and old men join us on the ramparts. The Trojan fighters crowd through the gates. Pen and our people ride in too. Only Priam stands outside. A few moments later, Hector races out of the mass of Greeks on foot. He must have been unhorsed, but he's so fast his feet seem to have wings.

Priam tries to draw his son into Troy. Hector pulls away.

Cassandra shouts, "Come in, brother! Come in! Save yourself!"

I doubt he can hear her, because I can't hear Priam and Hector, who are pantomiming an argument. Finally, Priam gives up and enters the city. The gate groans shut. Warriors press onto the ramparts with us. I can't see Pen and the others.

Hector lounges near the wall, waiting for the enemy to reach him. He scratches behind his ear and slaps his arm. A fly, I suppose.

Does he plan to bargain for a truce with the Greeks? No more spoils for us, then.

Or does he think he can turn the whole Greek army by taking down one of their heroes?

The Greeks arrive. Arrows rain from the ramparts. Grinning, I take out my bow and join in the shooting. When I pull the string, my ribs ache faintly, but I can shoot. The Greeks back out of range before I hit anyone.

One warrior detaches himself from their mass, dismounts, and runs toward Hector. I wonder if this is Achilles, the man Cassandra says will kill her brother.

I shoot at him, as does every other archer. My first arrow bounces off his huge shield. As if I were hunting, I aim my next arrow at where his neck is about to be. I let go and know the shot is true.

The arrow flies toward its mark.

But at the last instant, it dips and hits the shield. How did that happen?

Pops ping out as every arrow suffers the same fate. A Trojan archer shouts, "Die, Achilles!"

If I can kill him, what a trophy I'll win—a shield that draws arrows to itself.

A wind blows two clouds apart. A sun shaft shines on

only Achilles, outlining him in light. I blink at the bright-
ness of the golden crest on his helmet.

Cassandra digs her fingers into my arm. Her nails are
sharp. I'm her friend, so I endure.

Hector, who seems to have shrunk, backs away and
runs along the wall. Like a herding dog, Achilles drives
him toward the plain and the waiting Greek army.

Achilles presents his back to us. I fit another arrow and
loose it. It catches a lucky wind. He will die.

At the final moment, as if an invisible foot comes down,
my arrow drops to the ground.

As one, Greek archers nock their bows and wait. Hector can't escape. I'm astonished that Cassandra's prediction
is about to come true.

But Achilles gestures, and they lower their weapons.

Is he playing with Hector? Does he mean to let him
live?

I cover Cassandra's fingers with my other hand. Her
skin is ice.

Hector veers away from Achilles and streaks toward
Troy. This time I'm sure he wants to enter. I hear the gates
scrape open.

Both of them are running faster than I think anyone
can. In an impossible burst, Achilles almost catches Hector
only a few yards from the gate and forces him to turn.

Why don't the Trojans come out and help him?

The two diminish in the distance, angling away from Troy and the Greek army.

Cassandra recites in a voice that sounds like a crow cawing:

> *"The constellations will rise tonight.*
> *Waves are rolling on the ocean now.*
> *Somewhere, a wife stands at her loom,*
> *weaving a himation*
> *her husband will never wear."*

Hector and Achilles come back and go forth three times. The Trojans on the ramparts shout encouragement to Hector but don't rush to his aid. I join in for my comrade-in-arms, in hopes of fighting at his side soon. Cassandra is silent.

Achilles' face is a mask of rage: eyes wide, nostrils flaring, lips drawn back, mouth gaping. Hector's face is intent and red with effort.

On the third return, Hector smiles and turns his head to the left. His lips move as if he's speaking to someone though no one is there. I can't hear what he says because of the shouting Trojans on the ramparts with us.

Cassandra cries over their voices, "It must be a vision, Rin—godsent."

Hector stops and waits for Achilles. The two are in

profile, so I can see their faces. They speak. Hector is motionless. Achilles' arms cut the air angrily.

They back away from each other. Achilles hurls his spear. Hector ducks and the spear flies over his head. Hooray!

I gasp. Achilles' spear arcs back into his hand. I look to Cassandra for understanding, but her face is still.

Hector hurls his spear, a true throw that strikes the center of Achilles' shield and would have gone through any other shield to its target's heart. The spear clangs off. Hector's lips move again, and he turns to empty air. Almost comically, he falls back a step and another. If Cassandra was right about the vision, did it just vanish?

Hector raises his head to the ramparts, searching, I think, for his wife and Nax.

Tears stream down Cassandra's cheeks.

It isn't over for him. Warriors could still rush out of Troy to help him.

He draws his sword as Achilles raises his spear and heroic Pen gallops out of Troy.

Brave Pen! Showing the Trojans how to be a warrior. I yell our battle cry. She shoots arrow after arrow, which don't touch their mark though I know her aim is true.

Achilles throws his spear and Hector falls. I've lost my comrade-in-arms.

But Pen, her battle-ax raised, is upon the Greek to

avenge Hector's death. Strike hard!

Cybele appears. My heart stops.

Achilles, as one might go at a fly, swipes upward with his sword. Pen is struck. Through my tears, I see blood spurt. She falls off her horse. I shriek.

Despite my yelling, I hear Cybele's mellow voice. "You will fight on my side now. Thank you for your courage. Your friends will miss your arrows."

Thank you, Cybele, I think as I sob. Thank you for breaking my ribs and keeping me alive so that I may kill this Achilles.

8

Fighting halts again, this time for funerals. The Greeks are burying the hero that Hector slew the day before his death. Troy is grieving for Hector, though wicked Achilles took his body. We're mourning Pen, whose body we recovered without having to fight for it. I'm sad for Hector too.

Though I barely have the energy to mount Tall Brown, I return with the band to our camp. I hardly notice my tears. Pen is slung in front of me. I rest my hand on her chest as we go. Her horse follows mine.

After we've gone just a few yards, I realize that I'm queen, Pen's chosen.

When we reach camp and lay her gently on the grass, I say, "If I die, Lannip will be queen." It's my first act. The band needs to know who will lead them after me. I'm not sure if Lannip is the right choice, but if she's queen at least everyone will eat well.

The Trojans and the Greeks burn their dead, but we entomb ours in a burial mound called a kurgan. Using our battle-axes to carve out sod, we begin to dig a shallow pit. I send Zelke to the Trojans for stones and timber.

As I work, I marvel that I still have two legs and two arms. How can I be whole when I lost so much of myself the moment Pen died?

I hate that the kurgan will be here, so far from our other graves.

The sun sets on the last day Pen was alive.

Over dinner, people remember her. I take my bowl and move away. She'd laugh them out of their compliments if she were still here.

After we eat, we wash our bowls and our stewpot in the stream that waters the camp. Here, without dogs to lick them, the task can't wait until morning.

Then I lie on the grass. Sleep doesn't come. Who will be proud of me now? If I'm a good queen, the band will look up to me, but no one will be above me to be proud. Pen will be too busy helping Cybele.

If I can't sleep, I wish I could at least stop my mind from going in circles. When you lose someone you love and who loved you, you still love her, but she can't love you anymore.

My body feels heavy enough to pull me under the earth. I spend hours awake, often weeping.

In the morning, Pammon and several other Trojans drive oxcarts to us loaded with lumber and stone. Pammon says that Achilles hasn't returned Hector's body.

The Trojans are strange, but the Greeks are monsters.

I pity Cassandra, who must be grieving, as I am.

I haven't forgotten that she had prophesied the deaths of Hector and Pen, but I don't think of it. And I don't call to mind her prediction that I'll die in two weeks.

When Pen is buried, I'll visit Cassandra, but I'll sleep with the band until we go back to war and I kill Achilles.

Over the next two days, we build a chamber for Pen's body to rest in while her spirit is with Cybele. When it's finished, we spread Pen's leopard-skin blanket on the dirt floor and lay her on top on her back. I start crying again. Around her, we arrange her battle-ax, her sword, her gorytos, and her arrows. Her bow we keep in case one of ours breaks. Cybele doesn't want to leave us unprotected. I also keep her sack of potions, elixirs, and herbs. If one of us is wounded, we'll need them.

My eyes stream as I pull the gold plate off my gorytos and set it on the ground near Pen's head. Everyone in the band gives Pen something precious. If we had our wagons and the rest of the band, there would be much more. Still, we're not sending her to Cybele empty-handed.

When Pen has everything we can spare, we close the chamber door and pack sod around and over the chamber. The kurgan rises higher than my head. Grass and wildflowers will grow on it, but people in this flat land will realize that the small hill is no accident. If they know Amazons, they'll understand that a warrior is buried here.

The next morning, I ride to Troy to see Cassandra and learn if the war has resumed.

I see young men walking on the wide way inside the gate, so I know there's no fighting today. At the palace, I climb the stairs to the women's quarters and head for Cassandra's loom.

Few women are working. Hecuba isn't at her loom. Most women are there, but they're sitting, drooping in their chairs. I notice that their hair is wild and their robes are torn. Unbidden, the thought comes that this is why they need so much cloth.

Only Helen's hair is smooth and her robe unsullied. No men surround her today. She smiles pleasantly.

I see sudden movement. A dog barks. Someone—Cassandra!—rushes at the balcony railing. I run and catch her before she throws herself off.

Holding her bony shoulders, I guide her to her chair. She doesn't resist me. When I get there, Maera licks my leg.

Were her shoulders always bony?

When she sits, I look her over while she stares dully at my tunic. Her cheekbones stand out above gray hollows. Her head is bald in spots. Clumps of hair lie at her feet. Her forehead is bruised and swollen. Fresh beads of blood dot one arm, and scabs run down the other.

No one has been watching out for her, just as they didn't protect Hector.

I announce, "I'm taking her to our camp."

Helen calls, "Goodbye!"

No one else speaks. Cassandra holds my hand obediently and follows me out, along with Maera. I think my friend may be too weak to walk to the gate, but I walk slowly and she keeps up. When we get there, Maera whines, but sits. Outside Troy, I lift Cassandra onto Tall Brown and walk the horse to our camp.

When we're almost there, she says that Achilles still has Hector's body. "But Father will get it back in a few days. He doesn't know that he will."

I don't think he will, either. Achilles seems to want to wound the Trojans however he may.

"Father will bring him precious gifts in exchange."

I doubt we'll get any spoils from this war. As soon as I slaughter Achilles, we'll leave. If Cassandra wants to come with us, she'll be welcome.

As our guest at the camp, she's no trouble. She eats

Lannip's food and lets us remove her torn robe and dress her in a tunic and leggings. She even smiles when I put a tall hat on her head. When she stands, the tip comes to the top of my head.

After three days, she announces that Hector's body has been recovered. The next night, she leaves us to attend his funeral, but she promises to come back.

I'm not sure she will, though, so I wait half the night at the east gate for the funeral procession to return. Cassandra comes to me, walking like a wooden doll. In the procession's torchlight, I see her expression is wooden too.

The next day, she sits motionless near Lannip's cooking tripod. Her face shows nothing, while tears roll down her cheeks. That night, she doesn't move to lie down, so I sit with her.

"When I was little, Rin, he carried me on his shoulders as he used to carry Nax. I went to my first festival for Apollo that way. I was the youngest child there. When I was old enough to play in the streets, I used to go to the gymnasium to watch him wrestle. I think he liked for me to be there. When he finished a bout, win or lose, he looked to see me and grinned."

She lapses into silence.

I say through a tight throat, "I never saw him be anything but good. And he had a light heart." I wouldn't be Cassandra's friend if not for him.

"You understand. I wish everyone in the world could know what we lost." She pats my knee. "I'll try to sleep now."

Her health improves over the next week. She eats whatever we put in her lap and sleeps near me at night. She rarely speaks.

Meanwhile, Lannip and the others work with me on my swordplay and my handling of the battle-ax. My ribs hardly complain.

Once they approve my skill with the weapons, they set up pretend skirmishes and all come at me at once. Whenever one of them gains the advantage, they stop and tell me what I did wrong.

I learn that I have to look everywhere at once. While I'm battling one foe, I have to watch for the next. The battle will be deafening. I can't rely on my ears to warn me. Greek armor is thick. I should imagine I'm felling a tree.

"A tree that can jump away from you," Lannip adds.

Gradually, I improve. I use the speed that youth gives me. Accidentally, I deliver a terrible blow to Serag's thigh, though she laughs away the pain.

Lannip makes a lesson out of this too. "No unintended strikes! Hit where and when you mean to. Don't waste your strength."

She tells me the band's strategy before Pen died, and we decide to adopt it again. It's a way to continue to shoot as long as possible, since we're superior to the Greeks with our bows and arrows.

But Lannip says again and again that we don't know how Greeks think. "Fighting us isn't like fighting them. We can't prepare you for what they may do."

"Achilles' shield seems charmed," Zelke says. "There may be more like it. Be careful!" She adds, "All of us!"

I decide that I'll aim at Achilles' thighs. His shield seemed to pull arrows down, not lift them up. I have to just nick him, and the poisoned arrow will do the rest.

Cassandra says, "Achilles will die, but not in the coming battle and not at Amazon hands. Rin, you'll die soon after the fighting begins, and Achilles won't be your killer. He'll be an ordinary soldier, not especially strong or skilled, merely lucky."

Her ignorance makes us laugh and gives us the confidence we need.

She adds, "Your loss will deprive me of my only friend."

9

Cassandra returns to Troy the night before fighting resumes. In the morning, Aeneas, now the city's foremost warrior, leads us and the Trojans. Surprisingly, he's Cassandra's cousin, not a brother. He isn't worth much since he didn't help Hector and Pen.

We walk our horses to meet the Greeks, our pace slowed by the Trojan foot soldiers on our flanks. Aeneas has granted my request that the band and I ride at the center of his line. I reason that's where Achilles will be among the Greeks.

The Trojans are silent. I turn to wave to Cassandra on the ramparts, but I don't see her. Disappointed, I drop my hand. I'd have liked my friend to be there for my first departure for battle.

I'm more cheerful than I've been since before Pen died, glad for the chance to kill her killer.

But I told the band to strike him if they can. I want him dead most of all. I remember Pen's words about regret after killing an enemy. I'll be sad for the others I slay, but not for him.

Cassandra once recited a verse that she said came from her imaginary crows. I memorized it, changed one word, and made up a tune, which I sing:

> *"As sun sparkles on snowcap*
> *and blood-red poppies line a river,*
> *warriors ride to battle,*
> *singing their rousing songs."*

In Cassandra's song, instead of *rousing*, the word was *foolish*. The band hums along.

The sun pours endless heat. At least we aren't wearing iron helmets, as the Trojans are. Across my left shoulder hangs my gorytos that holds my bow and my poison-tipped arrows. My sword in its sheath and my battle-ax poke out of my belt. My crescent-shaped oak shield sways from leather loops on my left arm.

The morning advances. Finally, we see a band of gray and tan along the horizon—the sun glinting on Greek bronze and iron shields.

The Trojans howl their strange war cry: "Ya aya aya!" We shout, "Kiikiikaa!" When we stop our noise, the Greeks' "Alala alalay" reaches us faintly.

We don't spur our horses. The foot soldiers don't run at the Greek line. I'm reminded of evenings with the band, waiting for a meal to finish cooking.

The Greek front line mirrors ours: riders in the middle, foot soldiers on each side. The air above the Greeks is blurred by their long spears, which Trojans carry too. Behind us are sixty rows of Trojan fighters. Behind the Greeks, as I know from Pen, are four times that number.

Amazons shoot farther than anyone. Though I can't make out a specific target, I know I can reach the Greek line now. I nock an arrow to my bow. The war cries stop. I hear the thuds of our horses' hooves. I loose my arrow at the mass of Greeks. In the band, we all do. The Trojans wait.

I shoot again and again as we move forward. The Trojans too begin to shoot. Arrows come at us from the Greeks, but so far we're untouched.

A few minutes pass. The Greeks take shape in my keen eyes. I make out an exposed thigh. I shoot and see blood spurt. Later, I'll regret him. Now I see a golden crest, not in the front line—the coward, a few rows back.

Training and good sense keep me from rushing toward him.

After a few more yards, I pull a fresh handful of arrows from my gorytos and nock one. Lannip and I exchange glances. Yelling "Kiikiikaa!" we kick our horses. The band joins in. We divide and gallop along the Greek line, loosing arrow after arrow as only we can.

Tall Brown outstrips the others. Since I'm galloping along the mass of warriors hiding Achilles, I send an arrow higher than the others and hope that justice will guide it.

By the time I reach the end of the Greek line and turn Tall Brown, the Greeks and Trojans are rushing each other. The band is caught up in the fighting. I ride along the Greek flank, shooting and not stopping to see if warriors fall. I'm looking for an opening to Achilles.

Cybele appears before me. I hear an arrow whine. I'm about to die.

I scream, "Noooo!"

Someone or something shoves me off Tall Brown.

Cybele vanishes.

I land surprisingly lightly. For a moment, Cassandra's anxious face hangs over me. Then a man's arms pick me up. I struggle to get free and return to the battle.

A blast of wind picks us up. I go limp.

The two of us—no, the three of us—are borne above the ground. Cassandra's chin digs into the man's shoulder. She's holding him from behind, smiling and weeping. Terrified, I squeeze my eyes shut.

Cybele, what happened? Did I die? Why is Cassandra here? Am I being carried to your battlefield and to Pen?

Air whirs by.

Thank you, Cybele, for my life and for my death if it has come.

We slow. The wind weakens. The man lowers me onto grass.

Eyes still closed, I roll onto my stomach, afraid of what will happen next. I wiggle my toes and wriggle my shoulders. Nothing hurts.

Hands pat my hair and stroke my back. Whose hands?

"We did it!" Cassandra says. "She's alive. I touch her, and she really is!" She adds, "Eurus, I'm dizzy."

They're Cassandra's hands, still petting me. She goes on. "We did something. A sardine thing, but we did it. She can spoil it, but we did it."

She said I'm alive, but am I? I roll over and dare to open my eyes.

Cassandra and the man kneel over me. We're on a small lawn ringed by bushes and dwarf pines, but where are we?

I raise myself on one elbow. A stone digs into my skin, which I doubt I would feel if I were dead. I move my elbow off the stone. My bow is on the grass next to me.

Cassandra sits back on her haunches. "I *told* you you'd die." She grins at the man. "I've never been able to say that to anyone before. I'm less dizzy." She tells me, "I'm dizzy when I change the future more than a tiny bit."

I think her face will split if she smiles any wider.

He smiles back at her, a brawny man with a round nose and round cheeks, wearing a worn red himation although the weather is warm for a cloak.

There's an altar here, such as I saw in Priam's palace, but this one is made of granite rather than marble.

"Did I die?"

She lifts her chin, still grinning. "We saved you." To the man: "I could never say that before, either!"

"If I didn't die, then I wasn't going to." Even though I saw Cybele. I stand and put my bow in my gorytos. I still have plenty of arrows. "How far am I from the battle?" I have to kill Achilles, and the band may need me.

Cassandra jumps up. Her smile vanishes. She grabs my hand and starts to pull me.

I break loose. I'm far stronger than she is.

"If you return to the battle, Eurus and I may not be able to rescue you again."

The man—Eurus—says, "When I fail to save you, I'll blame myself." A hot wind blows across us. "But it will be your fault. And she"—he tilts his head at Cassandra—"won't visit me again."

I don't know what he's talking about.

He adds, to my wonderment, "Your Cybele has the advantage in her battle. She doesn't need you now."

Who is he?

He sees my confusion and announces that he's the god of the east wind. "A minor god," he adds.

Too much is happening. But it doesn't matter. What I have to do is clear.

"Rin," Cassandra begs, "please come with me. If you agree we're friends, come. It isn't far, and it won't take long, and if I fail at this, we'll bring you back to the Greeks, and Eurus will put you close to Achilles. I promise." She waves a hand at the sky. "In a moment, a hawk will fly by."

No, it won't. "It's too early in the day for a hawk to be hunting."

"Nonetheless."

A hawk flies over us, high in the sky.

"Don't you notice I'm always right?"

"By chance. You were wrong when you said I'd die." Ha! I have her there. "I'll go with you."

She takes my hand, then lets it go and hurries to the altar. On top, a big bowl and platter are littered with stems and pits, but a small bowl brims with walnuts. "Eurus, may I?"

He looks annoyed.

"Twice as many tomorrow. I promise."

He nods.

We start off down a path, Eurus following. A light breeze brushes us.

Anemones and bellflowers line our way. A lark sings. I smell laurel and glimpse other altars through the bushes. Cassandra veers left. We emerge into a larger clearing, where the altar is marble. The statue is made of black marble shot through with pink streaks. It represents a beautiful woman, taller than any of us. At her side are statues of a cow, a lion, and a peacock, standing in unlikely harmony.

Cassandra puts the bowl of walnuts on the altar then raises her arms as the Trojans do when they beg something of their gods. "Most beautiful goddess, you promised me a gift and said I could wait to ask for it. The time has come."

The wind stills.

The statue's pink streaks fade. Its eyes blink. Goose bumps stand out on my arms. The statue has become the goddess!

Her voice echoes, as Cybele's does, but her pitch is higher. "You *think* the time has come. What is the gift?"

Cassandra hesitates. "Er . . . This is Rin, an Amazon girl." She says in a rush, "Before, you wouldn't go against Apollo to lift my curse. But I ask you to lift it just on her, no one else, so that she can believe my prophecies. She isn't one of us. Apollo will lose nothing."

"If you please"—my voice squeaks—"lift whatever curse on the other Amazons who are here too. We're just twelve women." Whatever this is, I want us all to be part of it.

"If she isn't a worshipper, I can do noth—" Her face takes on a listening look. "Ah. I can." She turns to me. "Your Cybele doesn't mind if I give this gift. It's done." She vanishes.

My head hurts. My eyes burn. My ears ring.

Running through my aching mind is every prediction Cassandra has made and the truth of each, the likely ones and the far-fetched ones, from the hawk a few minutes ago to Pen's death—and mine.

The pain subsides. Cassandra can see the future. How could I not have realized?

If I had believed her, Pen would still be alive. I collapse on the ground, sobbing.

10

Cassandra rubs my back. A breeze plays around my head.

While I weep, questions pile up, but I can't stop crying.

At last, I do stop. I sit up and ask the most important one: "Do you know if the band is all right?"

"They will all survive today's battle, which will end soon. One is bruised but nothing worse. They won't last long, though."

They will! We're superb warriors.

But now I believe her.

"The Greeks are too numerous. You all should leave. Zelke will die tomorrow."

Tomorrow! I'm their queen. I must take them home.

Or send them. Achilles is still alive.

"What will happen to me if I fight tomorrow?"

"You'll probably die, but I don't know. Now that you believe me, I can tell you what I see, and you can do something else. You'll probably die anyway."

"Will I kill Achilles first?"

"I doubt it. Paris will kill him."

"Paris!"

Eurus says, sounding just as surprised, "Paris?"

She laughs. "I suspect a god will guide his arrow."

My next question comes out angrily: "Why didn't you save Hector and Pen the way you saved me?" She adored her brother. I loved Pen.

Eurus crouches, his face an inch from mine. His eyes are bulging. "She saved you. Have you thanked her?"

I didn't! I thank her and apologize. "But why didn't you save Hector?"

"I couldn't save either of them. Some god or goddess was there, helping Achilles, keeping him alive. I could tell because of what happened to your arrows." She's weeping.

Oh. His shield wasn't magical. One of their deities was at his side. Unfair either way!

Eurus pats Cassandra's arm.

"I hope Hector saw your mother. Otherwise, he died thinking no one came to his aid." She wipes her eyes. "Even if you and I weren't friends, I'd be grateful to the

Amazons forever for what she did."

Eurus says he's hungry. He points his chin at Hera's altar. "Greedy goddess."

The walnuts have disappeared, though the bowl remains.

Cassandra takes the bowl and we follow him back to his altar. As my guide, he points whenever the path forks toward a clearing and calls out the name of the immortal worshipped there. "In case you don't know, you're in the sacred grove."

When we reach his altar, he and Cassandra sit on it, their feet dangling. They smile at each other. She looks happy.

I stand in front of them and ask her, my heart fluttering, "Are you part goddess? Is he your half brother?" I've heard of such beings.

"No." She swivels her smile to me. "We're just friends."

"Just?" He sounds irritated. *"Mere* friends?"

I murmur, afraid to speak up to contradict a god: "There are no *mere* friends." I've learned that.

"Correct!" Eurus's vehemence makes a gust that tilts my hat on my head.

Cassandra blushes and changes the subject. "I'm so glad you're alive, Rin. I wonder if you'll see the crows now."

"There really are crows?" I wave my hand in the air to erase my words. "I'm sure there are crows."

Eurus says, "We must eat."

I notice my hunger. But there's no food.

The gentle wind that has been with us quiets.

Eurus and Cassandra jump off the altar. They watch me, their expressions merry.

I'd seen Hector and Andromache look cheerful together, much as these two do.

Cassandra says, "I don't approve of theft." Grinning, she adds, "Don't tell my mother what's about to happen, Rin."

A few minutes pass. My stomach rumbles.

The wind rises. Clusters of grapes soar to us and land on the altar. A walnut whirs by my ear. Ai! I raise my arms to protect my head as the air fills with flying food. Nuts click on the altar.

"Enough?" Eurus asks.

"Yes!" Cassandra says.

The wind dies. Walnuts, almonds, hazelnuts, grapes, figs, dates, and apples are scattered across the altar. Eurus is already biting into an apple. Cassandra lifts a grape to her mouth.

It's a day of marvels, so I eat, standing between them.

Speaking with her mouth full, Cassandra says, "Several farmers made a forced offering." She gestures. "He refuses to call it stealing."

The fruit is sweet, the nuts meaty. No bread. While we

eat, the air begins to smell of our meal. Eurus is breathing, and we smell what he ate!

Cassandra laughs. "The first time he came to life for me, I had brought him garlic. I don't do that anymore."

I laugh too, glad to be part of their camaraderie. But I have a question: "Do other Trojans see the future?"

"My twin, Helenus."

The one who visits Helen every day when there's no fighting, along with Cassandra's other brother, Deiphobus.

"Apollo didn't curse his gift, so people believe him. But he often lies, which they believe too. He'll betray Troy and be one of the causes of its fall."

"Troy will fall?"

She nods. "And burn."

I don't know why I feel sad. They're city people.

"What will happen to you?"

Her voice is calm. "I'll be a slave, and then I'll be murdered."

I gasp.

She smiles. "Before I'm murdered, I'll sail on a ship. I'll like that. Eurus will be the wind."

His brown cheeks tint red. "I'll try to keep her from being killed. I won't desert her."

She reaches across me to touch his hand. "I doubt he can change my fate, Rin."

But he's a god! I ask, "Could you always see the future?"

"No." Leaning against the altar, she starts a tale that I can barely believe. When she describes Paris's abandonment because of a prophecy, I blurt, "Your parents tried to kill their baby?" What terrible people! "Why didn't they leave Troy and take everyone with them? They could have lived the way we do, or they could have built another city."

Eurus cries, "Ho!"

Cassandra blinks. "They couldn't have thought of it." She shakes her head. "I didn't think of it, either, when I learned about his birth. We all might have been saved." She's quiet for a minute, then adds, "Only someone who isn't a Trojan could see it."

She tells me that Paris grew up on the mountain where he was abandoned. Then she starts to talk about what happened between getting her cursed gift and now.

I hold up my hand to stop her. The sun is low. "I have to go back to the band. We'll leave in the morning." As soon as the words fly out of my mouth, I feel sad.

And cowardly. I swore to be Cassandra's friend and to be Hector's comrade-in-arms. Hector is gone, but Cassandra is not. "Please come with us." We can teach her to be useful.

She jumps on the altar and looms over me. "I am a princess of Troy. Would you desert your band to save yourself?"

"I'd try to save us all." Which she isn't doing. On

impulse I say, "Spend another night with us. You can tell the band what happened to you." What if there's a way to help Troy without going to battle again and making her prophecies come true? "Now that they know the truth, they'll want to find out."

She agrees to come, and Eurus invites himself along.

Better, he blows us to them.

Pen would have known what the result of that would be.

11

When they see us hurtling toward them, everyone rushes to their horses. Serag needs help mounting. She's injured! They gallop away. Pen's horse and Tall Brown follow them.

The band is no match for the east wind. We overtake them and Eurus's wind hems them in. Their struggles against his gale might look funny, except for their terrified faces.

I realize, as I should have before, that they think I died on the battlefield. They believe Cassandra's prophecies now, and she predicted my death. I can't guess what they imagine they're seeing. Cybele never sends ghosts to the living.

"Cassandra saved me," I shout. I gesture for Eurus to quiet his wind. He does and I announce that I'm alive.

As one, they gallop off. I ask Eurus and Cassandra to

wait. "They're brave. They'll come back."

We return the short distance to the camp, where Eurus busies himself starting a fire and blowing it into a blaze.

The stars are coming out when Lannip rides to us.

"Rin?"

"Cassandra saved me," I repeat. "Cassandra and Eurus"—I gesture at him—"knocked me out of the way of the arrow that was going to kill me. A Trojan goddess has allowed us in the band to believe Cassandra's prophecies. Only us."

Lannip's chest rises and falls as she pants. "Can I— May I touch you?"

I nod.

She dismounts, edges toward me, extends an uncertain finger, and touches my arm. "Oh!" She pokes it. "Ah! We couldn't find your body."

In the low light, I make out that she's crying. We hug.

"I don't want to be queen." She hugs Cassandra too, and nods at Eurus. "I'll tell everyone they can come."

They're afraid at first, but soon we're all laughing and embracing. Cassandra and Eurus, both looking surprised, are pulled into the knot of us. I doubt the band understands that Eurus caused the windstorm that delivered us here.

They tell me that Serag fell off her horse when the enchantment was lifted and she could believe Cassandra's prophecies.

"Zelke saved me," she says. "I'll be fine."

Everyone else had been able to keep fighting—with difficulty. Their heads hurt just as mine had.

We spread our blankets near the fire—for light, not heat—and sit. The band makes room for Cassandra and Eurus. Lannip tells me of the battle after I left it. Among them, they killed twenty Greek warriors with their battle-axes. They don't know how many died from their arrows.

I feel sad now for the warrior I killed.

"More tomorrow," Zelke says.

"No." I rise on my knees. "Cassandra predicts you'll die tomorrow, and we'll all be killed eventually." I pause. "I saw Cybele, but she vanished before she spoke to me. Cassandra and Eurus pushed me out of the way of the arrow."

"There are too many Greeks," Cassandra says.

"They fight differently from us," Lannip admits. A note of accusation creeps into her voice. "Cassandra, your warriors could fight at our side more, but they don't. They don't protect us or let us protect them."

"The Greeks and the Trojans talk to each other before they fight." Khasa laughs. "Today two of them decided they were friends. They hugged and traded armor." She laughs harder. "The Trojan gave away his gold armor in exchange for bronze. Meanwhile I killed two Greeks."

Zelke says, "No wonder this war has lasted so long."

Lannip nods. "If we could survive, we'd get our plunder years from now."

"Troy will lose," I say.

No one moves or seems to breathe.

After a moment, Lannip says, "Will Achilles live to see it?"

When Cassandra says that Paris will kill him, Serag snorts. "No wonder we didn't believe you before."

Even Cassandra laughs. "I suspect a god will help him."

Lannip says, "Gods interfere?"

Serag jumps up. "Did a god make Pen die?"

"A god or goddess helped Achilles kill Hector," Cassandra says. "Otherwise, Pen might be alive."

A shocked silence follows this.

After a minute, I ask if anyone is hungry. They all are. We have dried meat, but I ask Eurus if he can blow four rabbits our way.

The air stills. I say, "Eurus is the god of the east wind. He and Cassandra saved me." I add, "I liked that interference."

A small whirlwind spins to us, with four fat rabbits hopping in its midst. In an instant, hands catch them and snap their unlucky necks. The whirlwind subsides, and the band waits uncertainly.

At the same moment, Cassandra says, "The east wind is a lesser god," and Eurus says, "I'm a lesser god." They smile at each other. This time, Eurus blushes.

Their pleasure makes me smile too. I wonder how long they've known each other—and how well—to happen to say the same thing at the same time.

They remind me of the shyness of some of my cousins and some boys, when the bands get together at Cybele's rock.

Eurus adds, "The great gods are behaving badly. I'd never act as they do."

Cassandra cries, "Crows!"

They're real!

Several in the band reach for arrows. Crow is tasty!

I yell, "Don't shoot them!"

In the dark, they're denser and a bluer black than the night. One lands on my head, one on Serag's, who yelps, and one on Eurus's. The crows squawk with a Trojan accent:

> *"On a mountain, a shepherd sleeps*
> *while a lion eats his sheep.*
> *King Priam cannot save his flock.*
> *Amazons, leave while you can!"*

The crows lift and fly away. Though I was prepared, fear is drumming in my ears. Band members cling to one another.

12

When the crows don't come back and no other miracles occur, I relax, and band members let each other go.

Eurus says, "I enjoy helping mortals, and I can always get food." The air quiets again.

I warn everyone. We don't have to wait long for a delivery of fruit and nuts, such as we had in the sacred grove. No one dares to touch them.

"Cassandra was telling me her tale, but I stopped her because it was getting late." I take a fig. "The beginning is very strange. Would you tell all of us over dinner?"

"Yes."

Brave Lannip reaches for an apple. She bites and chews. "Mm. Sweet!"

Everyone seems to exhale at once. People help themselves. Lannip busies herself skinning and butchering the rabbits. We sit again and wait while she starts cooking in a pan atop a tripod over the fire. She sits too when the pieces are sizzling.

I summarize what I've been told so far and add that the Trojans didn't think of leaving their city when its downfall was predicted.

Cassandra picks up the tale. As she goes on, I'm shocked at the behavior of the god Apollo. I'm surprised that Cassandra's twin, Helenus, also received the gift of seeing the future, and I'm stunned at his evil.

My friend doesn't boast about her attempts to save her city, but Eurus boasts for her. I was wrong to think she'd done nothing. We all say she was right to throw boiling broth at Helen.

Lannip announces that the rabbits are done. Cassandra and Eurus eat together from Pen's bowl.

We listen for hours, long after the rabbits and Eurus's bounty are gone. As queen, I decide that a sleepless night doesn't matter, since we won't be fighting in the morning.

But when Cassandra tells us about the Greek king Agamemnon sacrificing his daughter, we all want to fight. Our lives in exchange for his seems just.

Cassandra says, "I doubt you'll succeed. His end—"

"You *doubt*?" Serag sounds annoyed. "I thought you knew the future."

She explains, as she did to me. "Once you believe my prophecies, you can act differently from what I predict. Little changes, though, won't make much difference in the end, but you may succeed in killing this warrior or that one."

She continues the tale. I weep when she tells us about changing the future and saving Troy and then having the future snap back. Others sniffle too. Eurus blows his nose gustily.

The sky is brightening toward dawn when Cassandra says, "Then the Greek ships arrived."

I've forgotten my body in listening, and seemingly we all have. We stand stiffly, stretch, walk a little way, and return to pick at the rabbit bones and eat the nuts and fruit we missed in the dark. Eurus's wind brings more fruit and nuts, no more rabbits.

Cassandra tells us the history of the war before we came. "The gods are in it too. Apollo told me he'd help Hector, and Father is sure Poseidon is helping the Greeks, who are seafarers even more than we are. Years ago, near the beginning, Menelaus wounded Paris and was about to kill him and end the war when my brother vanished. Before the day's fighting ended, I saw him in the palace, uninjured. I think Aphrodite saved him."

I'm surprised that these gods don't have their own

enemies to fight, as Cybele does—and amazed that they take sides among their worshippers.

Lannip asks, "Cassandra, what will happen next?"

"In three days . . ."

We sit again.

" . . . Paris will kill Achilles."

"Finally!" Zelke says.

Lannip adds, "The weakling will find strength."

I lie back on the grass and stare at the pale sky. Then I roll over to look at Pen's kurgan. Thank you, Cybele, for Achilles' coming death.

Cassandra waits for me to sit up again before continuing. "Next, Paris himself will be wounded. He'll go to Oenone, his first wife, the nymph."

Cassandra told us about her last night. I noticed then that a mortal can marry a goddess, at least a lesser one, which makes me wonder again.

"Oenone is a healer," Cassandra says. "I don't know what will happen between them, since I can't see the future of another seer or a deity, but Paris will die of his wounds."

"Will Helen mourn him?" I ask.

"She'll weep." Cassandra pops a walnut in her mouth. "I don't know if she'll be sad."

"With Paris dead," Serag says, "Troy doesn't have to fall, right? Helen can go back to her first husband."

"Deiphobus and my twin, Helenus, will want her. What

I see is that Priam will give her—"

At the word *give*, people snort.

Zelke bursts out, "She's no more than a satchel covered with gold and jewels. First this one takes her and she goes, then that one."

Cassandra continues. "Priam will give her to Deiphobus. But I think Helenus will try to keep that from happening. He may succeed."

My hair lifts in a breeze. Eurus says, "But your brother is only a sardine too."

Cassandra explains. "The goddess Hera told me that just a few mortals—"

Eurus interrupts. "Or even a mortal and a lesser god—"

"Can't change the future any more than a sardine can stop a whale or a sparrow can budge the moon. Eurus and I are sardines or sparrows, and so is Helenus."

I understand that we're sardines too, though Cybele might not agree.

"It would be just a small change for Helen to be given to my twin." Cassandra adds, "If she isn't, he'll help the Greeks. Still, the war will drag on.

"After that, the Greeks will think of a ruse to fool us. They'll build a giant wooden horse and hide forty warriors inside."

I imagine Tall Brown made much, much bigger. How beautiful.

"During the night, they'll bring the horse—which will be mounted on a platform with wheels—and leave it outside the gates of Troy. In the morning, a young Greek man will be there when we come out. He'll say the Greeks have given up and sailed for home. The horse is an offering for the goddess Athena and he himself was going to be sacrificed to her, but he got away. He'll add that the Greeks hope we'll leave it outside the city to rot, which will enrage Athena."

I ask, "Why isn't the goddess angry at the Greeks for using her this way?"

Cassandra shrugs. "I don't know. The man will be believed. I'll say he's lying, but no one ever listens to me."

We know.

"Laocoön, one of Apollo's priests, will warn them too. My father will heed him. We'll almost be saved, but then something will happen that I can't see—either Helenus or an immortal will act. The next thing I do see is that everyone is terrified. They rush to bring in the horse. I wish I knew why.

"At night, the warriors inside the horse will emerge and open the city gates to the Greek army. That will be the end of us. They'll set fires. Our warriors won't have time to arm themselves. The women the Greeks don't kill by accident will become their slaves."

"*You* will be enslaved?" Lannip says.

"By Agamemnon, the one who sacrificed his own daughter."

As I had earlier, everyone urges Cassandra to leave with us.

She refuses as she refused me. "Rin said she wouldn't leave the band if you were in danger. I won't leave my band, which is Troy."

Lannip stands and begins to dismantle the cooking tripod. We should leave soon, or we'll lose the coolest part of the day. But Eurus blows in even more fruit and nuts, and she sits again.

In a dreamy voice, Zelke asks, "What would happen if Paris didn't die?"

Cassandra leans toward her. "I don't think the gods will let his death be interfered with, but I don't know. I see only the future that will be, not the future that would be *if*."

I say, "How many sardines do you think it would take to stop a whale?"

Khasa laughs. "If they attacked its eyes? Or chewed its belly?"

"If they were sardines with their own special bows and arrows?" Serag is laughing too. "Amazon sardines."

I say, "We won't fight on the battlefield with the Trojans again. I won't allow it." Pen would approve, I'm sure. "But if we can find another way to keep Troy from falling, will there be spoils for us?"

No one moves. Even the breeze stops. I think Eurus is holding his breath.

"Yes, if Priam knows it would have fallen and you prevented it. Otherwise, I have a box of jewelry, mostly gold."

That will do. We won't have the shame of laboring for no reward.

"Cassandra, we'll help you," I say.

Eurus shouts his joy and sends a cool breeze that reminds me of home.

13

Everyone suggests what we should do. Cassandra pokes holes in each idea. We keep coming back to Paris, the great gods, and Satchel, our name for Helen, because anyone can march off with her. Paris is doomed, and the great gods, as Eurus assures us, will act according to their whims. Helen interests us most.

After an hour of talking, I stand and juggle three walnuts, keeping them in the air for a full minute. I grin, glad to be doing something physical and to not feel like a queen for a moment.

But I *am* queen, and juggling reminds me of Helen's acrobatics. "Pen said we could learn from Satchel. She's stronger than we are in some ways." Pen had told them about Helen's performance. "What if we ask her to join us after Paris dies?" I think how much I'd rather have Cassandra in the band.

Lannip doles out dried meat. "We should hunt soon." She turns to Cassandra. "If Satchel is gone, will the war end?" She remembers. "You can't tell. But do you *think* it will end?"

Cassandra tilts her head from side to side, seeming to imagine what will happen one way and then another. "The Greeks and the Trojans won't have her to fight over. I don't know if the great gods will care. But my brothers and the other men will pursue you to get her back."

Eurus laughs. "They won't catch you. The wind will be against them."

"What if she doesn't want to come with us?" I ask, while chewing hard. Dried meat is tasty but tough.

After a minute of general disbelief that a satchel wouldn't rather be a person, Serag says, "We'll have to persuade her there isn't anything to be afraid of."

"But there is," Zelke says. "We get hurt. Some of us die in battle or on raids."

Cassandra sounds shocked. "You wouldn't let her fight, would you? She could be treacherous."

"No, we wouldn't." I cut to the heart of my question. "If she doesn't want to go with us, should we just take her?"

It's up to me, I guess. But I want to hear what they think. We never accept slaves as spoils, and we don't take prisoners in battle.

Everyone speaks at the same time. They're divided. They all want to change Cassandra's fate, but no one wants to take Helen's freedom, even though she doesn't seem to care about it and has never really had it.

Finally, I say, "We'll try our best to convince her to join the band. If she won't, I'll decide what to do then."

This satisfies no one, not even me.

I add, "She seems to want everyone to like her."

"*Love* her," Cassandra says.

People protest.

"We don't even know her!"

"I don't like her, and I haven't even met her!"

"Pretend!" I say. Something we've never needed to do, something I'm not sure I can do. "It's good to learn new skills."

Zelke says, "Even if she comes with us gladly, she won't really join the band, right?"

I have an answer for that. "If she helps us, she will, and we'll give her a chance. If not, we'll find a village that will take her."

Lannip laughs. "Beware an Amazon bearing gifts."

"How can we talk to her," Serag asks, "if she's always in the women's quarters?"

Cassandra tells us that we'll have our chance right after Paris's funeral.

At dusk, Pammon comes to find out why we didn't ride to battle this morning.

I've planned for this. "Your warriors didn't even try to save Hector, your own hero. Only Pen went to his aid. They both might have lived if others had come."

"We thought—"

"We went with you yesterday. We fight as a band, always looking out for each other, but each Trojan fights as if he's an army by himself."

The band is nodding.

"If you'd told us that, we never would have come to Troy." I took a deep breath. "When we finish our mourning for Pen, we'll go home."

"What if we double your spoils?"

He'd already agreed we could take what we wanted.

"Corpses don't need spoils."

"How long will you stay here?"

I say my only lie: "The queen decides when official mourning is over. I haven't decided yet."

He kicks his horse and goes.

We wait for Paris to die. We hunt, though Eurus tells us he can bring more game than we can eat. Khasa suggests we raid the Greek camp for fun. She's only three years older than I am, and I'm tempted—until I see

Cassandra's frightened face.

The days that pass are pleasant, except for my grief over Pen, which swells and ebbs in waves.

Cassandra is skilled at skinning and butchering the game we bring back from hunting, though she's never done it before. She's slow, but her work is perfect. She laughs at our surprise. I think how rarely I've heard her laugh.

She looks up from a haunch of deer. "I peer into the future and watch Lannip. Then I imitate her. My hands aren't used to handling the knife, which is why I'm slow." She laughs again. "Some aspects of prophesying are useful."

"What if you happen to watch me one of the times when I cut myself?"

"I guess I'd cut myself too. Next time, before I start, I'll watch you all the way through to see."

Lannip smiles, seemingly proud to have told the seer something she didn't know.

We suggest other things Cassandra might be able to do. She says she doubts she has the strength to shoot very far or to manage our horses as we do. But she asks Zelke if she can try her harp. First, she plays—perfectly—Zelke's favorite ballad about a tragic raid, and then, frowning and smiling at once, she plays a melody we don't know, with an irregular rhythm and notes in a smaller range than we're used to, but the harmonies are surprising and beautiful.

We're quiet for a few minutes after she finishes, thinking about what we heard and appreciating it.

Then I blurt, "Could you make one of our bows?" The skill I still wish I could master.

She stares into the distance. "Yes, though it might take me as long as five years."

Everyone but Cassandra laughs when Zelke says, "We should kidnap *you* instead of Helen."

Tears stand in her eyes. "I wish I'd been born into your band." She turns to Eurus. "Except then I wouldn't ever have come to your altar."

He turns the dull red of his himation.

She touches his arm. "I wouldn't have your friendship."

At the word *friendship*, he purses his lips as if he'd eaten moldy bread.

Cassandra and I are friends, but she and Eurus are as close as the bricks in Troy's wall.

The seer knows the future but is ignorant about herself.

I grin. My thoughts are starting to sound like the crows.

Cassandra doesn't return to Troy. Three days later, in the afternoon, she tells me that Achilles is about to die. I hold my breath.

After a moment, she nods. "He's gone."

I feel dull relief but not the joy I expected. Pen is still dead.

A few day later, Cassandra sees Paris wounded in battle moments before it happens.

After another week, she foresees him die. At the time, I'm busy brushing Tall Brown and don't see her face.

But I hear her gasp. I turn. Paris?

Eurus stands with her. His hands grip each other. I realize he wants to hug her or do something to make her feel better. He flies upward, whips himself in a tight circle above her, comes down next to her again, in a crouch with his head between his knees.

When she puts a hand on his shoulder, he looks up, his face questioning.

She sees me watching and speaks to both of us. "Paris just died. I can't see him anymore." She lets Eurus go. "This brother and I didn't grow up together. I didn't know him well. He might have been a better man if . . ." She trails off. "The great gods and goddesses, Paris, Helenus, even my parents . . . I don't know which to blame."

"All of them!" Eurus stands.

I nod. Village people! Not Cassandra, my friend.

The next day, we follow our plan.

14

According to Cassandra, funerals are held a full day after the person dies and start as soon as it's dark. Paris will be carried to the cemetery in a horse-drawn wagon, followed by mourners—men first, then women and children. The cemetery is outside Troy, about a quarter mile farther than the sacred grove. There, his body will be lifted onto a pyre, and a fire will be lit. His ashes will be placed in an urn and buried. Then the mourners will go back to Troy, men first again. The sky will still be dark.

Our chance will come on the return. Cassandra will whisper to Helen that she wants to talk to her privately. Curiosity will probably succeed with Helen, and she'll go. If not, Eurus will be nearby to force her with his wind. The other women won't care that she leaves.

I ask Cassandra about evil Helenus.

Her cheeks swell in a long exhale. "I'm sure he'll be at Deiphobus's side, since he has to walk with the men. He'll probably be plotting to ruin our brother's chances at Helen. If he happens to look at her immediate future, he'll see what we're doing. If he concentrates only on Deiphobus, we'll be safe from him. He's our greatest threat."

Eurus says he can blow Helenus far away, but Cassandra holds up a hand. "Don't! He'll cry out and make an uproar. We'll be discovered."

Zelke says, "We can kill him to stop his noise."

I hear Cassandra's intake of breath. Everyone waits for me to speak.

I toss back my head. "Troy is still our ally. We can't kill one of its princes."

The night of the funeral is lit by a three-quarter moon. We wait far enough from the cemetery so that the Trojans won't hear our voices when we speak to Helen. Cassandra is with the mourners. Eurus hovers in the air above us, hidden by a low cloud in an otherwise cloudless sky. Cassandra has asked him to interfere only if she or the band is in danger.

While we stand silently, I worry what Pen's opinion would be. I imagine her in Cybele's camp between battles, watching me and disapproving. If she were alive, we'd be far from Troy by now. No matter how sad she'd feel for my friend, she wouldn't endanger us to save strangers from a bunch of selfish, felt-headed gods.

Wrong! I hear Pen's voice in my imagination or coming from Cybele's homeland. *Cassandra saved your life. We'd help her, Rinny-Rin.*

Several minutes pass before I can stop crying. Thank you, Cybele, for my mother.

Then I start weeping again because I wonder if Hector is watching us from the Trojans' Hades. He'd be happy that we're helping his sister. Even more, he'd want us to succeed so Nax can live to grow up. I wish I could tell him how glad I am to be Cassandra's friend. I wish I had told him.

The wind brings us Trojan voices singing to the music of their lyre and flute. Eurus must be blowing the sound to us because the distance is too great even for my sharp ears. The song is slow, and each note lingers. I weep again. The Trojans are good for something.

The singing and the instruments end too soon.

We wait. Cicadas hum. The air is dry.

I'm the first to hear footsteps. I paste on a smile and hope the moon isn't bright enough to show how false it is.

Cassandra and Helen are holding hands. Both are panting. They have no endurance. Cassandra's face is tight, but Helen's is serene, open. She's beautiful even in a torn peplos and without her jewels.

When they let each other go, I take both Helen's hands

in mine. "Welcome." Time to pretend. "We're glad you've come."

"Cassandra said you want to talk to me."

The band leans in to hear Helen's whispery voice.

She squeezes my hand. "We've both lost people we love."

I should have said that!

Her grip loosens, and I let her hands go.

"I told Pen how you could almost be a horse and about your jumping on one hand. She said you're stronger than we are, at least in some ways." Helen would be likely to recognize the lie if I suggested she was stronger in everything. "Pen said we could learn from you, Satch— Helen."

Someone cheeps with suppressed laughter.

Helen seems not to notice. "I doubt I could ever be as strong as you are."

This, I'm sure, is meant as a compliment, but I don't like it, and I doubt the others do, either. We're not fond of real or fake helplessness.

I keep going. "We're a small band, even though this isn't all of us." I widen my smile. "When someone dies, we find a new member, a woman who can make us even better."

"Me?" This comes out as a breathy squeal. "Become an Amazon?"

"Yes."

Lannip echoes, "Yes."

"You prefer me to her?" She touches Cassandra's shoulder.

Through lips that barely move, Cassandra says, "I won't leave my parents."

Helen doesn't let it go, though. "If she'd join you, would you take her over me?"

If she comes with us, we'll deliver her to a village as quickly as we can. Her need to be most loved would spread poison through the band.

"Both of you would be best of all."

Helen goes to each in the band and asks, "Would you be glad to have me?"

Cassandra and I exchange desperate glances. Every second increases the likelihood that Helenus will notice Helen's absence.

They all tell her *yes*. It's partly true. We'll be glad to save Cassandra, and if that means taking Helen, we're willing.

Finally, she returns to me. "I've longed for the companionship of women." Her expression is solemn. "I'll go with you and teach you what I know. Thank you for wanting me!"

"Wonderful!" My smile becomes real. I wonder if Cassandra sees her city saved, but her face is neutral. I reach out for Helen's hand again. "The horses are at our camp.

We'll leave as soon as we get there."

She slips her hand out of mine. "Without my jewels? Don't you want my jewels? People would have frowned if I wore them to Paris's funeral."

We love jewels, but not now.

Lannip chimes in. "We take spoils on our raids. You'll have jewels to choose from. In the band, we share."

She smiles widely. "I love you all! But I can't leave them. Paris and my other husband, Menelaus, gave them to me."

Everyone tries, but she can't be persuaded, not even when I tell her she can't join the band if she doesn't come now. Our conversation has convinced me that we mustn't take her by force, or we'll be ruined. I wonder if the jewels are just an excuse. She may really be afraid to stop being a village woman.

Helen goes back to the mourners. Cassandra comes with us to camp. I'm sure she thinks that she's again failed to save Troy, but we should have rehearsed more, been more persuasive, made Helen want to come with us. I'm the one who failed.

15

When we reach camp, I ask Cassandra, "Should we have taken her by force?"

She says what I already thought, "That might have saved Troy, but it would have ruined your band."

Khasa spreads her blanket. "Cassandra, you have the courage to stay with your city. Satchel wasn't brave enough to leave them, and they aren't even her people."

Cassandra laughs. "But my heroism stops at sleeping near her at home tonight. May I stay with you one more time and say farewell tomorrow?"

We're happy to have her. Eurus brings us snacks of perfect fruit and nuts.

After we eat, my full belly churns. I don't sleep much. In the morning I tell the band that I'm not leaving with them. They all argue with me. Cassandra argues longer and louder than anyone.

I let them. Then I say, "The Trojans are our allies. Cassandra is our friend. If I can help them, I will. I won't rejoin their army, though." Which would almost certainly get me killed. "I'll come back when it's over."

Zelke juts her chin forward. "Pen wouldn't—"

"Pen believed in me. Lannip, if I don't return by winter and you don't want to be queen, choose someone else."

They try to persuade me to change my mind or to let them all remain. I forbid them to stay. Then each of them urges me to keep only her with me, to protect me. I'm sure it's out of love for Pen, who wouldn't want me to die so young.

I shake my head until my neck hurts.

An hour later, they're gone. I feel like a tooth pried away from its fellow teeth.

Cassandra says that today Helen will be given either to Deiphobus or Helenus. "If Helenus gets her, Troy may be saved, and you can rejoin your band." She adds, "I want to be there. Maybe I can do something. Probably not." She raises her right arm.

Blushing again, Eurus picks her up with her arm around his shoulder, and his wind carries them both away.

I know nothing about affection between a man and a

woman. If the band were here, I'd ask Lannip about my friend and Eurus.

I lie back on my blanket and make my mind and heart as still and empty as the cloudless sky. Eventually, I stand.

Walking rather than riding, because I don't want success to be easy, I look for my next meal. The afternoon is almost over when I shoot a hare. While I butcher it, I ask myself what an Amazon can do that a Trojan wouldn't think of.

They fight. We fight.

They like spoils, and so do we.

They have their diswitted gods and goddesses, and we have steadfast Cybele. Thank you for being our goddess, who gave us our horses, our gorytos, our bow, and our knowledge of poisons and herbs to use against our enemies and for ourselves.

Poisons and herbs!

A plan begins to take shape. I can hardly wait for Cassandra to come.

But I also dread her coming, because she'll see the problems I've missed and will tell me my plan is impossible.

The next morning, she arrives with Eurus, whose wind is behind them, causing their legs and feet to jut ahead of them. Her peplos and his himation puff out as if they're living clouds. I laugh because they look funny and because I'm glad to see them.

Cassandra tells me that Helen put on all her jewelry when they got back to the women's quarters. "She talked for hours as if she thought me a friend, mostly gushing about how honored she felt that your band had invited her to join them. She said she'll be ready in case the chance comes again, but she's content now to know that not all women hate her. Then she listed every kind word that had ever been said to her. She even mentioned the dogs of Troy wagging their tails at her."

She's pitiable.

"In the afternoon," Cassandra continues, "while the trial went on between my brothers, she admitted she didn't want Deiphobus as her next husband. She'll have to have him, though. Helenus lost out, but he may yet do something." She tilts her head. "Is any rabbit left?"

She must have seen me bring it down when shooting it was still in the future.

I even saved a morsel of fat from the thigh for Eurus. His face softens when he sees it.

Over my meat and the extra bounty that he provides, I explain my plan.

"What if I were in the horse? I'm tall enough to be mistaken for a Greek warrior."

Eurus nods along with my words. Cassandra's eyes

never leave my face. Her expression gives nothing away. When I finish, Eurus and I wait. Only Cassandra's judgment matters. A fly lands on my nose. I brush it off.

Crows flap to us from the west, the direction of Troy. A crow perches on the head of each of us.

"Clouds lit from below,
trouble made by mortals.
Clouds stabbed by lightning,
Zeus having his say,
speaking nonsense in heat and noise."

Cassandra laughs. "*Crows* speak nonsense. Your plan sounds good. I can't tell if it will work." She stands and paces. "You have such concoctions? For sleep and wakefulness? Both?"

I nod.

She adds, "Mm. I don't like you going into the Greeks' camp."

The plan is tricky even though it's simple. I'll sneak into the Greek camp before the warriors stuff themselves into the horse. When they're about to, I'll line up to go inside with them.

Cassandra says that getting into the wooden horse will be one of the most dangerous moments. "Helenus will be in the camp. You'll be finished if he recognizes you."

"Why does he care anymore? He isn't likely to have Satchel, no matter what happens."

"I think he wants Troy to fall because Deiphobus will lose her then. And he's going to stay with the Greeks after the war."

Oh.

"You have some of their armor, right?" I ask.

Cassandra says they do. Spoils.

"It will disguise me."

"Yes." But she looks worried.

When a plan has Greeks and Trojans in it, anything can go wrong.

Cassandra says that after everyone is inside the horse, oxen will be hitched to its platform. Overnight, five men will lead the oxen and make sure the horse doesn't topple. The army will row themselves in skiffs to their ships and then row the ships to hide behind the nearest island.

In the morning, the horse will be discovered when Troy's western gate is opened.

"Can you yell when you see the horse? Otherwise, I may not hear you through the wood."

"Of course."

Her cry will be my signal to unstop the ewers that hold the concoctions. I'll breathe in and keep breathing in the one filled with a potion to keep me alert: rosemary, basil, lemon, mint, and snake venom.

I'll let Pen's sleeping elixir spread in the air.

Eurus says he can help with this part. He can trap a little wind in the ewer with the sleeping potion. "When you open the crock, the wind will waft the scent all over and keep it from fading."

The men will be dull in seconds and asleep in a minute. I thank him.

Their snores will tell me I can bellow the Amazon war cry. The Greeks may shift in their sleep, but alertness won't be possible. I'll keep roaring to let the Trojans know who I am and that the horse is no gift for their goddess. I won't stop until they attack it and find the Greeks.

Cassandra thanks me, speaking through tears. "Lately—because it's so close—I can't resist looking ahead. I see them slaughtering us. I see my father—" She breaks off. "But it's a good plan. Eurus, if it fails, will you blow Rin to her band?"

If I'm alive, but she doesn't say that.

He promises but I won't let him, and I'm sure he'll agree. I won't leave her to her fate. When her murderer attacks, I'll be there if I can be.

Cybele, thank you for making me loyal. Even if loyalty will kill me.

16

According to Cassandra, the horse won't be built for three months. First, Helenus has to betray Troy and prophesy twice for the Greeks. When they do what he says and still aren't victorious, the warrior Odysseus will think of the horse. Until then, fighting will continue, but it will halt while the horse is built and when their plot is carried out. The Greeks will ask for the truce, they'll say, in order to hunt and fish. The Trojans will welcome the break to do the same.

I yawn. "If Cybele were the Greeks' goddess, she'd make events move more quickly."

Cassandra laughs. She tells me to savor the time left.

But I can't. I miss my band. Our yearly gathering on

Cybele's island is coming, and I'm unlikely to be there.

The Trojans think I've left with the band. I don't want them to see me, so I stay in our camp while Cassandra sleeps in the palace.

She and Eurus come to me daily.

Once, he blows us to nearby Mount Ida, where I admire chasms, forests, and a rainbow of wildflowers. He lands us on the bank of a lake where Cassandra swims and I flail my arms and manage to keep my head above water until Eurus's wind stirs up waves. I go under and come up sputtering.

Cassandra paddles in place while Eurus stands on shore. They both laugh at me, but I never see him swimming, either. Cassandra demonstrates several ways of moving through the water—on her back, side, belly. She says side and back are easiest. I don't try. I want to learn every skill an Amazon needs, but we don't need this one.

We spend lazy days in the sacred grove. Eurus and Cassandra teach me a game called knucklebones and spend half an afternoon laughing at my clumsiness until I spend the other half gloating over Cassandra's slowness and mocking Eurus for having to use his wind to beat me.

They tell me about the Trojan gods and goddesses and their antics. If I didn't know Eurus and hadn't seen Hera, I would scoff at all of it.

* * *

A week before construction begins on the horse, Cassandra peers for hour after hour into the future, seeing and re-seeing the days to come at the Greek camp. She says that warriors will volunteer and line up to climb into the horse not long before it leaves. "No one will want to be shut up for a moment longer than they need to be."

The Greeks will tuck themselves into the belly. The horse's legs will be solid wood as will be the head and neck. The horse will be painted with a scene of a festival procession.

Cassandra says, "The side seams of the hatch will be hidden by the folds and hem of a worshipper's cloak. The worshipper will be a stooped old man, so the outline of his curved back will disguise the upper seam. The painter will be clever."

During the night, a day before I'm to leave, Eurus steals an assortment of Greek armor and weapons from Priam's storage rooms. He wafts it all, along with Cassandra and himself, to my camp. She has things for me too, including a Greek tunic. I can't wear my leggings, which mark me as an Amazon.

Eurus spreads the gear on the ground, including a large water jug.

I take off my felt hat because I know what must be done, a thing an Amazon would never do, but a village woman often does. Cassandra says her preparation is very good, made of mashed leeches that have been pickled for two months.

This does not comfort me.

But I can't pass myself off as Greek with red hair. My pale skin is bad enough.

First, she uses my scissors and cuts my hair to just below my ears. Then she brushes the leech mush into my hair. My scalp itches. The mess has to stay on for about an hour. I dig my fingers into my palms to keep from scratching.

Meanwhile, Cassandra stoops over the armor and points at this and that. She looks up at me. Her face is mischievous. "I'm outfitting you as a Myrmidon. Some of them are freckled too. No one pays attention to a Myrmidon."

"Why not?"

She straightens. "It's a long story, but Zeus turned ants into people for Achilles' grandfather. The ants' grandchildren were Achilles' soldiers until he died. Now Agamemnon commands them. They're very dull—like ants probably are—and their armor is brown. They rarely talk, but when they do, it's always about what they ate for their last meal or what they'll have for their next one."

I think I'd like the Myrmidons. I'm not chatty myself.

At last, I rinse my hair in the stream that runs beside the camp. Cassandra and Eurus pronounce me a brunette.

He looks away while I don the Greek tunic, which reveals the ibex tattoo above my left knee. We're not happy about this. Greek and Trojan legs aren't decorated.

"It's too hot for a cloak," Cassandra says.

"Maybe no one will look at my legs." This can't ruin everything!

Eurus suggests covering the spot with mud. He vanishes and returns after a minute or two with mud in his fists, paler mud than I've ever seen.

This succeeds until, after a few minutes, the mud dries to sand and falls away.

"I can keep my shield over it." Even I don't like this idea. I'll be holding my shield in an unnatural way, which will also be noticed.

We stand silently. Both of them stare at my legs. I feel embarrassed.

Finally, an idea arrives, a painful one. Without asking their opinion, I sit on my folded blanket on the ground and scrape my knife over the tattoo and beyond its borders, back and forth until beads of blood pop out.

"Rin! Stop!" Cassandra cries.

I continue. "My tattoo will not spoil the plan." When I think I've done enough, I fetch a handful of salt from the supplies Lannip left for me. Ignoring the smarting, I blend the salt with Eurus's sand and rub the mixture into the wound.

The lines of the tattoo are dimmed by my red and angry skin.

Eurus, who may never have felt pain, erupts in laughter. "It's perfect."

Cassandra's eyes are wet. "Thank you!"

He adds hopefully, "Maybe it will ooze with pus."

Cassandra and I laugh. He looks puzzled.

By now, it's twilight. We dine on leftovers from my last hunt and Eurus's endless bounty. I sleep as if I have no cares. If I die, I will have done my best.

The morning is cloudy. I put on the tunic and over it a tarnished bronze cuirass, which presses into my chest. The greaves over my shins and calves rub when I take a few steps. Amazons don't wear them. And the sandals flap. The cork sole is bigger than my foot, though Cassandra picked the smallest pair. Scratchy laces wind around my big toes and tie around my ankles.

The helmet, though, pleases me, especially its copper crest, which reminds me of the feathered crest of the hoopoe bird on our plains. The nose and cheek guards disguise me, I'm sure. I hear Pen's voice in my mind: *Rin, is that you?*

Cassandra says, "You won't be the only youth. Others won't have a beard yet, either."

I point out that I'll never have one. She laughs and hands me a wooden shield, round rather than crescent-shaped like ours. I sling on the strap that holds my gorytos.

"No!" Cassandra holds out a Greek bow and quiver of arrows. "The gorytos will stand out more than the tattoo."

"I can't fight without my gorytos."

Cassandra puts down the weapons.

"If you need to fight," Eurus points out, "we're lost."

This is true, even though I want to argue.

"The gorytos will draw attention. Someone will try to take it from you." Cassandra smiles. "Your bow is desired by Greeks and Trojans." She chuckles. "One or two might prefer having it to marrying Satchel."

I take the quiver and the enormous Greek bow.

Cassandra has brought a mirror of polished obsidian. Stepping back, she holds it so I can see my whole self.

A Greek warrior faces me. My eyes are in shadow. The cheek guards cover the corners of my lips, making my expression spiteful. I smile, which calls a rabbit to mind. Don't smile!

"You make a credible fighter." Cassandra puts the mirror away.

I nock an arrow and draw back the string. The bow is so stiff it's almost useless. I aim it away from Cassandra and Eurus.

After I shoot, I don't have to go far to collect my arrow. "I'd starve if I had to hunt with this." I try again, and the arrow flies fast and far.

Eurus laughs at my confusion, giving himself away.

"Don't do that!" I don't want his help with my shooting.

We have hours before I need to leave in mid-afternoon. I remove the uncomfortable armor and practice with the bow, making little progress.

Finally, the time comes. I don the armor again.

Cassandra tells me to take the water jug that Eurus brought. "He'll leave you at a stream that's near the camp. The water in the jug will give you a reason for having left and for returning." She adds, "Avoid Helenus. Watch for him every moment. If you see him, move away."

"I will."

She hugs me, releases me, and hugs me again. "Before you came, I didn't know what friendship was."

I say, "I didn't guess a village woman could be a friend or be brave or save my life."

We hug one more time.

Eurus coughs.

I hang the ridiculous bow across my left shoulder and push the strap of the misshapen shield over my left forearm. My own arrows are in a quiver on my belt behind my foreign sword. The vials of sleeping potion and wakefulness potion hang in a pouch between the two. I push my helmet into my right armpit. With difficulty, I hold both my spear and the water jug in my right hand.

Cassandra tells me that I am the image of a young Greek warrior. A moment later, she adds, "No. Your posture is too good. Slouch!"

I ask Eurus to blow me slowly to the Greek camp (though faster than I can trot), so I'll see the route that the wooden horse will take. I want to know the ups and downs along the way. He picks me up.

A hundred things can go wrong. I may never see my friend again.

Or my band.

17

I savor the fresh wind as Eurus blows us along. Cassandra has warned me that inside the horse, the air will stink of sweat, farts, and bad breath.

The land below is flat but furrowed, with grass here, dirt there. The wooden horse will have a bumpy ride and will have to ford a stream halfway to Troy. From our height, I see the ocean ahead, striped with foam. The horizon is broken by the masts of the Greek fleet and, behind them, by an island with two hills. After the horse leaves for Troy, the Greeks will board their ships and hide behind the island.

Before we descend, I see the horse. I've been eager for this, but it's a horror to a lover of horses. Garish in its paint, and so stiff! It seems to lack knees or ankles. Just enough of a horse to show what it's supposed to be.

Eurus stops far enough from the river that we won't be seen and sends his wind ahead to make sure no one is there. The riverbank is deserted, so he takes me.

I hear the camp in the distance, voices calling and a rumble of beasts moving.

"You have the gratitude of a lesser god for helping her. You know . . ." Eurus trails off.

"You love her."

"It's hopeless."

I was right! "The crows might say something surprising about hope."

"And about luck. Good luck." He whisks himself away.

My stomach is uneasy. I put down my shield and fill the jug. I can't hold the jug and the spear without spilling water, so I half empty the jug. It's just for show anyway.

Then I think, as none of us had before, how odd I'm going to look. A Greek, living at the camp, wouldn't take his spear, his helmet, and his shield with him to fetch water.

I leave the jug.

The simplest explanation is that I had gone to relieve myself. I might take my spear because of snakes, which are drawn to latrines—although my knife would do. I can't think why I'd have my helmet and shield.

And I have no idea if I'm coming from the direction of the latrine.

I walk briskly. Swallowing a nervous giggle, I wonder, in case someone speaks to me, what a Myrmidon would have eaten at his latest meal.

The first Greek I see is currying his horse. His weapons and armor lie on a blanket a few feet from him. I can kill him easily.

He looks up when he hears me and smiles. "Hello, lad."

I've stopped noticing the Trojan and Greek accent, but now I'm aware of it again. *He'o, 'ad.*

I'll give myself away if I speak! Instead, I nod.

I see him take in that I'm a Myrmidon. He returns to his work.

I keep myself from grinning. Thank you, Cassandra.

The camp bustles. My eyes rake the scene, searching for Helenus, but I don't see him.

Men eat porridge from wooden bowls. Others sit in circles, playing dice. Cries and groans ring out. Some lead horses and oxen to the beach and urge the beasts onto skiffs. Many pack their belongings into sacks.

A crowd of warriors in battle dress, as I am, cluster near the wooden horse. The hatch hangs half-open. A team of a dozen oxen has been harnessed to pull the horse.

Helenus isn't among the waiting men. A few are Myrmidons. I stand with them and put on my helmet. Now I look like everyone else.

To the side of us, not in our line, is a man I recognize

305

because Cassandra has described him: Agamemnon, the Greek king who will be her captor and the cause of her death. My heart picks up its pace.

He towers over the Greeks and pulls his shoulders back. Some might call his face handsome. Not I. His nostrils are big enough to admit a fly. His deep-set eyes seem to be holes. He's smiling, giving him a greedy look.

Striding back and forth, he says in a voice that booms from his big chest, "Men, you will be courageous beyond others for entering the horse. If you die in its belly, there won't be final deeds of yours to sing about. But if you are reborn from it alive and Greece is victorious, you'll get double spoils and double the captives to choose among."

Captives? Slaves!

"Take with you our hopes and . . ."

The rest is drowned out by cheering. A rope ladder unrolls from the hatch. A Greek, not in armor, scrambles down. I surge with the others toward the hatch. A warrior climbs up.

I position myself in the middle of the line that forms. We advance. Two warriors are ahead of me, then one, then I grasp the ladder.

A man pushes me out of the way. "Your elders first, lad."

When he's high enough, I try again and am brushed aside again. I wait. Everyone seems to think he is older than I am. Finally, I'm the only one left. I start to climb.

"Wait!"

I know the voice. Helenus's hand circles my ankle in its greaves. I kick, but he holds on.

He says, "I have scores to settle in Troy, Agamemnon. I want to be with the first in the city." He whispers to me, "I saw you come into camp, and there's a scrape hiding your tattoo. Tell my twin this is the destiny I choose."

I bunch myself up to shove him away, but Agamemnon tilts his head for me to stand aside.

I've failed!

Helenus rises into the horse. The rope ladder is pulled in.

How will I escape going on a ship and joining the Greek army?

The hatch door is shut, though a bit of tunic sticks out. Helenus's voice comes through the wood. "Wait." He pulls the cloth in.

I marvel at how the seams of the hatch have vanished. And I'm surprised that his voice carries so well through the wood.

Agamemnon puts his arm around my shoulder. "Come, lad. We're off to the ships. You'll still be in on the fighting."

We walk together toward the beach. Two warriors come to him with questions. He lets me go.

Can I walk away? Who will notice me? Everyone is occupied. Someone always needs the latrine at the last minute. I wish I knew where it is.

The man currying his horse hadn't challenged me before, so maybe it's that way. I start back from the beach toward the stream. Two steps. Five.

Someone calls to me. "Lad!"

I pretend not to hear.

A man rushes to me. "We need a rower."

He sees my face, which is tight with my need to get away. He thinks what I hoped he would. "Hold it. You can go off the ship." He takes my arm.

He puts me on a skiff at the second row of four benches. Fifteen warriors, carrying their armor and weapons, board. The skiff sinks until it rides just a few inches above the sea that laps against its sides.

The man ahead of me cries, "Row!"

I pull hard. I don't want to be caught because I'm weaker than the others. We hold our course toward the ships.

Too late for me to profit from it, a lesson arrives: I failed to learn everything I could from the Trojans. If I had let Cassandra teach me, I'd be able to swim. Shame floods me.

Cassandra's crows dive out of the sky. They face me from the shoulders and head of the rower ahead of me. He keeps pulling, seeming not to notice. The crows caw:

"The mouse, who shies at shadows, stays alive,
but mortals, challenging the sun in the sky,
are dazzled by their own bright minds
and flounder, waver, die."

I suppose they're predicting my death for trying to save Cassandra. They're probably right. The Greeks will discover me eventually. If they don't realize I'm a girl, they'll kill me. If they do, they'll enslave me. I hope they don't realize.

18

In just a few minutes, we reach a ship. I have to wait again for my elders to climb a rope ladder. The beach is so close that even I can probably swim there, but someone will dive after me if I try.

My nose is stuffy. I force myself not to think of Cassandra, Eurus, Troy, Pen, or my band.

When we're all on board and the skiffs are hauled in, I'm put to rowing again, placed in the mid-level of oars. The top level sits on benches on deck. My level is on deck too, sitting on beams that hold the ship's sides in place. The third and last level is below the deck. Thank you, Cybele, for not putting me in that murky dark.

I take off my armor and place it at my feet with my shield, spear, and ridiculous bow. The men who aren't

rowing sit on the deck in groups of friends. The Myrmidons sit together, looking as contented as sheep in a
meadow.

Ugh! A few men hang their behinds over the ship's side
to relieve themselves, as the man who took me thought I
needed to do.

The sails aren't raised, I suppose because the distance
is short. A drummer and a piper mark the rhythm of our
rowing. The ship resists and then begins to move. Everyone
sings a begging prayer to Poseidon, their god of the sea:

> *"Oh Poseidon, lord of leviathans!*
> *Of the tossing waves!*
> *Of brine and foam!*
> *Cup this ship in your vast hands!*
> *Let us ride the bucking sea!"*

I wonder why we're bothering to row instead of leaving
it all to Poseidon. I hum and move my mouth and remember a not-begging song to Cybele. I recite it in my mind:

> *Thank you for your gifts:*
> *our bow and strength to pull it,*
> *horses to milk and ride,*
> *a band to hunt and fight beside,*
> *your army to join when we die.*

The island is about twice as far from shore as Cybele's island is and, in the dusk, seems twice as big. Small and not very distant, really, but an endless way for someone who doesn't swim.

Our ship is among the first to circle the island. We're told to stop rowing. A rower goes to the bulwark and drops anchor. The ship bobs in light swells. Another ship draws in barely a yard from us.

A man with a basket walks from warrior to warrior, handing out thick slices of bread. I swallow mine in three bites. Hunger doesn't make it tastier.

The rower behind me touches my shoulder. I jump and then turn.

Smiling but with raised eyebrows, he holds out half his bread. "Myrmidons are always hungry, and you're a growing lad."

I nod. By way of thanks, I stuff it all in my mouth and grin with bread spread across my teeth.

He grimaces and looks away.

The sky darkens. The night is bright with stars and a half-moon. More bread is given to everyone. Flasks come out. Here and there, men sing softly in groups. Lamps are lit. Men laugh and argue.

Three men in a cluster list—by name!—the Trojans they're eager to murder. All of Cassandra's remaining brothers (except her traitorous twin) are on the list, including Polydorus, who is still too young to go to battle.

I ball my fists and squeeze.

One gloats, "Proud Queen Hecuba can clean my wife's pots and pans."

A man says thoughtfully, "Andromache is a beauty."

I think about jumping overboard. I won't let myself be enslaved, and if I must die, I'd rather it be by drowning than by the hand of a Greek. I don't want them to have felled two Amazon queens.

From the other side of the deck, Agamemnon's deep voice calls, "Cassandra is for me."

My stomach seems to turn over. I didn't realize he was on this ship. My friend's death has begun though it's probably still weeks or months away.

Agamemnon adds, "You are all on notice. She belongs to me."

I shudder. No one argues.

Is there anything I can do, other than drown myself?

A seed of an idea forms. The island is close enough that I can splash to it. With luck, I can hide there. The Greeks will think I deserted. I can wait for them to bring their prisoners while I practice shooting with their terrible bow and plan a way to rescue Cassandra.

I can't do anything until the Greeks sleep, but they don't. Glee over the coming massacre spreads. The voices grow louder and more excited. Each word seems to be a tiny arrow piercing me.

Oh! I have a remedy! The vials of sleeping potion and wakefulness potion I was going to use in the wooden horse. The sleeping elixir should bring slumber to these Greeks. It had worked on everyone in the open air the night I'd broken my ribs.

But the breeze here is stronger than it was in the grass-lands and may blow the scent away.

The man who gave me the bread says he wants to be the one to kill Cassandra's father.

First, I open the wrong vial. I bite down on my yawn and push the stopper back in. My pounding heart keeps me awake as I pull the stopper off the right one and hold it to my nose. The snake venom stings! I am as alert as I've ever been.

With my free hand, I unstop the sleeping vial while remembering that Eurus put a little wind in to spread the scent. Thank you, Eurus! I hope your wind doesn't join the sea breeze!

I wait.

The bread giver yawns loudly. His yawn is catching! I hear several more. The voices drop and sputter out. Men curl up and begin to snore. I wait until no one stirs, and then I wait a little longer.

Finally, I stand. I leave the spear and my armor and prop the sleep vial against the cuirass, hoping the remedy will continue to do its work. I sling the bow across my shoulder. The quiver is at my waist. I thrust my hand through the strap at the back of the shield, unwilling to leave myself defenseless, though if I need it, my life will probably be lost.

Barely breathing, I pick my way among the sleepers. Only a few yards off lies the rope ladder, folded neatly on the deck where we boarded.

Maybe the Greeks' Poseidon sends the higher swell that makes me stagger into an outstretched leg.

Agamemnon's leg?

I manage to keep the wakefulness vial to my nose.

"Zeus!" An ordinary Greek. He raises himself on an elbow.

The man next to him stirs too, then rolls over.

My shield! My excuse is to relieve myself, so why take a shield?

"Watch yourself!" The first man closes his eyes, his head still resting on his elbow.

I wait for him to gather himself and jump up, but he starts snoring as he slumps down. Thank you, Cybele and Eurus.

While my heart calms, the sea calms too. I get to the ladder without disturbing anyone else. One-handedly, I hang the loops in one end of the ladder on hooks in the ship. Gently, I feed the ladder over the side. My shield thuds against the hull. I freeze again, but no one wakes.

I inhale once more from the wakefulness vial and hold my breath while I stop it and return it to my pouch. Then I throw one leg over the side of the ship and find the top rung of the ladder. The other leg follows. I lower myself to the second rung. In a wave's trough, the ladder bows out from the ship. I hang loose in the air. My hands ache with the tightness of my grip.

Below, the sea never stops moving. My stomach rises into my throat.

The ship lifts into the next swell, and I'm slammed into the hull.

I hold on, but I'm so frightened I stop descending. Pen would be terrified too, I think. Anyone would be. I remember the leviathans the Greeks sang of. Are they right below, opening their jaws?

Pen would know how to quell her fear. The rolling sea might remind her of our grassland in a strong wind.

I lower myself and slip into the water as smoothly as into my leggings. The sea is warm as spit.

Instantly, my arrows float out of the quiver. While kicking my feet and flapping one hand into the water, I manage to grab three.

The seawater holds me up, as the lake water on Mount Ida did not. I wonder why.

How will I get to the island with one arm in the shield

strap and one hand gripping the arrows?

I let the shield go. It floats.

I try to imitate Cassandra's smooth strokes. My arms strike the water and splash loudly. I kick desperately. The island is no closer, the ship no farther away. The shield drifts nearby.

A large swell comes and smothers me. Water fills my nose and mouth. Cybele appears only on the battlefield or I think she'd be here.

I come up sputtering, my free hand gripping the shield, which may have saved me. Can I use it?

My arms circle its rim, holding it with both hands, even my right, which still has the arrows. I kick too energetically. We buck, but forward, toward the island. I steady my kicks. The shield helps me keep my head up. We progress.

Soon, I reach the island.

19

The shield changes my plan. With its help I believe I can reach the mainland. I don't know how I can save my friend, but at least I'll be with her again.

The woods on the island are too thick for me to make my way through, so I go around on the stony beach. If I were to list what I hate, first would be the memory of Achilles, second Agamemnon, and third these Greek sandals. The island is small, but my feet smart by the time I reach the other side.

Troy is four miles from the sea. My feet will be bloody by the time I get there—if I get there.

The water feels sweet on my feet when I wade in. The sky is graying toward dawn. I hold the arrows I saved between my teeth and grip the shield more comfortably.

The swells are gentler on this side. I'm an experienced sea kicker now anyway. If I have the chance, I will learn to swim and make the band learn too.

Five Greek warriors went with the oxen that pulled the wooden horse. I reason that a skiff would have been left for them and they'll be headed this way. We may pass each other on my way to Troy. I wish I hadn't left my spear behind.

But when I reach the shore, no skiff waits. I decide that the five have hidden themselves and the oxen somewhere near Troy. Why travel the distance twice if they don't have to?

I tuck the arrows into my waist and set out at a trot, but after only a few minutes I have to loosen the sandals' straps. My ankles are bleeding. The soles of my feet are blistered. I set off again, but the rubbing is worse. I take off the sandals and hurl them as far as I can. Barefoot, I have to pick my way carefully, and I'm limping. Still, it's better. The sky is turning pink.

Finally, I see Troy. Not much farther, the horse takes shape, standing almost as high as the city wall. A few minutes later, I hear voices in the distance.

When I limp to the wall, a crowd is gathering between the horse and the gate. Cassandra and Eurus stand apart from the others. His hand rests on her shoulder. She must have already shouted to me and heard no response.

If not for the horse and the Greek man Cassandra said would be here, I'd be noticed: a girl with cropped hair, bloody feet, wearing a Greek tunic. But no one turns my way, except Cassandra and Eurus.

I've grown so used to her knowing what will happen that I forget she can't foretell my future anymore, or Helenus's. When she sees me, she smiles as widely as she did after she saved me.

She runs to me. "I was sure the Greeks had killed you."

She's happy for me, though her own end is assured.

She adds, "We were doomed anyway."

I can't think of anything hopeful, so I hug her. Then I look around.

Helen stands under the horse and smiles up at its belly.

The Greek man—the liar—is speaking to Priam. He's a slight young man with a wispy beard. ". . . that's how they treat me! King, you're known for your kindness. Will you take me in?"

Priam nods. "You've suffered enough."

An elderly man, leaning on a walking stick, approaches the king. Two young men follow him.

"Sire?"

Priam turns. "Yes, Laocoön?"

I remember what Cassandra said. The old man must be Apollo's priest. My heart flutters. Cassandra squeezes my arm.

"My sons and I doubt this man's tale."

People nod.

The old man goes on. "I feel Apollo at my elbow, urging us not to trust him."

One of the sons says, "What harm can come from leaving the horse outside for a single night? It won't rot that quickly."

In a moment will come the event that Cassandra couldn't foresee, that she believes will be sent by a god or accomplished by Helenus, that will terrify everyone.

Priam nods. "Caution is always wise. Let your sons—"

The earth beneath us rolls as if we were on the sea. Cassandra, Eurus, and I back up against Troy's wall. My heart feels about to burst out of my chest.

People run wildly—toward the horse, away from it, into Troy's gate. A man picks Helen up and runs with her away from Troy. Last of those racing to the city are the priest in the arms of one son and the other at their side.

Ai! A chasm opens a few yards from our feet. Oh no! Two serpents rise from it. I jump up and down with fear. Each is as long as a Greek ship, purple-scaled, with a mane of fire and spears for teeth. Side by side, they surge after the Trojans dashing to the gate.

Laocoön shouts, "Poseidon!"

One serpent swallows the priest and the son holding him. The other gulps down the second son.

The serpents dive. The earth closes. The grass is undisturbed, as if there had never been a cleft.

Those outside Troy shout and shriek. I struggle to catch my breath.

Cassandra is holding her head and swaying. Eurus's dark face is ashy.

Frantically, the Trojans push the horse toward the gate. Dozens of men are needed. Their muscles swell with effort. At the gate, the horse's head clears the stone ceiling by only a few inches.

Helen runs toward Troy, holding the hand of the man who had her.

Cassandra lowers her arms and stops swaying. "Rin, I think that was Poseidon's doing. Sea serpents are his, and he loves the Greeks."

And kills for them!

"Go to your band. When I'm on the ship with my captor, I want to think of your freedom."

"Soon." I'm lying. Between now and tonight when the Greek army comes, I'll fetch my gorytos and more arrows so I can fight.

The three of us lag behind the crowd entering Troy. I hear distant drumming. I wonder if the Greek and Trojan immortals are starting something else. What's left for them to ruin?

Inside the city, Maera races to Cassandra. The horse

fills the narrow street. How close can I get to it? Silently, I curse the Greek bow.

The Trojans wheel the horse to the plaza outside Priam's palace. A brazier is brought out. Incense is burned. A man shouts a prayer, begging Athena to forgive them for hesitating. Three men hurry into the palace and return with drums, a lyre, and a flute.

I start away from Cassandra and Eurus, but she sees me and follows. Eurus and Maera come after her.

"Rin!"

I wait for her.

"Don't!"

"Hector told me to be your friend."

"He didn't mean for you to die for me."

"I hope to save us." I edge nearer to the horse. My bare feet sense faint tremors. After I take a few steps, I stop to see if anyone is watching me. No one is. They're all concentrating on the horse or their prayers. I move in. Stop. Step. Stop. Step.

At last, I'm a mere dozen feet from the horse on the side where the hatch is. I draw one of my three arrows from my waist and hold it at my side.

I look around. No one pays me heed.

Slowly, slowly, I raise the Greek bow, nock my arrow, draw back the string against the stiff wood, using all my strength. I release it, knowing my aim is true.

I hope to hit someone through the seam in the hatch. Best if the someone is Helenus.

But Eurus—the dizzard!—sends his wind to speed my arrow and give it power. The wind throws it off its path so that it strikes the middle of the hatch and is buried uselessly in the wood.

Someone shouts, "She attacked the offering!"

Feet thud. Maera barks.

As fast as I can, I pull out another arrow, yelling, "No, Eurus!"

A hand circles my arm.

It's over. I failed.

But I yank myself free, run in closer, fit the arrow, pull back, release.

A bloody line appears along the seam.

"She wounded it!"

"Forgive us, Athena!"

People surround me and hold me. A terrified silence falls.

Again, I feel a pulsing under the paving stones. A monster sent by the immortals is rising up for me!

A man's voice comes from inside the horse, "Leave it be. It's just a scratch."

"Hush!" Sounds like Helenus.

⚕ 20 ⚕

People cry out: "She wounded a god!" "That was no god!"
"I'll get a ladder." "I heard a Greek voice!" "I heard Helenus. Where is he?"

The hands release me.

Cassandra squeezes through the crowd to me. She
clings to my arm. "Troy is saved. I'm so dizzy. I don't think
it will be undone this time. Don't let me fall."

I support her. Thank you, Cybele.

People turn. The drumming is loud now—horses'
hooves.

Two men turn out of an alley, bearing a wooden ladder.

Lannip and the rest clatter down the wide road toward
us. Maera and other dogs bark. The riders dismount and
push through to me. I've never seen such joyous faces.

I'm sure my face mirrors theirs.

Lannip begins. "Your hair! We couldn't—"

I hold up a hand for silence, and she stops.

The ladder is carried through the crowd. Deiphobus, Helenus's brother and rival, climbs up.

Helen stands between Priam and Hecuba. Her first husband and her current one are about to meet, but she's smiling at us—at my band and me.

From the top of the ladder, Deiphobus feels along the seam and finds the wooden latch. He lifts it.

The door opens. Helenus catapults out into his brother. The ladder topples. The two are on the ground, fighting.

But Helenus is lifted by a wind, then carried along the street and beyond. I hope Eurus is sending him so far that he can never come back.

We leave Maera at Troy's gate. At our camp, Cassandra tells us what will happen. The warriors from inside the horse and the man who told the tale about it will be held as hostages. Priam will use them to arrange a truce, which will end the war. He'll have the wisdom, despite Deiphobus's rage, to give Helen to Menelaus, her first husband.

No one will ask her what she wants.

I say, "Helenus told me to tell you he was choosing his destiny. But why did he force me away from the horse and climb in himself? He wasn't going to get Helen, so why did he care?"

Cassandra smiles. "He probably believed—correctly—that you had a way to reveal the horse trick, which he thought would mean Deiphobus would keep her. He couldn't tolerate that." She turns to Eurus. "Where did you send him?"

"To the other side of the river Oceanus, where there are no ships to bring him back."

Cassandra says, "Thank you! Hatred devoured him."

"Now my offerings will keep coming." Eurus laughs.

Cassandra laughs too. The two can't stop laughing. The band discovers that gales of laughter can be real. We bunch together.

Afterward, we spend the afternoon and the night at our camp. Lannip and I hunt together and bring down a young stag, which she cooks delectably. Eurus contributes ripe figs for dessert.

In the morning, knowing that everyone agrees, I again ask Cassandra to join the band. I tell Eurus he can be with us as often as he likes. Of course, whether I say so or not, he can be. I can't order the wind about.

He's angry again! "You want me?" He paces. "I'm not always a helpful wind. You'll get a bungler!"

Cassandra smiles. "I looked into the future. Not too far. I don't want to see my new death or the deaths of any of you. I won't use my gift, except to learn how to be a band member, but in the future, I see I'm happier than I've ever been."

Smiling too, I say, "You'll have to give up bread."

"I like bread! But I'll manage without it. I see that I'll help Barkida and Gamis make your bows." She turns to Eurus. "You'll often be with me." She blushes.

He looks at her face. "What?"

Her blush deepens.

"What!"

She doesn't answer.

"We'll marry?"

She nods. "In a few years." Laughing, she adds, "Or I'll marry another god, because the groom is invisible in my prophecy."

Amazons don't usually marry, but I'm jumping with happiness. Band members hug Cassandra and even Eurus, who sends a mischievous wind to lift our hats and drop them back, askew.

Cassandra assures us, though I hadn't thought of it, that she won't stay in her wagon and never come out once they're wed. "I'm no longer a village woman."

Delighted, we snap our fingers over our heads. Eurus says a wind god wouldn't want a stationary wife.

Finally, she says she has to tell her parents that she's leaving with us. I remember Helen going back for her jewels and wonder, even now, if my friend will return.

But in a few hours, she does. Pammon is with her, leading an ox that's hitched to a cart. Maera is in the cart, wagging her tail atop a mound of spoils: Greek armor, a dozen swords, seven spears, bolts and bolts of linen and wool woven by Trojan women.

And a loaf of bread for everyone. Cassandra's joke, I'm sure.

When the cart stops, Maera jumps out and rushes to Cassandra, tail wagging.

Pammon clears his throat. "King Priam regrets the loss of your queen. He recognizes her valor in attempting to save the hero Hector. All of Troy thanks you, Queen Rin, for revealing the Greek deception. We hope you'll come to our aid again if need be."

"We may call on you in turn," I say, "as allies do."

He looks surprised. "I'll tell the king what you said."

I let him go. He leaves the ox and the cart for us.

When he's gone, Eurus offers to blow us all to the rest of the band. "I'm better at blowing people than I used to be." A note of pride enters his voice. "I'm experienced."

Half in the band are grinning. The others look afraid. I know what Pen would say.

I thank him. "We hope you'll come with us on our slow journey and learn how we live." We can't have him or Cassandra solving our problems with their powers. "But would you show the ones who want to find out how it feels to fly on the wind?"

He does. In the end, everyone except Zelke takes a turn.

We spend another night at the camp. In the morning, we pack and leave, with Maera riding in the cart.

Cassandra mounts Pen's horse and a laughing Eurus jumps up behind her.

He tells us how funny it is for the wind to ride a horse. "I'm not putting any weight on the beast."

Cassandra says, "Thank you, Cybele, for this Amazon band."

Three crows perch on her horse's mane:

"Moles hide from the sky.
Trojans huddle behind their high wall,
but bored Apollo, liking surprise,
releases Cassandra to the Amazon queen."

They fly off.

I say, "The band is home, wherever we are. You're home now." I'm home.

A NOTE FROM THE AUTHOR

I was nine or ten when I first encountered Greek myths in *Mythology: Timeless Tales of Gods and Heroes* by Edith Hamilton. Nowadays I question the book's title. What about the goddesses, who were just as important as the gods? What about the women and girls, the heroines? For example, there was Thisbe, who may have been Shakespeare's source for Juliet in *Romeo and Juliet*. She braves a lion! And let's remember Atalanta, the hunter and wrestler who brings down the boar that ravages the kingdom of Calydon.

One of the myths I loved was a little known one, about the origins of Achilles' soldiers, the Myrmidons, who come up in *Sparrows in the Wind*. The Myrmidons started out as ants! I wonder about that transformation. Did they become big first—gigantic ants—and then human? Or vice versa?

Did they understand what had happened to them? Did they enjoy being human?

The myths were like fairy tales to me—all action and never a dull moment. The myth of Cupid and Psyche even has the same basic plot as the fairy tale "East of the Sun, West of the Moon," and it's similar to "Beauty and the Beast." Creatures like Cerberus, a three-headed dog, and the Minotaur, a bull-human combo, populate myths, as fairies, ogres, and dragons inhabit fairy tales.

Neither myths nor fairy tales in their original form reveal the minds and hearts of their characters the way modern novels do. In the myth of Cassandra, she's a tragic figure because she foresees the fate of Troy, the people she loves, and her own murder, and no one believes her warnings. The myth tells us she's sad, but nothing else. What does she think? What kind of person is she? What does she do? What *can* she do?

My job is to consider these questions.

To help me cogitate, I read two books about daily life in ancient Greece, although ancient Greece is more recent than the events described in the Trojan War. But I couldn't find a book about daily life that far back. Since I was writing fantasy and not historical fiction, I figured I could use what I learned as I saw fit.

Because the books cover such distant times, I found little about gestures and manners. I used what there was, though, which is why characters toss back their heads rather than shaking them to indicate *no*, and why they express appreciation by snapping their fingers over their heads—which seems to be coming back into fashion.

In *Daily Life in Greece at the Time of Pericles* by Robert Flacelière, the section called "The Status of Women" begins, "In Athens, the wives of citizens enjoyed no more political or legal rights than did their slaves." Whoa!

They lived indoors, going out only for religious festivals, and their husbands mostly spent their time outdoors. They rarely had a reason to speak to each other!

When Paris divorces Oenone simply by leaving her, that reflects the practice at the time. In ancient Greece, the man would also have had to repay his ex's dowry—to her father, not to her. But in the earlier era of the Trojan War, there would have been no dowry. Instead, the groom would have paid a bride price to her father at the time of the wedding, so he would have had nothing to refund.

The Trojans are the enemies of the Greeks in the myth of the Trojan War, but the two peoples worship the same gods, speak the same language, and seem to share the same customs. It isn't much of a leap to guess that their women are treated the same way.

If Cassandra is under a kind of house arrest, along with every other girl and woman, and that's normal, how could she even think of trying to save her city?

A poet called Homer is said to be the creator of at least part of the story of the Trojan War. No one is certain exactly when Homer lived or if he lived at all, but scholars are sure that if he was a real person, his day was more than two thousand seven hundred years ago. That's a long time! Not much of his writing survived. The portion about the Trojan War that's come down to us is called *The Iliad*. It starts long after the fighting began and ends with Hector's funeral, though the war continues after that. We know the rest of the saga from later ancient poets. The entire tale probably started as spoken poems that were eventually written down.

If there's so much uncertainty about Homer, was there a Trojan War?

We don't know.

It's clear from archaeological digs that there was a city called Troia by the ancient Greeks, Ilium by the Romans. The city had as many lives as a cat. It rose and fell at least nine times. Some reasons for its collapse were earthquake, invasion, fire, and war. It kept being rebuilt because it was a hub of trade, ideally located where the Scamander River met the Aegean Sea, which today separates Turkey and Greece.

Could one of Troy's downfalls, around 1200 BCE, have been caused by fire following both a forced entry and a battle? Maybe.

Is the Trojan horse mythological or historical? What do you think?

Let's talk about Helen. Out of curiosity, I googled "most beautiful woman in the world" and found lists of the so-called most beautiful. There were websites that named this particular woman or that one, but opinion differed.

The women online didn't look alike. There wasn't, for example, a perfect nose that each of them possessed to one degree or another. Same for skin color, lips, chins, eyes. Or height, say I at fifty-eight inches short.

Did everyone back then agree that Helen was the most beautiful, or did just Aphrodite think so? In *The Iliad*, Cassandra is said to be Priam's prettiest daughter. (In another spot in the same epic, her sister Laodice is given that honor.) And in a third part, Cassandra is compared favorably with Aphrodite, the goddess of beauty. Even Homer couldn't make up his mind!

When I started thinking about the Trojan War, I remembered that, according to the myth, Amazons come to Troy's aid near the end. I had imagined an army of Amazons, but according to the myth, there are just thirteen women. They arrive after Hector dies but before Achilles does. He kills Queen Penthesilea, but later. I moved the chronology around, as fiction writers are allowed to do, especially if we confess!

In my story-planning stage, I didn't think there had ever been real Amazons. I was merrily making things up when a friend told me about a fascinating, scholarly book, *The Amazons: Lives and Legends of Warrior Women across the Ancient World* by Adrienne Mayor.

They were real! Amazons were nomads over a vast territory, from parts of eastern Europe to western China. They didn't have a written language, so they couldn't leave records (which is why they were thought to be imaginary). The ancient Greeks wrote about them, but they also wrote about monsters that never existed. Now, with DNA testing, archaeologists are discovering that some skeletons of warriors, long thought to have been male, were female—Amazons.

Even though they didn't write, they were by no means primitive. Amazons were part of a larger people called Scythians, and Scythians were high-tech back in the day. They entered the Iron Age early. Their trousers may have been the first tailored clothing ever. Most of all, their composite bows were such a marvel that they're still being made. Though the bows are small, they deliver as much power as a much bigger bow. And since women generally are smaller than men, the Scythian bow allowed Amazons to be great warriors.

I didn't make up the gorytos, either. The combo bow case and quiver allowed Scythians to shoot faster. It's true too that they put valuables into kurgans (tombs) with their fallen warriors, and they never interred the dead person's bows, which took years to make. The Amazons needed them!

I didn't invent the tattoos, either. Scythians were tattooed.

But *Sparrows in the Wind* is a fantasy, so I did make up a lot. For instance, there's no evidence that Amazon women didn't live in tribes with men. They often did, and they fought alongside them.

And I invented, just to have fun, their way of naming horses and dogs by color, size, and age. Real Amazons gave their horses names, exactly as we do, but horses were so important that sometimes people were named after them! (I have no idea about dogs.)

If we put the women of Troy and the Amazons side by side, their lives couldn't be more different. And yet, we can imagine how the mythical Cassandra and my imaginary Amazon girl could achieve miracles together. Cassandra has knowledge, and Rin has confidence and a habit of action. Both are kind and affectionate and want to save the people they love. It's an unlikely friendship, but it's perfect!

ACKNOWLEDGMENTS

How lucky I am to have the enthusiasm of my editor, Rosemary Brosnan! You are the wind in my sails! I depend to the limit on your thoughtfulness, responsiveness, and discerning eye to bring out the best in my stories. Many thanks also to your delightful and dedicated team, especially to the ever-helpful Courtney Stevenson! My gratitude also goes to Mary Flower for her careful copyediting.

Lucky again! My agent, Ginger Knowlton, is my bulwark. I depend on you for your judicious advice on the many choices that come up and, of course, for your nonpareil negotiating skills.

Many thanks to my friend, writer, journalist, and translator, Liuyu Ivy Chen, who set in motion my learning about the Amazons. Without you, I would have written a very different and much less informed book!

Thanks to Bonna D. Wescoat, interim director of the Michael C. Carlos Museum, for answering my inquiry and recommending Adrienne Mayor's *The Amazons: Lives and Legends of Warrior Women across the Ancient World.*